GUANYA PAU

broadview editions
series editor: L. W. Conolly

Zobah at a funeral feast. Photographer: William C. Siegmann.

GUANYA PAU
A Story of an African Princess

Joseph Jeffrey Walters

edited by Gareth Griffiths and John Victor Singler

broadview editions

Library and Archives Canada Cataloguing in Publication

Walters, Joseph J. (Joseph Jeffrey), d. 1894.
    Guanya Pau : a story of an African princess / by Joseph Jeffrey Walters ; edited by Gareth Griffiths and John Victor Singler.

(Broadview editions)
Includes bibliographical references.
ISBN 1-55111-365-1

    1. Vai (African people)—Fiction.   I. Griffiths, Gareth, 1943-   II. Singler, John Victor
III. Title.   IV. Series.

PR9384.9.W35G83 2004   823   C2004-905018-4

Broadview Editions

The Broadview Editions series represents the ever-changing canon of literature in English by bringing together texts long regarded as classics with valuable lesser-known works.

Broadview Press Ltd. is an independent, international publishing house, incorporated in 1985. Broadview believes in shared ownership, both with its employees and with the general public; since the year 2000 Broadview shares have traded publicly on the Toronto Venture Exchange under the symbol BDP.

We welcome comments and suggestions regarding any aspect of our publications – please feel free to contact us at the addresses below or at broadview@broadviewpress.com.

North America
Post Office Box 1243, Peterborough, Ontario, Canada K9J 7H5
3576 California Road, Orchard Park, NY, USA 14127
Tel: (705) 743-8990   Fax: (705) 743-8353;
e-mail: customerservice@broadviewpress.com

UK, Ireland, and continental Europe
NBN Plymbridge, Estover Road, Plymouth PL6 7PY UK
Tel: 44 (0) 1752 202301   Fax: 44 (0) 1752 202331
Fax Order Line: 44 (0) 1752 202333
Customer Service: cservs@nbnplymbridge.com   Orders: orders@nbnplymbridge.com

Australia and New Zealand
UNIREPS, University of New South Wales
Sydney, NSW, 2052   Australia
Tel: 61 2 9664 0999   Fax: 61 2 9664 5420
email: info.press@unsw.edu.au

www.broadviewpress.com

This book is printed on 100% post-consumer recycled, ancient forest friendly paper.

Advisory editor for this volume: Professor Eugene Benson

Typesetting and assembly: True to Type Inc., Mississauga, Canada.

PRINTED IN CANADA

Contents

Acknowledgments

The late Bill French, legendary owner of the University Place Bookshop, Manhattan, New York, brought *Guanya Pau* to Singler's attention. The quotations from Episcopal missionaries appear courtesy of The Archives of the Episcopal Church USA in Austin, Texas. We are grateful to Jennifer Peters, archivist, and the staff for their assistance. We are also grateful to the archivists at Oberlin College and the West Virginia Collection at West Virginia University and to Margaret White at the Penick Archives in Winston-Salem, North Carolina.

We also wish to thank the following for their kind assistance: The Rev. Canon E. Bolling Robertson, head of the Cape Mount Mission from 1945 to 1971; Alan Schaplowsky at Columbia University Library; librarians at New York University, the University of Michigan, and the New York Public Library; Guinevere Roper and Todd Bolton at Harpers Ferry National Historical Park; Dr. Levi Zangai and Atim Eneida George for research at the Maryland State Archives; Dr. Jeanette Carter for research at the Library of Congress; Francis O'Neill and Donna Williams at the Maryland Historical Society; the Rev. Paul Coke, Dr. D. Elwood Dunn, the Rev. Emmanuel D. Hodges, the Rev. Dr. Gary W. Kriss, James B. Lumei, Dr. Jane Martin, Moses Nagbe, Dr. Mohamed Nyei, Marilyn Robertson, W. Feweh Sherman, William Siegmann, Dr. Linda Susman, Warren Susman, Dr. Luciano Varaschini, and E. Boakai Zoludua. We also wish to thank Carolyn, Michael, and Aneurin Griffiths for their help in preparing the manuscript.

We also wish to thank Oxford University Press for permission to reproduce a chart of Vai script characters and an example of Vai writing, both from John Victor Singler, "Scripts of West Africa," in *The World's Writing Systems*, ed. Peter T. Daniels and William Bright (New York, 1996) 593-98.

Introduction

1. The Text of *Guanya Pau*: The History of its Publication

The Historical Significance of *Guanya Pau*

What makes this small text so significant? After all, it is only 81 pages long (in this edition) and its author, Joseph Jeffrey Walters, with characteristic modesty, describes himself in the short introduction as merely "an undergraduate" who "cannot hope to be able to make a valuable contribution to Literature" (75). What is so important about this text is that it remains the earliest complete text we have of a fictional work in English by an African. Published in 1891, it predates J.E. Caseley Hayford's autobiographical and polemic novel *Ethiopia Unbound*, which was published in London in 1911 and which is cited in many places as the first long African fictional text in English. Thus, Singler's discovery of *Guanya Pau* in 1985 set back the date for the earliest complete, surviving African fictional text in English by twenty years.

In 2002 Stephanie Newell edited and published an even earlier, though incomplete, fictional text, recovered from the pages of contemporary Gold Coast newspapers, entitled *Marita, or The Folly of Love*.[1] This was published in serial form in the early Cape Coast newspaper *The Western Echo*, starting on January 20, 1886. Of course, in the nineteenth century Africans were writing extensively in English, appropriating and transforming the language to their own ends and purposes. They edited newspapers, published articles, wrote books, preached and published sermons, wrote reports and travel accounts, published occasional verse and wrote histories. Many poems, short stories, and even fragments of longer fiction such as the Newell text also appear in the newspapers of the period. But *Guanya Pau* is still the earliest African long fiction in English to have been published in book form and to have survived as a whole, making it of great historical importance.

---

1 Stephanie Newell, ed. *Marita, or the Folly of Love: A Novel by A. Native* (Boston: Brill Academic Publishers, 2002).

Singler became aware of the existence of *Guanya Pau* when William P. (Bill) French, owner of the University Place Bookshop in New York, showed him a catalogue reference to the book. Singler found a copy of the text on microfilm at the New York Public Library. Since then, a copy of the original edition has been found in the Special Collections section of Oberlin College, Ohio, where Walters studied and took his bachelor's degree in 1893, and a second copy in the University of Michigan library. These are the only copies we have found so far, though there may be others in the collections of the many US colleges and libraries whose catalogues we have not been able to search. The only subsequent republication we have been able to determine is in the periodical *The Liberia Recorder*, which issued the novel in serial form in Monrovia in late 1905 and early 1906. Only some of the issues have survived.[1]

Through corresponding with the librarians at Oberlin and at the Episcopal Church Archives in Austin, Texas, Singler discovered that Walters had attended the Episcopal Church's Cape Mount Mission school in Liberia and had, after graduating from Oberlin, been the superintendent of the mission. Singler had taught at the same school from 1971 to 1975. Singler published the first article about the text in an academic journal in *The Liberian Studies Journal* in 1990. He had previously published an article in *The Daily Observer*, a Liberian newspaper. Singler and Griffiths had begun work on a fully annotated edition and were negotiating a contract for that edition when Oyekan Owomoyela's edition was issued by the University of Nebraska Press in 1994. Owomoyela had contacted Singler in August, 1992, to request a copy of any work that he had published on Walters. However, he did not alert Singler to the fact that he planned to use that material to work on his own edition of *Guanya Pau*. The publication of Owomoyela's edition effectively closed the Singler/Griffiths project down for several years as it seemed to them that a second edition would be difficult to justify to a publisher so quickly after the first.

There are a number of serious limitations to the Owomoyela edition. It consists of a simple facsimile of the text, based on a photocopy of the original text obtained from Oberlin College. There are

---

1 We are grateful to Jane Martin for bringing the republication of *Guanya Pau* in the *Liberia Recorder* to our attention and making copies of the relevant issues available to us.

no detailed notes on the text, and no substantial archival searches appear to have been made in preparing this first modern edition of the text; the short (16pp) foreword draws heavily on the material in the 1990 Singler article. Given the importance of the text in the history of English writing in Africa, it seemed to Singler and Griffiths that, despite the existence of the Owomoyela edition, the text deserved a more fully annotated and researched publication.

They also felt that Owomoyela's characterization of the text as "[sharing] the prevailing Christian prejudices against the heathen" (xiv) was too simplistic. Recent theoretical accounts of mission discourses and cultural patronage argue for a more complex and ambivalent relationship between mission discourses and indigenous agency.[1] While Owomoyela's edition acknowledges this ambivalence, it does so by drawing heavily on Singler's earlier comments in the 1990 article. The present edition also tries to locate the degree to which Walters's text negotiates between the mission agenda and a complex of local and external agendas in late nineteenth-century Vai society. Its presentation of the Poro (men's) and Sande (women's) secret associations is a case in point, which will be dealt with in detail later in this introduction.

The First Publisher of Guanya Pau

Despite Walters's religious convictions, and his long association with the Episcopal Church, Guanya Pau was published in 1891 by a secular publisher, Lauer & Mattill of Cleveland, Ohio. We have not been able to find the records of the publisher, if they have survived at all. But from the surviving contemporary books which they published, held at the Cleveland Public Library and elsewhere, it is clear that they specialized in religious texts, primarily directed towards the strong German Lutheran community in Cleveland and its vicinity, and in genealogical and family histories of the same community.[2]

---

1 See in particular Gauri Viswanathan, *Outside the Fold: Conversion, Modernity and Belief* (Princeton: Princeton UP, 1998).

2 The only full-length study of the Cleveland publishing trade in the period does not contain a reference to Lauer & Mattill. See Russell Duino, *The Cleveland Book Trade, 1818-1912: Leading Firms and Outstanding Men* (University of Pittsburgh PhD dissertation, 1981). We also found no records of the company in the Cleveland Public Library. However, texts published by them which have survived bear out our characterization of their publishing profile.

Guanya Pau's Intended Audience

Who did Walters envisage as his readership? In his preface Walters beseeches his "lady readers" to support the project of educating African women. He clearly intends the book mainly for an audience of women, and American churchwomen especially. Walters probably had in mind a readership from the Oberlin community. Oberlin, as the first co-educational college in the United States, had an ongoing commitment to the education of women; moreover, it was also a place known for its commitment to the education of African Americans. In addition Oberlin and its community strongly supported foreign missions. For all these reasons it was an ideal location for Walters's developing views on African women and their role, and provided a natural audience for *Guanya Pau*.

The second likely audience would have been Episcopal Church women. In the period after the American Civil War

> the Women's Auxiliary became the primary avenue of support for the Board of Missions. As the first church-sponsored organization for all Episcopal women, the Auxiliary raised money and recruited workers for the mission field. Its members wrote and published mission education programs and trained the teachers who spread this knowledge throughout the church. For many laywomen, work in the Auxiliary was their first step into a world outside the home.[1]

Julia Emery, the woman who led the Women's Auxiliary, corresponded regularly with the women missionaries at the Cape Mount Mission, Walters's alma mater. The fact that the book is aimed at women is also reflected in the selection of the frontispiece. The portrait is identified as Queen Ranavalona of Madagascar. It symbolizes the central role of women and womanly concerns in the text that follows.[2]

---

1 Mary Sudman Donovan, *Women's Ministries in the Episcopal Church, 1850-1920* (Columbia University PhD dissertation, 1985) 115.
2 Ranavalona played a historic role in restoring Christianity to Madagascar and in the subsequent struggle to keep her country both independent and Protestant in the face of French colonial assault. Given the popularity of the Queen in American Protestant missionary circles at the time, her portrayal as the frontispiece for *Guanya Pau* poses the interesting question

The Relative Lack of Notice the Text Received When Published

In an 1893 article/letter in the *Oberlin News* (See Appendix E6), Walters states that "The people for whom I am soliciting are the Veys, a tribe of Africans I introduced to my Oberlin friends in my little book 'Guanya Pau'." There is little evidence that the book sold many copies to anyone. No notices of the publication of *Guanya Pau* have come to light in the press of the time. Searches in Episcopalian publications, particularly *The Churchman* and *The Southern Churchman* (a journal in which Walters's sponsor Bishop Penick published extensively in the 1880s), failed to discover any mention of the text. Searches in relevant interdenominational and Congregationalist newspapers have also failed to discover any contemporary notices of it. Freewill Baptist publications seem less likely sources since, although this was the orientation of Storer College, where Walters first studied on arriving in the US, he had no ongoing connection with that denomination. Further searches may uncover such a notice, but the evidence would seem to suggest that the publication did not get much publicity or reach a wide audience. The *Oberlin Alumni Catalogue* publication contains a note indicating that Walters wrote the text "to help defray his college expenses."[1] We know from the Oberlin archival records that Walters worked to pay for his education. The records indicate that scholarship students were routinely

---

of whether Walters himself or the publisher selected the image. While there is no means of establishing this conclusively, the choice of Queen Ranavalona is so apposite to the book's general message that it is likely Walters either chose it or approved the choice. Here was a woman at the head of an "African" nation, which, by wedding its past with a refinement provided by Protestant Christian ideals of education, hard work, and justice across the races and sexes, had achieved a modernized but still essentially African-controlled society. Walters's own goals, as expressed in his life and in *Guanya Pau*, are not dissimilar, and his stated intention in the Preface is clearly congruent with this, when he beseeches "his lady readers" to support the project of educating African women and giving them a role in their country's future. As he says, "I feel assured it will not fail to rouse the sympathy of those who read it, the women especially, in behalf of their unfortunate sisters in that dark land" (75).

1   *Oberlin Alumni Catalogue* (Oberlin: Oberlin College, 1936). Despite the publication's late date, this information probably reflects an earlier entry, since alumni catalogues frequently reproduce earlier material, and it would not be consistent with their practice to invent something as specific as this.

employed as yard boys or as general laborers. It is possible that Walters's health had already begun to deteriorate in a way that would have interfered with his ability to do this kind of work and may have encouraged him to seek another source of income through the publication of this book. But whatever pecuniary motive he may have had, he was also clearly a passionate believer in the ideas the book espouses. George Hinman, an Oberlin classmate, notes in his obituary that Walters was "always ready to speak for what he considered the truth, and his burning eloquence frequently stirred the souls of his hearers, whether in the society hall or the larger public assembly."[1] Walters was capable of passionate and successful promotion of the causes in which he believed before audiences, but it seems that he was far less willing and able to promote himself and his published work. Hinman describes Walters's character and behavior in the following way:

> Mr. Walter's (sic) life was one of genuine helpfulness to those whose hearts were open to read its lessons. He never put himself forward. He was a most perfect gentleman, refined, courteous, modest and retiring in the presence of those whose prejudices forbade an intimate acquaintance. (288)

Refined, courteous, modest, and retiring are not the attributes of the successful promoter.

The Oberlin archives contain only two references to *Guanya Pau* from Walters's lifetime, one in a history of the college activities in the College yearbook in his final year, and the other in the letter cited earlier that appeared in the *Oberlin News* in November, 1893.[2] Just as we have been unable to locate any references to *Guanya Pau* in religious publications, so we have found no notices in the Oberlin campus paper or town newspaper of the period. This is striking in that books by Oberlin authors were routinely reviewed in these publica-

---

1 George Hinman, "In Memoriam," *Oberlin Review* (6 February 1895): 288. See Appendix F2.
2 Apart from the mention of *Guanya Pau* in the list of Walters's achievements in the 1894 edition of *Hi-o-hi*, the Oberlin yearbook, this is the only evidence that Walters's short fiction was known at Oberlin until Bishop Penick, responding to a request for information from the College after Walters's death, mentions that Walters had been the author of "various articles and a little work Guanya Pau" (Oberlin, Charles C. Penick, 28 January 1895, to Azariah Root).

tions and given prominence.[1] Searches in the Cleveland press for the period have also so far failed to turn up notices. All in all, it is a meager record for such an important event as the first published fiction in English in book form by an African.

2. Patronage and Agency in Nineteenth-Century Mission Texts

Guanya Pau and Mission Texts by Nineteenth-Century Christian Converts

The role of missions in the production of texts in Africa has been crucial. In a recent memorable phrase, the eminent historian of South African missions Norman Etherington has referred to "The Missionary Writing Machine."[2] There is little doubt that missions and missionaries from Robert Moffatt, David Livingstone, and Mary Slessor to a myriad later, if not lesser, men and women produced an inordinate amount of written and printed material. Missionaries, of course, introduced printing to Africa as well as writing down many African languages for the first time. They did both primarily in order to evangelize and convert Africans. As a result the dominant concern of Protestant missions especially was to ensure that the Bible was available for their converts and potential converts.

Conversion, Culture, and Missions

It is difficult to decide how much the mission "patron" exercised direct control over the texts published by converts. In some cases the control was almost total, to the extent that the "subject" had no agency, and was simply the pretext for the authentication of the mission amanuensis's own ideas and attitudes. But at their best these mission texts gave Africans the chance, often for the first time, to speak and let their own voices be heard by those who had stereotyped them and their cultures as savage and heathen. Despite the possibility of such appropriation, the majority of these texts re-inforced denigratory stereotypes of Africans and their societies. These negative attitudes continue to be a feature

1 For example, the *Oberlin Weekly News* of April 16, 1891, has a review of "An Interesting Book by an Oberlin Alumnus." This is an account by F.A. Hazeltine of his travels entitled *A Year of South American Travel: Letters from the Plate Countries and Brazil* (Philadelphia: J.P. Lippincott, 1891).

2 Norman Etherington, "The Missionary Writing Machine in Kwa-Zulu-Natal," *Mixed Messages: Missions, Textuality and Culture*, ed. Gareth Griffiths and Jamie S. Scott (New York: Palgrave, forthcoming).

of mission discourse well into the twentieth century. In fact, the descriptions of a savage, barbarous, "dark," and benighted Africa conditioned the ways of speaking and writing of most Africans who used mission forms and audiences to get their message over to Americans in the late nineteenth century. Walters's text is not immune from this. The very idea of conversion and of the discourse of modernity that it involved made this inevitable. In Liberia many missionaries—and African-American Settlers too—used highly pejorative terms to describe Africa. So, despite its occasional complicities, it is against this uncritical acceptance of such views that Walters's more complex text needs to be judged, and against these it comes off well as an example of a text that escapes from the more stifling forms of control and achieves a certain independence and self-assurance as it embraces a positive vision of many aspects of African culture.

Thus, Walters's dissenting voice against the Vai treatment of women is complemented by his dissent from the prevalent mission tendency to present Africa and Africans as wholly "benighted," the term used by the first Liberian Settler bishop of the Episcopal Church, Samuel Ferguson, in a letter to Walters in 1893.[1] As Singler's article showed in 1990, "there is ample evidence that Walters was very much his own person, appalled by the abuse of women in Vai society yet fiercely proud of his Vai heritage, thoroughly Christian (Christianized) yet able to laugh at the missionaries' imperfect adaptation to Africa"[2] It is this which makes it necessary to see Walters as someone who was both a convinced Christian convert and, at the same time, a passionate advocate of African values. Converts were not people who simply "left" one culture to enter another.[3] In becoming a Christian, Walters did not cease to be Vai. For Walters, Christianity and Christian values were tools to alter Vai culture for the better, not an excuse to reject his culture entirely in favor of a superior European culture. Judged against the period and the texts that surround his, we can now form a more just and balanced view of his work. Although he rejected many contemporary African practices, notably polygamy, and was eager to embrace many aspects of Euro-

---

1 Archives of the Episcopal Church [AEC], RG 72 45, Samuel Ferguson, April 20, 1893, to Walters.
2 John Victor Singler, "The Day Will Come: J.J. Walters and *Guanya Pau.*" *Liberian Studies Journal* 15.2 (1990): 125–34.
3 See Gauri Viswanathan, *Outside the Fold: Conversion, Modernity, Belief* (Princeton, Princeton UP, 1998) for a useful discussion of the complex condition of the converted "native."

pean culture, he was also a passionate believer in Africa and its future and a strong advocate for Vai culture in its broader aspects.[1] He champions the Vai past and asserts his belief in the potential of his people for the future. Despite his conversion, Walters was never less than "his own man" and remained, as the text clearly shows, an advocate for Africa and Africans within a model of their Christian "perfectibility" throughout his brief and tragic life.

The Extent and Nature of the Mission Control of *Guanya Pau*

One of the clearest examples of Walters's independence comes at the end of Chapter XV of *Guanya Pau* when he relates the story of the song sung by the Vai canoeists when he accompanied a missionary to a village to preach. He notes that the songs of the Vai can be made to "suit the occasion" and in illustration of this recounts how the paddlers sang the following rather pointed refrain:

> Oh God man, your face is white, your hair is straight, you can read and write and speak God palava. My face is black, my hair is curly. I can neither read books nor write letters nor speak God palava. But by the devil, if the canoe upsets I know who would get first to land. Oh white man, you better learn to swim, you had better learn to swim. (135)

This is passed over without comment by Walters, but his silence resonates.[2]

---

1   The form of polygamy practiced by the Vai and in West Africa generally is, more precisely, *polygyny*. However, we follow popular usage—and Walters—in using the term *polygamy* to refer to the practice.

2   What may well be the missionary's telling of the same story is to be found in a letter that the Rev. John McNabb sent back to church officials in New York soon after his arrival at the Cape Mount Mission in December, 1878. "Such are the people whom[,] accompanied by one of the boys from our mission who served as interpreter, I visited this afternoon and passing through another heathen Vey town, we arrived at a friends by the lakes side who kindly furnished us with two men and a canoe in which [we] sailed to our destination. As in a lively manner these man paddled us over the surface of the "still waters." 'Twas strange & pleasant to listen at one of them compose an impromptu song about myself. It ran somewhat thus, I am carrying a white man over to Krew Town, chorus Krew Town thrice repeated" (AEC, RG 72 54, John McNabb, c. Dec., 1879, to Kimber).

Mission discourses and mission literary forms such as the "release narrative" have a distinct and strong influence on this short novel.[1] Despite these influences from such standard mission forms on the text's construction, its sentiments contrast strongly with the uniform presentation of African society as barbarous in most mission discourse in the period. In fact *Guanya Pau* incorporates many positive signifiers of Africa, not least being a number of very positive descriptions of the landscape that stress its luxuriant and beautiful features.

The traveler, away out in the forest, if his provision gives out, need not famish. Almost at any time of the year the woods have a liberal supply of fruits and nuts—walnuts, colanuts, hickory-nuts, troves, several kinds of plums, wild plantain, figs, monkey-apple and fruit, persimmon, lady-finger, alligator-pear and pepper, etc., etc.; if no brook is near, from which to quench his thirst, a large vine can frequently be found that has in its hollow abundant supply of cool, sweet water. (111)

While it is necessary to assert the positive elements of *Guanya Pau*, it is equally important not to overstate the claim for the independence of Walters's text. Its limitations are those of its time. So, for example, the development of Africa that he envisages depends upon the introduction of modern reforms based on European practices.

The Africans have not yet awakened to a full consciousness of their worth. It needs only the application of the scientific principles to the illimitable resources of that wonderful land which are lying dormant, to make her rival the most affluent of her sister continents. (111)

But we might notice that even here the verb he employs is "rival" not "serve."

Walters perceives changing the attitude of the Vai—both men and women—as to the role of women in society as central in this devel-

---

1 For a fuller account of "release narratives," see Gareth Griffiths, *African Literatures in English: East and West* (London: Longman, 2000) 50-70, and Gareth Griffiths, "Appropriation, Patronage and Control: The Case of the Missionary Text" in *Colonies, Missions, Cultures in the English-Speaking World: General and Comparative Studies*, ed. Gerhard Stilz (Tübingen: Stauffenberg Verlag, 2001) 13-23. The latter article, though published later, was the earlier account of this important and widespread missionary form.

opment, and so it is to the reform of women's treatment that he directs his polemic tale, so that the potential of Africa can be realized.

We need then, finally, to try to be clear as to the extent to which it remains a text constructed within mission forms and under mission control and the extent to which it succeeds in escaping these controls. First, although the society from which Guanya Pau flees is presented as rich and diverse, marred principally by a specific failing—its treatment of women, rather than a general benightedness and barbarity—it remains in need of reform. But, despite this, we should note that the support for the reform of women's position is voiced by figures that the narrative places within African society itself. Neither Guanya Pau nor her lover Momo, both of whom object to polygamy, do so in the story because of Christian influences. So they are not presented as the product of Christianization or of missionary influence. In fact, Guanya does not find out that Momo has gone to the Christian town until she reaches Tosau Island (Chapter XX), where a woman tells her of the existence of the Liberian settlement and that Momo has gone there. One final point of distinction needs to be made. Guanya Pau never encounters a Christian or a Christian church in reality. But she does have two dreams. In the first she falls asleep and is threatened by the spirits of the river whose waters she polluted earlier in the day. She wakes from this nightmare and falls asleep again. This time she finds herself in a town where the population is happy and well-dressed, where families are clearly monogamous ("a man and woman walking arm in arm, children passing in high spirits" 144) and where "everything seems to be in gala day." Here she sees a Christian service taking place, though she does not know what it is. At its climax she realizes that one of the men at the service is Momo, and he recognizes her and embraces her. The moment is both the culmination of the romantic search, and the only moment when Guanya engages directly with the Christian world, into whose embrace she is, metaphorically, accepted in the dream—"'Guanya Pau,' he cries, and folds her in his arms. Amid sobs and tears the fainting girl lisps, 'Momo,' and awakes" (146).

Guanya and Momo's reformist impulse is presented as self-generated from within the internal possibility of the reform of the values and practices of Vai society itself. The text does not lay any stress on the missionary presence as offering anything but a distant and largely unknown example of an alternative social structure, and when Guanya Pau runs away it is not in order to reach this alternative world. Most significantly, the world of the Christian is never reached, except in an obliquely symbolic way. At the end of the narrative,

Guanya and her companion are detected and placed in a canoe to be taken back to Kai Kundu, the man whom she refuses to marry. To escape they cast themselves into the lake and drown. "After a minute Guanya Pau came to the surface and said pathetically: 'This is preferable to being Kai Kundu's headwife.' Then she sank to rise again at the last day, when the seas and lakes and rivers shall give up their dead" (153). This ending clearly invokes the closure of the classic "release" narrative where baptism is also a form of narrative "death." But here no mission has been reached, and the "baptism" is invoked only symbolically in the mind of the Christian, American audience. There is a kind of sleight of hand here, which is an important feature of the text's presentation of the Christian world to which Walters had given his public allegiance. Christianity is presented throughout in similarly oblique ways. For example, early in the text Guanya and Jassah are praying to the Gregrees (or spirits) to help them. They come out into the open air having "disrobed themselves of those [beads] which would give a clue to their identity" and, "after invoking the Gregrees to protect them from harm ... with uplifted hands, looked up into the sky and made a deep, prolonged sigh" (93). Walters then enters the narrative as direct commentator and speculates as to whether or not it was "our God they thus invoked in the silent recesses of their souls." There is a long speculation on this possibility, ending with the query as to whether or not their eyes are uplifted "to the hills from whence cometh our help." The frequent mention of God introduces Him into this scene and keeps him before the mind of the Christian, American reader. The denial that follows does not entirely efface the impression of God's presence. Walters's answer, "I trow not" (93), allows him to engage in an even longer lament for the fact that many parts of Africa have never been "told the old, old story of Jesus and His Love" (93). This implies that it would have been better had the girls been converted and thereby able to appeal to the Christian God. But that is not the case. Walters could, of course, have chosen to make it so, had he cast his narrative differently. The simple fact is that he chooses to make his heroines Borneys (neophytes of the Sande) and they end the novel as such, not as converts. That narrative fact, and the choice of its Christian convert author in making it, clearly distinguish the novel from those more overtly controlled mission release narratives in which narrative closure is achieved by conversion, and whose concern is with the arrival at a Christian finale, not at all with the African world journeyed through. Walters, like other mission authors, however, does show much wrong with African societies. But there is one significant difference. However flawed Walters finds Africa on specific matters such as the treatment of women and however much in need of enlightenment and reform as a result, its role is to be reformed and preserved not merely denied and discarded.

3. The Dominant Themes of *Guanya Pau*

Women, Marriage, and Vai Society

The Status of Women: Polygamy in Guanya Pau

The condition of Vai women is Walters's main theme in this short polemic fiction. *Guanya Pau* strikes a very modern tone, especially when the heroine declares that "the day will come" when Vai women will refuse to accept their inferior status. Despite this, Walters's overall attitude to women is the product of the feminist discourse of the high Victorian period, and of Walters's mentors at Oberlin, who emphasized the need to educate women for their special roles. The chapter on the education of women from the Victorian text *Friends in Council,* from which Walters took his prefatory quotation, shows the kind of limitations that the age placed on the idea of women's "liberation" and education.[1] For Walters women "constitute the prop and stay of the national fabric"(75). But they do so for the reason Victorian accounts generally praise women. Women are the moral arbiters of a nation's fate or, as Walters puts it, "no country can become great until it has pure, true, virtuous women" (75). In Victorian moral discourse women exercise power primarily in their marital roles as wives and mothers, restricted by this to the private sphere. What may account for our sense of the modern tone of *Guanya Pau* is that Walters's Africanness makes the domestic politics of the role of women part of a broader politics of African recognition.

Like his mission patrons, Walters is adamantly and unambiguously opposed to polygamy, as the text of *Guanya Pau* shows. His pronouncement that "*Polygamy must be wiped out of the land*" leaves us in no doubt of this (75). But Walters never simply echoes the ideas of his mission patrons. He has his own set of concerns, and these are differently nuanced. Although he shared a general objection to polygamy with his American mission colleagues, he put his own very distinctive emphasis on these concerns in *Guanya Pau.* The American

---

1   See Appendix A, "The Education of Women," from *Friends in Council.*

missionaries seem mostly concerned with adult polygamists, as we will see below, but Walters's text does not emphasize this concern. It is the practice of the forced betrothal of "girls when three and four years old" (75) that Walters specifically targets.

The Polygamy Debate in African Christian Missions and in *Guanya Pau*

It is useful to consider the wider contact of mission attitudes to polygamy to contextualize Walters's response further. For European and American missions, there were a number of African cultural and social practices that were seen as synonymous with "paganism" and "savagery." These included ritual human sacrifice, polygamy, and, after they had given up the practice themselves, slavery and slave owning. By the late nineteenth century the focus was strongly on the latter two: polygamy and slave ownership. While it might be thought that the mission authorities would have been more concerned to eliminate slave owning than polygamy, the attention of missionaries to Africa in the nineteenth century centered on polygamy.

Episcopal missions in Liberia regarded polygamy as a barrier to a full Christian conversion, hence to baptism. But there were practical difficulties in enforcing this attitude. For example, in February 1883 the Rev. William Fair presents a carefully argued case for admitting polygamous African converts to baptism. He describes polygamy as practiced among the Grebo in the southeastern part of Liberia. Fair notes that current mission policy has a strong negative effect on Africans:

> Protestant and Roman missions generally have demanded that all wives but one shall be put away. What does compliance with such a demand involve? The breaking up of home, the separating in many cases of a father from his children or a mother from her offspring, who even to a heathen mother are dearer than life. The demand is as unreasonable to them as it would be for a Minister in a Christian land to require that, in order to be admitted to Baptism, a man must get rid of his one and only wife. "[1]

---

1 William Allan Fair, "Polygamy in West Africa; and How to Abolish It." *The Spirit of Missions* 48 (1883): 95.

At the Cape Mount Mission the Rev. John McNabb seems to share concerns for the Vai similar to those Fair had expressed from his experience with the Grebo at the Cavalla Mission.[1] In fact, a comparison of his comments with those of Fair and McNabb might even suggest that Walters took a stronger line against polygamy than the Episcopal missionaries who trained him.[2] If so, why? Walters's text, as we have argued above, was clearly aimed at the Christian women's audience in America. For American churchwomen, the issue of polygamy would have been much more clear-cut than for missionaries in the field like Fair and McNabb, struggling with the need to raise conversion rates. Also, while Fair and McNabb both concentrate on the conversion of men in their accounts, Walters's focus in *Guanya Pau* is entirely on women. The issue of "forced marriage" is at the heart of Walters's concern in *Guanya Pau*. For Walters the concern is not whether the ban on polygamy will make mission work more successful but the effect of polygamous marriage on the social condition of African women. Although *Guanya Pau* is opposed to polygamy, in discussing that institution it stresses above all the degree to which women are subject to a process by which they are married against their will to men to whom they have no personal attachment. Such a concern would clearly resonate with the audience of American women for whom the book was intended. Yet it is clear that Walters is not just pandering to this audience and that he passionately shared their views on this subject.

Child Betrothal, Women's Agency, and Vai Marriage Practices in
Guanya Pau

The departure of Vai marriage practices from European-American Christian norms entailed more than the simple fact that a man could have more than one wife at the same time. Possibly the most salient

---

1   The Episcopal Church sent its first missionaries to West Africa in 1836 to work among the Grebo in Cavalla at Cape Palmas 300 miles down the coast from Cape Mount. When Episcopal missionaries went to Cape Mount in 1878, they concentrated on building a school. Consequently, they encountered far fewer of the issues that polygamy raised for adult conversion. Moreover, because the Grebo do not practice child betrothal, nothing in the Episcopal Church's initial African encounter prepared its missionaries for the custom of child betrothal as practiced by the Vai.
2   Walters's treatment of polygamy does include some positive elements. Kai Popo, Guanya's father, for example, exemplifies a "good" polygamist.

difference, certainly the one against which Walters argued with the greatest vehemence, was child betrothal, the practice by which pre-adolescent girls, even toddlers, could be betrothed by their parents.[1] Child betrothal was such common practice among the Vai that Ellis, writing in 1914, noted, "Very few girls in families of standing are not engaged long before they enter the 'Greegree Bush.'" The "Greegree Bush," or Sande school, was the girls' school that every Vai girl entered, usually when she was between six and thirteen in age. See "Bush schools and traditional education" below.[2]

When it came to marriage itself, a Vai girl, once she was a Sande initiate, could be married as young as thirteen years of age. Guanya Pau herself was fifteen. Thus, in our discussion of Vai marriage, we refer to the bride as a *girl* rather than a *woman*.

Traditional Vai marriage is an alliance between families, and the arrangement is between a man and the girl's parents, not between a man and his future wife. The economic aspect of marriage in Vai society is central, both when child betrothal is involved and when it is not. The transaction was mutually beneficial to the man and to the bride's family. The latter received the money of the dowry.[3] Their son-in-law received a woman with whom he might have children and, simultaneously, a worker. Further, "the more wealth a man acquires, the more wives he will have."[4] The wealthiest of Vai men would have many wives, twenty or thirty or more.

In the case of child betrothals, the dowry was often paid on a lengthy "installment plan," with a man providing goods and possibly some money over the years and—in the case of a less well-to-do man—living with the parents and working on their farm for them.

---

1   In theory it was possible for a man to "engage" a pregnant woman's unborn child. If the woman gave birth to a girl, then the infant was immediately betrothed.

2   George W. Ellis, *Negro Culture in West Africa* (New York: The Neale Publishing Company, 1914) 57. While it is possible that Ellis is overstating the frequency of child betrothal, child betrothal was clearly common practice among the Vai.

3   Walters reports that the man who wished to marry Guanya Pau "was comparatively wealthy, according to their standard of wealth, and was therefore able to pay a handsome dowry for her of about $300 in wood and ivory. The average dowry is between fifty and one hundred dollars" (85-86). On the basis of other accounts, it is clear that these figures are significantly inflated (Svend E. Holsoe, *The Cassava-Leaf People*, 12).

4   Svend E. Holsoe, *The Cassava-Leaf People*, 13.

In sum, marriage, particularly marriage linked to child betrothal, involved both economic advantage and the building of alliances. It was a social not an individual matter.

Still, it was not the case that girls were without any voice whatsoever. When child betrothal had not occurred, a girl would ordinarily have the right to accept or reject a suitor. There was often parental pressure and even intervention, but the girl had a voice. Chapter VI of *Guanya Pau* presents such an instance: the acceptance or rejection of Prince Musah is left up to the young girl whom he wishes to marry, but her guardian frames the choice in a way that will yield the outcome he seeks.

The existence of the possibility of a choice for some created a situation in which others—themselves deprived of choice by, for example, their having been betrothed when very young—might object to the man to whom they were given. Thus, opposition like Guanya Pau's to her prospective marriage to Kai Kundu was, in type if not intensity, a byproduct of the institution of marriage among the Vai. (When a girl was married against her will and resisted, as occurs in Chapter VI, the leaders of the Sande would put pressure upon her to accept her situation, even meting out punishment if she persisted in defying her husband.) However, if Guanya's unhappiness with—and resistance to—the man selected for her is recognizable in the context of the Vai society of her day, her opposition to polygamy is not. Marriage *was* polygamy. There were men who practiced monogamy in Guanya's day, but they did so out of poverty, not from a commitment to a moral ideal.

Vai society is strongly hierarchical. As a consequence, any assessment of status within a polygamous household must reckon not only with the man but also his head wife. In describing a Vai man's wives, Holsoe states:

> The first wife he marries will remain his head wife during his and her lifetime. It is she who is responsible for any subsequent wives he marries, and it is with her that he consults concerning any matters involving the household. Often a woman will encourage her husband to take extra wives thereby lessening her work load and also providing herself with company while carrying out chores.[1]

---

1   Svend E. Holsoe, *The Cassava-Leaf People*, 13.

Walters's presentation of head-wife status is unrealistic, little more than a fillip in marriage negotiations; in three of the five situations in *Guanya Pau* in which head-wife status comes up, it is something being given to a pretty young Borney, the nineteenth-century Vai version of a "trophy wife." In Walters's presentation of polygamous marriage, he presents the arrangement as a negative one for all the women involved. He minimizes the important distinction between a head wife and other wives. In suggesting that the only reason why a woman would perpetuate the system of polygamy is because of ignorance (87), Walters obscures the fact that, for head wives at least, a polygamous marriage might be a means for achieving considerable status and power.

A further point about Vai marriage is that society required that a girl be a virgin at the time of the marriage. As Walters states:

> ... after you have gotten the woman, if you find that she is not a whole hundred per cent., like any other transaction, she can be restored and the money refunded. The custom in some sections is that when a man takes unto himself a wife, a report of several guns testifies that he is pleased with her, and no salute signifies displeasure, and to-morrow morning she may be seen with her little bundle making her way back to her mother's house, to await another chance for disposal. (86)

Perhaps not surprisingly, while Walters objects to polygamy, child betrothal, and the dowry system—all of which he sees as demeaning to women—he is not at all critical of the Vai emphasis on a bride's virginity. With regards to Borneys, he comments:

> As a rule these girls are respected and cases of unchastity are comparatively few.
> I believe I can truly say that cases of mortal turpitude are more frequent in America than it is among these heathen people. (89)

Here, Vai emphasis on female virginity at the time of marriage practice coincides with Victorian Christian ideals. (And, as in Victorian societies generally, there is no equivalent pressure on men to remain chaste before marriage.)

Slavery, Vai Society and *Guanya Pau*

The International Slave Trade and the Vai

The presence of European traders directly affected the political balance of the Vai region. The Portuguese had begun trading along the Vai coast in the late fifteenth century, seeking gold, ivory, and malaguetta pepper in return for salt and tin. In the sixteenth and seventeenth centuries, English, French, Dutch, Danish, and Swedish traders all engaged in commerce with the Vai, with the Dutch establishing a factory at Cape Mount early in the seventeenth century.[1]

Late in the seventeenth century, the focus of trade shifted to slaves. Vai participation in the international slave trade started slowly, but— once begun—the slave trade quickly became the most important component of trade with Europeans, and it remained so throughout the first half of the nineteenth century. Holsoe states, "The main source of slaves appeared not to have been the immediate people along the coast because only occasionally would an individual be sold into slavery and then only as a commutation of a death penalty for some grievous offense. Instead, most of the slaves were brought from the interior...."[2]

With the British abolition of the trans-Atlantic slave trade in 1807, the dynamics of the trade in Vai society changed.

> With the increased danger involved in shipping slaves, the price per slave rose sharply, and it became imperative that waiting slave vessels be loaded with great speed.... The Vai adjusted their economic priorities and slaving system to meet the new circumstances. What had been a casual system, in which slaves were only one among many products exported, now shifted to a system focusing on the collection of slaves.[3]

The primary port for slave trading within the Vai region shifted from Cape Mount to Gallinas at the northern edge of the Vai coast, particularly when Spanish and Brazilian traders settled there in the

---

1 Svend E. Holsoe, *The Cassava-Leaf People*, 59, 98.
2 Svend E. Holsoe, *The Cassava-Leaf People*, 106.
3 Svend E. Holsoe, "Slavery and Economic Response among the Vai (Liberia and Sierra Leone)," *Slavery in Africa: Historical and Anthropological Perspectives*, ed. Suzanne Miers and Igor Kopytoff (Madison, U of Wisconsin P, 1977) 293.

1820s. (The slaves who successfully rebelled aboard the *Amistad* had been shipped in 1838 from Gallinas.)

While almost all the slaves exported from Vai ports came from regions far into the interior, the Vai area itself was subject to a chronic political instability that the international slave trade only intensified. Local chiefs waged war, in part to gain or retain access to the slave routes and ports, and European slavers contributed arms to the fray.

Domestic Slavery Among the Vai

Any discussion of the Cape Mount region in Walters's day that considers only the Vai and their Gola and Mende neighbors leaves out a major part of the population, quite possibly a majority, namely the domestic slaves held by the Vai. Whether the institution of domestic slavery among the Vai evolved from the caste structure of society in the Mali Empire or instead arose only after the international slave trade came to the Vai region, domestic slavery was central to Vai economy and society. Holsoe comments that "the Vai, like many other societies in this region, defined wealth not in terms of material goods or land but rather by the number of individuals whose services they could control."[1] This characterization held throughout the nineteenth century and into the twentieth, with slavery among the Vai not suppressed by the Liberian government until the 1930s. There were no censuses in Liberia during this period, but a census of Sierra Leone in the 1920s showed that in the Vai chiefdoms of the two districts in Sierra Leone that bordered on the Cape Mount region the percentage of the total population that was enslaved ranged from 50% to 60%.[2]

The Vai word for someone who is not free is *jɔŋ* (pl. *jɔnnu*); this designation encompasses "indentured laborers, pawns, and domestic slaves."[3] The status of indentured laborers and pawns was distinctly different from that of domestic slaves. Being an indentured laborer or

1 Svend E. Holsoe, "Slavery and Economic Response among the Vai," 287. "[T]he number of individuals they could control" includes wives as well as slaves. Holsoe continues: "Thus, the Vai were concerned with acquiring large numbers of wives as one means of increasing the number of dependents."

2 John Grace, *Domestic Slavery in West Africa, with Particular Reference to the Sierra Leone Protectorate* (London: Frederick Muller, 1975) 172.

3 Svend E. Holsoe, "Slavery and Economic Response among the Vai," 289.

a pawn was, in theory at least, a temporary condition. An indentured laborer—a male—was held until such time as he could work off a debt that he had incurred. Similarly, a pawn was a relative of a debtor and was held in servitude until the debt was repaid.

Domestic slaves, on the other hand, were in permanent servitude. Their enslavement came about because they had been captured in war, because they had committed a grievous crime, because they were born to an enslaved woman, or because they had been purchased from neighboring peoples. (Holsoe notes that freeborn Vai captured in war were not enslaved; they were either ransomed or killed.)

> Although domestic slaves formed a separate social category, their treatment varied depending upon the character and social position of their master, the nature of their work, and the time period in Vai history.... Some Vai felt complete contempt for slaves and treated them accordingly. They thought of them as unclean and had no more contact with them than was necessary. Harshness sometimes occurred on the institutional level: slaves were often buried alive at the funeral of an important master, and slave babies were sacrificed in ceremonies when crocodiles, who were believed to be the embodiments of ancestors, were honored.[1]

The Treatment of Slavery in *Guanya Pau*

There can be no doubt that, if asked, Walters would have declared himself deeply opposed to slavery. Vai involvement in the international slave trade had continued up to 1850, and domestic slavery was a central feature of Vai life throughout Walters's lifetime. In *Guanya Pau* Walters uses the Vai word for "slaves," *jonkais*, (literally "slaveman" plus the English plural), but he translates it as "servants" (83).

---

1   Svend E. Holsoe, "Slavery and Economic Response among the Vai," 290–91. The reference to the sacrifice to a crocodile comes originally from Thomas E. Besolow, *From the Darkness of Africa to the Light of America* (Boston: Frank Wood, 1891) 33. See Appendix C. Walters also mentions the sacrifice of infants to a crocodile. As observed in a note for p. 139 of *Guanya Pau*, however, Walters presents the sacrifice as a voluntary act by free women, not—as all other observers have it—the forced sacrifice of slaves' children. Walters's evident misattribution may be motivated by a desire to mention the sacrifice as an example of heathen practice while at the same time avoiding mention of Vai slavery, as he does throughout the text.

He only uses the word five times in the course of *Guanya Pau*, and only one of these acknowledges that the Vai held slaves. In Chapter XX Guanya tells Jassah that she has learned from the sympathetic woman at Tosau Island that, in the Christian city down the Beach, "even if a slave goes to them, his master dare not go and ask for him" (150). Thus, the theme of slavery is noticeably absent from the pages of *Guanya Pau*.

On the other hand, *Guanya Pau* does engage with the issue of slavery metaphorically to represent the plight of women. On two occasions Walters compares the plight of freeborn Vai women to that of slaves (pp. 87 and 105). In making this comparison between slaves and freeborn wives, Walters is not alone. John Grace, describing domestic slavery in Sierra Leone at the end of the nineteenth century (and focusing on the Temne and Mende), writes:

> Slaves had to perform the heavy, the unskilled and the unpleasant work in the community; even though freemen sometimes also had to share in this work the heaviest burden fell on the slaves.
>
> In some cases, particularly among the Mende, slaves shared this burden with wives who were little better than slaves. Captain Carr [a colonial official] thought that ... a wife was really worse off than a slave.[1]

Holsoe details the differences between wives and slaves with regard to inheritance among the Vai of Tewoh, the area that provides the setting for much of *Guanya Pau*. A man's slaves—as part of his personal property—would go to his younger brothers and sons.

> ... [A] man's wives can also be inherited, should they themselves agree; for at the husband's death a woman has a choice. She can either agree to accept her new husband or return to her own family. But should she do the latter, she will have to leave her children behind and her own family will be responsible for returning her dowry to her husband's family.[2]

---

1 John Grace, *Domestic Slavery in West Africa*, 169. Captain Carr lived in Bandajuma District, further into the interior than the Vai region. His comments are contained in the Chalmers Report, an 1899 compendium on slavery in Sierra Leone that is cited by Grace.

2 Svend E. Holsoe, *The Cassava-Leaf People*, 11.

The lack of engagement that the text displays to the Vai involvement with the international slave trade and with the practices of Vai domestic slavery shows that, despite mission attitudes, Walters is loath to dwell on the negative side of traditional Vai culture. In fact, he seems prepared to ignore or gloss over many negative aspects of that culture, especially the practice of slavery.

The Poro and Sande[1]

Poro/Sande as a Force for Social Conservatism

Central to Vai society and that of surrounding ethnic groups in Walters's day were "compulsory all-tribal organizations for men and women," known in much of the region and in scholarly literature as the Poro and Sande respectively.[2] Warren d'Azevedo notes:

> The peculiar form of secret society known as Poro appears to have emerged as a crucial institution in defense of traditional principles of ranked-lineage authority.... In a highly mobile and diversified adaptive situation, the Poro provided a sacred and secret arm of political authority and intergroup diplomacy that helped to maintain stability through appeal to the gerontocratic and hierarchical principles derived from the ideal model of the ranked-lineage structure of the past.[3]

d'Azevedo's comments apply to the Sande as well. Further, recent research confirms d'Azevedo's assessment that the secret associations function centrally and crucially to re-inforce existing status relationships. In the Vai Sande, the leaders hold the positions that their

---

1 We write this section as non-initiates of the associations we describe. We have not sought to learn or present the societies' secrets. It should be pointed out that, while the Poro and Sande are secret associations and while the "bush schools" are off-limits to non-initiates, each society has had a highly visible face. Many association activities are open to the public, for example, the coming-out ceremonies of Sande school graduates. In the early 1970s Singler attended such a coming-out ceremony in response to a printed invitation sent out by a graduate's parents.

2 Warren d'Azevedo, "Some Historical Problems in the Delineation of a Central West Atlantic Region." *Annals of the New York Academy of Sciences* 96 (1962): 516.

3 Warren d'Azevedo, "Some Historical Problems," 516.

mothers held and *their* mothers before them.[1] Thus, absolute loyalty to the Sande necessarily becomes fealty to a social order in which some families are perpetually in charge.[2]

In the nineteenth century (as well as, to a much diminished extent, today), the Poro and Sande governed life among the Vai and their neighbors. Membership extended to all members of local society, including slaves.[3] In terms of politics and military alliances, various nineteenth-century commentators attest to the power of the Poro. And, as Adam Jones observes with regard to Gallinas (a Vai-Mende area) at that time: "It is virtually impossible to assess how important the political role of the Sande was. The only information we have on this subject is from accounts written by male non-Africans." He notes that "[t]he head women of the Sande ... had considerable power while their school was in session."[4]

Bush Schools and Traditional Education

The Poro and Sande bear the responsibility to educate Vai youth for full participation in society. The terms "Poro" and "Sande" themselves are widely used to refer both to the secret associations and to the "bush schools" that they sponsor. Along the same lines, reflecting the societies' educational roles, Walters refers to them as "*Boys'* Gregree Bush" and "*Girls'* Gregree Bush" (84, italics ours). Every adult member of society was a graduate of the sex-appropriate school; in this regard, it is virtually certain that Walters was himself a Poro graduate.

Traditionally, the Poro school lasted four years, the Sande three. They alternated; thus, a town's Sande school would commence every seven years. The girls who entered the Sande varied in age, but most would have been between six and thirteen. (A Poro member speculated with us that one criterion in determining the age at which a

---

1 See Svend E. Holsoe, "Notes on the Vai Sande Society in Liberia," *Ethnologische Zeitschrift Zürich* 1 (1980).

2 See Carolyn H. Bledsoe, *Women and Marriage in Kpelle Society* (Stanford: Stanford UP, 1980).

3 Svend E. Holsoe, "Notes on the Vai Sande Society," 100.

4 Adam Jones, *From Slaves to Palm Kernels*, 182. Similarly, Bishop Penick reports with regard to the Sande, "if the tribe decides to go to war, that declaration of war is not complete until it has been referred to the women and they pass upon and approve it" (Charles C. Penick, "The Devil Bush of West Africa," *Fetter's Southern Magazine* 2.2 [1893]: 229; see Appendix B).

girl entered the Sande was the agricultural obligations that faced her. Girls too young to work would not be accepted.) The "camp" where the first phase of the Sande was held was a mile or so from town; it was called *jí kɔɔ*, literally "under water."[1] That is, as each girl entered the "bush school," she was being taken, figuratively, under water. During this stage, a Sande girl would undergo clitoridectomy, and, "she also was likely to receive scarifications ... on the lower back."[2]

Subsequently, the girls would move from their isolated bush location to an enclosure just outside of town, inside a fence (known in Vai as a *bòndò*). During the period in which they lived inside the *bòndò* and were permitted to go out in public, they were, in the terminology of *Guanya Pau*, Borneys. They were still students, not yet initiates. They had gone into the bush and not yet come back (or gone underwater and not re-emerged). In that way, even if they went into the world, they were not yet of the physical world. This seems to explain the Borneys' tendency to keep their eyes to the ground. Their appearance reinforced their separateness, their otherworldliness. They reappeared covered in kaolin, wearing white cloths and/or aprons around their waist.[3]

Other items of clothing set the Borneys apart from ordinary society. In *Guanya Pau*, Walters states: "On entering the Gregree Bush they [Sande girls] are given a peculiar kind of beads and a small horn for the neck, which they are required always to wear. As a rule these girls are respected and cases of unchastity are comparatively few" (89). The connection between the two sentences from *Guanya Pau* is this: the horn contained medicine whose purpose was to prevent molestation by men. "In the past, if the girl's horn fell to the ground and was seen by a man, it was required that he be killed. If the horn dropped and the girl did not report it, she would become sick and infertile."[4]

In the final phase of the Sande school, the girls would go through further training in preparation for their emergence from the school. This training would include their initiation into the Sande Society itself. Finally, at the end of their training, their graduation from the school was three days of public celebration. Upon the ceremonies'

1 Augustus F. Caine, *A Study and Comparison of the West African "Bush" School and the Southern Sotho Circumcision School* (Northwestern University MA thesis, 1959).
2 Svend E. Holsoe, "Notes on the Vai Sande Society," 100–01.
3 Svend E. Holsoe, "Notes on the Vai Sande Society in Liberia," 101.
4 August F. Caine, *A Study and Comparison*, 72, and Svend E. Holsoe, "Notes on the Vai Sande Society," 102.

completion the girls are permitted at last to return to their families as "full-fledged marriageable women."[1] In Guanya's day, if the graduate had attained puberty, marriage would often follow almost immediately.

Zobahs *and the* Gregree Bush

Like much about the Poro and Sande, the bush schools were conducted in extreme secrecy. This secrecy reinforces the spiritual component of Poro and Sande, which mediate between the supernatural and natural worlds.

The terms that Walters uses in *Guanya Pau* reflect the spiritual and supernatural aspect of the Poro and Sande. As noted, he refers to them as the "Boys' Gregree-Bush" and the Girls' Gregree-Bush." Jassah tells Guanya, "I promise you that sooner than betray you, my darling Guanya, may the Gregrees curse me" (87). As part of the same conversation, Guanya reveals to Jassah that, after Kai Kundu visits her, "I shall run away and search for some other land, or if the Gregrees will, perish in the attempt" (87). Then, in Walters's description of the Sembey Court, the Court is surrounded by "a rustic fence with here and there curiously twisted bunches of Gregree" (107). Thus, *Gregree* refers both to the spiritual forces that control the universe and to the amulets that embody these forces' power, and the *Gregree Bush* schools are sites where representatives of the *Gregrees* qua spiritual forces train young people for responsible entry into the world. A comparable duality of meaning attends the term *Zobah*. Walters describes the Zobah as a masked figure: "Their attire consists of a black gown, reaching to the ground, a false-face, a headdress two feet long, carrying in their hand a plaited brush" (89). In the course of Guanya and Jassah's travels, when the girls are caught and Guanya is interrogated about her identity, she is asked, "Were you ever a Borney? if so, where and who were your teachers?" (125) Guanya responds by citing her alma mater and by naming "as one of her teachers a Zobah who was a prominent figure there and whose reputation was known throughout the Marphar..." (The interrogator in this sequence is herself a Zobah, not a masked figure but rather a high-ranking Sande official.) Thus, a *Zobah*, whether appearing as a masked figure or as an elderly woman, is a high-ranking Sande official. This implies, in turn, that a high-ranking Sande

---

1   Svend E. Holsoe, "Notes on the Vai Sande Society," 104.

official—whether in human or masked form—has powers that pertain to the forces of the universe and to their manipulation through "medicine."

Walters's Opposition to the Sande

Walters makes reference to the Poro (the Boys' Gregree Bush) only in the first few chapters of *Guanya Pau*. In contrast, he makes extensive reference throughout to the Sande (the Girls' Gregree Bush). He has to do so if he is going to write about Vai women: "Throughout a woman's lifetime Sande influences every aspect of her physical, psychological, and social development."[1]

As might be expected of the convert, Walters views the spiritual component of the Sande with a Christian's scorn, yet—crucially—this is not the focus of his opposition to the Sande. Early in *Guanya Pau*, he presents a story of its founding that makes "Pandama-Pluzhaway, the Devil's brother-in-law" its founder: "Upon Pandama-Pluzhaway's return to earth he instituted the Gregree Bush and appointed certain old women at its head" (88). That story alerts the reader to the intrinsic evil of the Sande (from Walters's perspective) without explaining what makes it evil. Beyond that, Walters makes reference to the European practice of referring to the *Zobah*, when in the guise of a masked figure, as a "Country Devil" (a term that has survived into modern Liberian English). Walters also has a chapter (XVI) in which Guanya Pau twice commits grave sacrilege, first by stepping into a sacred pond and then, "by a childish noise," disturbing the local war-god, "an alligator of tremendous and scary proportions." Each of Guanya's blasphemies ought to have incurred disaster for her and the townspeople, but nothing untoward happens. Indeed, in terms of spirituality, only by Guanya's impunity does Walters have a Christian worldview prevail over the Sande one.

Walters is both vigorous Christian and—it seems clear—proud member of the Poro. He presents the Poro positively in *Guanya Pau*. The organization, he writes, "is said to owe its founding to Guanya Pau's eminent father" (88). The Poro and Sande share their belief system. If the convert to Christianity is to maintain a positive view of the Poro, he is compelled to de-emphasize the supernatural aspects

---

1 Sylvia A. Boone, *Radiance from the Waters: Ideals of Feminine Beauty in Mende Art* (New Haven: Yale UP, 1988) 15.

of secret associations, whether Poro or Sande.[1] If the fundamental animism of the Poro/Sande belief system is not the basis for Walters's opposition to the Sande, then what is it?

Two explanations present themselves. The first involves the power with which the Sande acts to preserve the *status quo*. Thus, Bledsoe follows d'Azevedo in asserting that the Poro and Sande "strengthen patterns of stratification within the larger society."[2] Walters's frustration with the Sande in this regard is evident from Guanya's remark to Jassah: "The truth is, my friend, my mother and the other women ... are satisfied with this state of things, because *they know of no better. They accept them as being absolutely necessary to the life of society*" (87; italics Walters's). Thus, unyielding in their resistance to change, the leaders of the Sande stand in the way of the marriage reforms that Walters sees as essential for the salvation of Vai women.

Given the reformist social focus of *Guanya Pau*, this conservatism alone could stand as the basis for Walters's antipathy for the Sande. However, a second possible cause must also be considered, namely the indomitable power of the Sande. As noted, the Vai women's and men's secret associations are closely linked to the secret associations of the Vais' neighbors, the Mende and Gola. Boone's description of the Sande among the Mende could surely have been applied in its entirety to the Vai Sande of Walters's day:

The Sande Society is ubiquitous in Mendeland—where there are women, there is Sande. Throughout a woman's lifetime Sande influences every aspect of her physical, psychological, and social

---

1 We are aware of only two possible causes for viewing the Poro differently from the Sande (from a nineteenth-century perspective). One would be to see marriage among the Vai as strictly a women's domain, hence outside the purview of the Poro. However, such a view seems unsupportable; in the same way that the Sande trains girls to be wives, so the Poro trains boys to be husbands. The second way would be Christian objection to the clitoridectomy that every Sande girl undergoes. However, it is not certain that the Christians of the day would find the procedure objectionable, and we have no way of finding out the views of Walters and the Christian missionaries to Cape Mount in this regard. Not surprisingly, Walters makes no mention, not even the most oblique one, to clitoridectomy in *Guanya Pau*. Further, there is no evidence that, during the period that Walters was a student at the Cape Mount Mission, the missionaries there were aware of it. As we discuss, the Sande was, after all, a *secret* society, and the early missionaries seem largely unaware of its practices.

2 Carolyn H. Bledsoe, *Women and Marriage in Kpelle Society*, 65, and Warren d'Azevedo, "Some Historical Problems."

development. Sande was there before she was born and remains when she is gone; it shapes a woman, influences her every thought and action, endows her with her identity and personality.... Sande is the guardian of the women; their spokesman, shield, protector, battling to give women life space, power, health, love, fertility, self-expression. And, as it guards and cherishes the women, they in turn rally round it and hold its standard high.[1]

While Walters is passionate in his desire to promote gender equality among the Vai, he is yet hostile to the organization in which Vai women's power resides. (A curious mirror image obtains in *Guanya Pau*: the book's two central female characters are virtuous yet the Sande is evil; on the other hand, with the exception of Guanya Pau's deceased father and the young man whom she wishes to marry, all of the book's central male characters are brutish and wicked yet the Poro is good.) Walters's opposition to the Sande may reflect a wider ambivalence by Vai men towards it. After all, it constituted a source of power for women over which men exercised no control. At the individual level, this empowerment manifested itself in the belief, widely held among the Vai in Walters's day and subsequently, that in the Sande bush school girls "learn the art of poisoning food to keep husbands in line."[2] Along similar lines, Bishop Penick, in his 1893 article "The Devil Bush of West Africa" (Appendix B), reports the Sande's practice of using poison to punish "unusually cruel" husbands.

As we have noted, Walters approved of the Poro but disapproved of the Sande. Possibly Walters's opposition to the Sande represents a convergence of the attitudes of Vai men with the attitudes of missionary Christianity. After all, the Sande represented the one part of Vai society—and the one part of Vai women's lives—that Vai men could not control. It is possible to see opposition by a Vai man to the Sande as arising out of frustration born of powerlessness in this domain.

A further point about the Christian response to the Vai Poro and Sande is worth making. In the early days of the Cape Mount

---

1 Sylvia A. Boone, *Radiance from the Waters: Ideals of Feminine Beauty in Mende Art* (New Haven: Yale UP, 1988) 15.

2 George W. Harley, *Notes on the Poro in Liberia* (Cambridge, MA: Papers of the Peabody Museum, 1941), and Carolyn H. Bledsoe, *Women and Marriage in Kpelle Society*, 65. A Vai member of the Poro told us of something that was similarly subversive without being murderous: in the Sande, he said, girls learned how to escape detection when cheating on their husbands.

Mission, the missionaries seem not to know how to respond, or even that a response might be appropriate. Just as the Episcopal missionaries' four decades of experience at Cape Palmas among the Grebo gave them no preparation for the practice of child betrothal that they encountered once they established the Cape Mount Mission and began their work among the Vai, so the same was true concerning the Poro and Sande; there was nothing analogous in structure, function, or power among the Grebo. The missionaries at the Cape Mount Mission were seeing something that, from an Episcopalian perspective, was entirely new. Not only was it new, it was secret. Further, rather than the missionaries telling Walters and other Vai Christians what to think about the Poro and Sande, the opposite seems to have occurred. Certainly in the case of Bishop Penick's article "The Devil Bush in West Africa" (Appendix B), the congruence of views between the article and *Guanya Pau* seems to owe more to Walters than to the Bishop. That is, with regard to the secret associations, especially to the view that the Poro served a valuable civic function as a unifying entity, Walters's views seemed to have shaped Penick's.

4. The Vai and the Cape Mount Region

The Vai Country[1]

The Vai live on the Atlantic coast, in what is now Liberia and Sierra Leone. To the extent that Walters makes use of real place names and topography, *Guanya Pau* takes place in the Liberian part of Vai

---

1   A note on orthography: When spelling Vai person and place names in English, we have used the following conventions:
    <eh> for ɛ, the vowel in English *pet*
    <oh> for ɔ, the vowel in British English *caught*
    <ng> for a nasal consonant at the end of a word.
    The most comprehensive and authoritative source on the history and culture of the Vai in the Cape Mount region, i.e., the setting of *Guanya Pau*, is Svend E. Holsoe's 1967 Boston University PhD dissertation *The Cassava-Leaf People: An Ethnohistorical Study of the Vai People with a Particular Emphasis on the TewO Chiefdom*. Information found there forms the basis of this section. (In quoting Holsoe, we have adjusted the spelling of Vai names in keeping with the orthographic conventions outlined above.)

country, near the Mafa River and Lake Piso in Grand Cape Mount County (Walters's "Marphar" and "Pisu"). "Vai country" is in fact ethnically mixed, inhabited by Vai, Gola, and—to a lesser extent—Mende.

The "Cape Mount" of "Grand Cape Mount" is the dominant land formation along this stretch of the Atlantic coast. It is a peninsula with a high hill—the "mount"—near its tip. The Atlantic borders Cape Mount on one side, and a large lake—the Piso—borders Cape Mount on the other. The Piso connects to the ocean by what is referred to locally as the "bar mouth."

In the historical literature relating to the region—and in modern usage—the term "Cape Mount" has two different meanings. More narrowly, it refers to the communities near the tip of the peninsula. This includes the Vai village Fanima as well as—from 1856—Robertsport, the African-American Settlers' community. More broadly, it refers not only to the peninsula but also to a large region interior to the Atlantic and Lake Piso, including the area drained by the Mafa River, which flows into the lake. "Cape Mount" in the larger sense is reflected in the Liberian political designation, "Grand Cape Mount County." In the discussion that follows, we use "Cape Mount" to refer to the area at the tip of the peninsula. When we mean the larger area, we specify it as the "Cape Mount region."

The Vai, the Gola, and the Mende

The Gola were the first to settle in the area. Then, in the sixteenth century, the disintegration of the Mali Empire in the savanna region sent people from that area further south. One such group of people were the forebears of the modern Vai. The disruption of the Mali Empire prompted re-alignment of peoples living near the Empire as well. As groups from the Empire moved south (though not traveling so far as the Vai), their arrival triggered movement further south by those whom they were displacing. In this way the Mende and related groups arrived in what is today Sierra Leone and northern Liberia. One part of the Mende settled near to the Gola, not at the coast, but near it.

Portuguese trading along what is now the Vai coast began even before the Vai had settled there. Competition for trade with Europeans—especially trade in slaves—shaped relations among Vai polities and between these and those of other groups from virtually the arrival of the Vai on the coast all the way into the middle of the nineteenth century. (See "The international slave trade and the Vai.") Even when trade with Europeans declined, as it did after international slave trade halted in the region, the habit of political instability and intermittent warfare continued. Thus, in the part of Vai country where *Guanya Pau* is set, the most recent war prior to the book's publication was the Pahn War (in Vai, *kpaŋ*), which lasted from 1878 to 1882. (See the Notes for p. 82 of *Guanya Pau*.)

The Settlers

Western attention to Liberia tends to focus on the African Americans who immigrated there and their descendants, but these Settlers play only a bit part in *Guanya Pau*. Walters makes reference to "Liberians" only twice, in Chapters I and XX. Still, Walters's views of the Settlers and the nineteenth-century history of Vai-Settler relations merit comment.

The political entity Liberia had come into being as a white American solution to an American problem. It was intended to be a place where free African Americans could enjoy the rights of citizenship being denied them in the United States. Further, whites hoped that the African Americans who went to Africa could help to Christianize the continent. In the words of Henry Clay, "Every emigrant to Africa ... [would be] a missionary, carrying with him credentials in the holy cause of civilization, religion, and free institutions."[1] The scheme to bring Liberia into being was extremely expensive. The funding for it came almost entirely from southern slaveowners (who saw free African Americans as a direct threat to the preservation of slavery). The nature of the venture's American support and the perils that faced the first people to immigrate to West Africa meant that few African Americans actually went there, whether they were already free or—as was more often the case—emancipated on condition of immigration to Liberia. The governing organization, the American Colonization Society, first placed African Africans in what became Monrovia in 1822. Over the next 21 years, only 4,571 African Americans immigrated to Liberia, and of these only 2,388 were still alive and living in Liberia at the time of the 1843 census. (Shick calls the mortality rate "shockingly high" and questions the morality of those who, in the light of such a death toll, continued to send African Americans there.)[2]

---

1 *African Repository* 5 (1829): 208.
2 Tom W. Shick, *Behold the Promised Land: A History of Afro-American Settler Society in Nineteenth-Century Liberia* (Baltimore: Johns Hopkins UP, 1980) 27.

Although the Cape Mount peninsula was only fifty miles up the coast from Monrovia and the Settlers wished to establish themselves there, this was slow in happening, both because of the region's political instability and ongoing warfare (exacerbated by slave traders) and the small number of Settlers present in Liberia. The Liberian government—independent as of 1847—established the settlement of Robertsport at the tip of the Cape Mount peninsula in 1856, receiving 100 emigrants from the United States that year and another 216 the next year.

In his discussion of the history of the Vai in the first chapter of *Guanya Pau*, Walters bemoans what he sees to be the decline of the Vai and their valiant leaders. He comments that "one reason for the present degeneration of the Veys is due to their alliance with the Liberians who fight their battles for them" (81). The Settlers did assist particular Vai leaders on several occasions. Moreover, in the years since the Settlers had been living at Cape Mount, the Vais *had* declined, in strength and independence, particularly those in the Mafa and Piso regions where *Guanya Pau* takes place, i.e., Tewoh and neighboring chiefdoms. However, as Holsoe points out, it is necessary to place the weakened position of the Vai in a larger perspective.[1] In the decades immediately preceding the arrival of the Settlers, it had been the Atlantic slave trade and European slavers that had buttressed Vai military strength and economic prosperity. Thus, it was the end of the Atlantic slave trade, brought about at the local level by British involvement, that had begun the diminution of Vai power, not the use of Settler armies to fight Vai battles, as Walters asserts in *Guanya Pau*.[2]

The second aspect of the Settler presence relevant to *Guanya Pau* is Robertsport as quite literally the city of Guanya Pau's dreams, a place where

a man has but one wife, and woman is held in the highest esteem and respect. All that I saw in my dream is correct. They are God's people, who have God-men to do nothing else but to speak God palaver to the people. She [the woman on Tosau Island] said that

---

1 Svend E. Holsoe, *The Cassava-Leaf People*, 229.
2 At the same time, however, Walters's lament is part prophecy. Two years after the publication of *Guanya Pau*, war broke out again in the Vai region. (This is the war to which Walters refers in the documents in Appendices E6 and E7.) It was to last for ten years and to launch a series of events that brought the Vai fully and utterly under Liberian government rule. (Svend E. Holsoe, *The Cassava-Leaf People*, 231.)

even if a slave runs away and goes to them, his master dare not go and ask for him. She told me that she has helped some girls of my spirit to go there, and hear that they are in school, learning to read and write, who have given up their Gregrees and medicines, and have laid their hearts down to the American religion. (150)

The Cape Mount Mission is on the side of the Cape "mountain," above Robertsport. Walters as a student would have known Robertsport and its citizens, and there were a few Settler children in attendance at the Mission school. While in Liberia, Bishop Penick was embroiled in a dispute with the Settler clergy of Monrovia over church governance, and Walters would probably have been aware of this and other conflicts between the missionaries and the Settlers. None of this seems strongly relevant, however, to his description of Robertsport in *Guanya Pau*, for the model for Walters's city on the Beach is not so much "real" Settlers in the "real" Robertsport as it is the saints of God in the New Jerusalem.

5. Joseph Walters

The Search for Joseph Jeffrey Walters

There is very little record of Joseph Walters's life in Africa, especially of the years before he traveled .to America. Even where there are records, questions persist. In the discussion that follows, we first summarize the information that we have been able to assemble about Walters's background and early years. Then we look at each of the places where Walters studied—the Cape Mount Mission, Storer College, and Oberlin College. It is possible, we argue, to see the way in which the people and principles of these institutions influenced Walters and *Guanya Pau*. But it remains the case that *Guanya Pau* is very much Walters's own book. As we have tried to show, *Guanya Pau* proves to be like Walters himself, Vai as well as Christian.

Walters was born in the 1860s, according to Bishop Charles C. Penick, the Episcopal prelate who brought Walters to the US.[1] Penick stated further that he supposed Walters's place of birth to be on or near Cape Mount, i.e., the region at the tip of the peninsula. If Walters's birthplace had not been on the peninsula itself, then it would presumably have been in the area surrounding Lake Piso or interior to it.

---

1 Oberlin, Charles C. Penick, 28 January 1895, to Azariah Root.

By Walters's own account he was Vai. In the introduction to *Guanya Pau*, he describes himself as "one ... who has coursing through his veins the same blood as those for whom this book pleads, and who has consecrated his life to the evangelization of his people" (75). While writers might misidentify themselves for various reasons, there is no reason to doubt Walters in this regard. Ware, in her 1954 study of the Episcopal schools of Cape Mount, likewise identifies Walters as Vai; her work is based on interviews with Cape Mount elders.[1]

Beyond Walters's assertion of his Vai heritage in the introduction of *Guanya Pau*, the body of the book itself repeatedly confirms his Vai ethnicity and, further, his status as a Poro Society initiate, both by its demonstration of an insider's knowledge of Vai culture and language and by its favorable appraisal of the Poro Society.

The source of Walters's western names is apparently the Cape Mount Mission. Students there were routinely assigned western names at some point prior to baptism. All the students were financed by scholarships. Each scholarship was given a name, either that of the donor or of some person whom the donor wished to honor. In the earliest years of the Cape Mount Mission, it was apparently not unusual for the name of the scholarship to become its recipient's western name. In the search for an alternative source, we investigated the possibility that the provenance of Walters's name was "local," i.e., was somehow Vai or Settler in origin. However, in all the years since we began our efforts to "locate" Walters in 1985, we have never been able to find a Cape Mountainian—in the county seat Robertsport, in the national capital Monrovia, or anywhere else—who had ever heard of a Walters in Cape Mount. This argues that Joseph Jeffrey Walters was the only Walters in Cape Mount, that he received the name from the Mission not from his family, and that the name died with him.

The Cape Mount Mission was founded early in 1878. Walters traveled to America in March, 1883. Walters refers to the Mission as "my *alma mater* where three years of my life was spent when a boy & where I received the first incentives to a higher & nobler life."[2] Walters's three years would have fallen in the period from 1878 to 1882, with the academic years 1880, 1881, and 1882 the likeliest.

1 Rachel J.N. Ware, *Episcopal Schools, Cape Mount* (Cuttington College, Liberia, Bachelor's thesis, 1954) 5.
2 AEC, RG 72 69, Joseph Walters, Annual Report and Scholarship Record, 1894; see Appendix E9.

Although it is not certain, what may be a reference to Walters occurs in an article that Bishop Penick wrote for the Episcopal Church's publication for American children. It begins in the following way:

MISSION NOTES
A LETTER FROM CAPE MOUNT, W. AFRICA

Dear Children:

The missionary's study is a curious place, not so much for the books and furniture thereof, as for the talks had and battles fought therein. Let us take a scene to-day. The hour is 10 A.M. My boy Joe, who is a general help, comes to the door, and says, "Here is Robert."[1]

The letter makes no further mention of "Joe." Rather, it recounts the Bishop's struggles first with Robert ("a Christian ... with sufficient education to read his Bible and write an English letter, yet with such low cunning as to attempt to deceive with a complication of falsehoods") and then Jessee ("the Mission's incorrigible," characterized by Penick as a liar and a thief).

Penick's "boy" is clearly his houseboy. As for "Joe" vs. "Joseph," all the references to Walters at the two American schools he attended are to "Joseph," even informal ones at Oberlin, but the Bishop sometimes referred to Walters as "Joe," as for example in a letter to the Mission Board in New York in which he indicated where the Board officials were to send "Joe Walters" upon the latter's arrival in New York from Liberia.[2]

---

1   Charles C. Penick, "A Letter from Cape Mount, W. Africa," *Young Christian Soldier and Carrier Dove* (14 May 1882): 100.
2   AEC, RG 72 59, Charles C. Penick, 31 March 1883, to Kimber. During the early years of the Cape Mount Mission the Episcopal Church's missionary activities were administered out of Bible House, the Church's headquarters in New York. Domestic and foreign missions were run separately, with the Rev. Joshua A. Kimber in charge of foreign missions. In 1885, the Church placed the domestic and foreign missions under a single administrative officer, the Rev. William S. Langford (Mary Sudman Donovan, *Women's Ministries in the Episcopal Church, 1850-1920* [Columbia University PhD dissertation, 1985] 48). Kimber continued to be directly in charge of foreign missions. Thus, while all letters sent to Bible

In all Penick brought three boys from the Cape Mount Mission to the US for further study "under his own charge."[1] He enrolled each of the three at Storer College in Harpers Ferry, West Virginia. Lewis Penick Clinton arrived in the US in 1884, a year after Walters, and followed him to Storer. Pela Penick was younger than Walters and Clinton and did not enrol at Storer until the end of the 1880s. In correspondence in 1884, Bishop Penick states, "The ... two boys Lewis & Pela are under my direction being orphans left to me."[2]

The bearing of Clinton's and Pela Penick's histories upon Walters is that Bishop Penick seems to have brought to the United States those to whom he felt personal ties. Apparently, he brought "his" boys, whether they were his wards or his servants and whether they were the Mission's finest students or not. In this he was not alone. The Rev. and Mrs. Curtis Grubb, missionaries at Cape Mount from 1878 to 1881, brought their young housegirl Nettie with them to live in the US when they returned home.[3]

A final point about Walters involves his age, particularly as compared to that of Lewis Clinton. There is more information about Clinton's age, and it suggests that he was born in 1865 or 1866. A comparison of Walters's and Clinton's careers at the Cape Mount Mission, at Storer College, and then at US colleges (Clinton graduated from Bates College in Maine in 1897) strongly suggests that Walters was approximately three or four years older, born in roughly 1862. That in turn makes *Guanya Pau* the work of someone who was nearing thirty rather than the college sophomore's usual twenty.

House prior to 1885 by Cape Mount missionaries went to Kimber (or to Miss Julia C. Emery, head of the Women's Auxiliary of the Board of Missions), letters after that date sometimes went to Langford as well.

1 "Bishop Penick on the Negro," Boston *Herald* (3 December 1893): 22.

2 AEC, RG 72 59, Charles C. Penick, 15 April 1884, to Kimber. Clinton had been entrusted to Penick's care in 1878 in Grand Bassa when he was en route from Cape Palmas to Cape Mount to found the Mission. Pela had been entrusted to the Bishop's care in 1878 as well. Regarding Clinton, see D. Elwood Dunn, *A History of the Episcopal Church in Liberia, 1821-1980* (Metuchen, NJ: The Scarecrow Press, 1992) 120. Regarding Pela Penick, see "A Letter from Bishop Penick," *Young Christian Soldier and Carrier Dove* (2 March 1879): 55.

3 AEC, RG 72 54, Packard Cole, 30 October 1882, to McNabb.

The Cape Mount Mission

The founder of the Cape Mount Mission was Bishop Charles C. Penick. Like the other priests who served at the Mission in its early years and like most Episcopal missionaries to Liberia in the nineteenth century, Penick was a Virginia native. He resigned the rectorship of a church in Baltimore to become Missionary Bishop to Cape Palmas and Parts Adjacent, i.e., Liberia. Consecrated bishop in 1877, Penick arrived in Liberia in December of that year. After going first to Cape Palmas for a brief visit, he then moved up the coast to Cape Mount to establish the Episcopal Mission there.

The Vai, the dominant group in the Cape Mount region, had cachet among the Settlers and westerners more generally owing to the fact that they had their own writing system. (See Appendix D, "The Vai Writing System.") An 1880 article in the *African Repository*, the journal of the American Colonization Society, states: "The Veys ... are, in many respects, the most interesting tribe on the African Coast. They are distinguished as the only tribe on the continent of Africa which has invented an alphabet." The article continues: "In their ability to hold epistolary communication in their own language, written in letters of their own invention, this tribe forms an interesting exception to the tribes on the African continent, and, indeed, they belong to the very few exceptions among all the tribes of mankind."[1]

As Penick himself wrote in 1880 in explaining why he had selected Cape Mount for the new mission station: "Many and flattering representations had been made by various parties from time to time, both as to the healthfulness of the locality and the intelligence of the people. Moved by these and other smaller considerations, we selected a position on Cape Mount, and established a Mission there in 1878."[2]

The school began at once and grew rapidly. The Mission school's curriculum sought to provide a basic Christian, western education, as indicated by the Rev. Curtis Grubb's 1880 account of a typical day at the Mission:

School [opens] with singing a hymn, recital of the Apostles Creed, and prayer. Then follows reading of the Bible in classes under the several teachers. Bro. McNabb and I taking a week about in open-

---

1   *African Repository*, August 1880, reprinted in *The Spirit of Missions* 45 (1880): 317.
2   Charles C. Penick, *Our Mission Work in Africa*, 9.

ing the school and hearing the first Bible Class, recite a verse a piece usually the same verse, upon which we make such remarks as we think proper. Then the class reads part of a chapter which [we] explain as God gives us grace for the occasion. This occupies about an hour from nine till ten oclock, then follows the Spelling, Arithmetic, Reading, Geography, and Grammar Classes, which with a fifteen minuit recess continues till about half past twelve oclock. When Miss Lottie Hogan instructs the school for an hour in singing which closes the school exercises for the day.[1]

Students were expected to do manual labor as well. Grubb's account continues:

The Bell is rung at two oclock, (P.M.) And the boys are put to work on the farm under their respective headmen (or rather boys), till four oclock, when the Bell is rung again. And they come in and get ready for evening prayers, which are held ten minuits after five, after which the[y] eat their dinner, carry their wood and water and rest for the night.[2]

That the language of instruction at the Mission was English was never questioned. The missionaries preferred it, and—from all accounts—so too did the students and their parents. (For parents, a child's knowledge of English held potential economic benefit in trading with Europeans.)[3] Student interest in learning English

---

1 AEC, RG 72 50, Curtis Grubb, 25 October 1880 [?], to Kimber.
2 AEC, RG 72 50, Curtis Grubb, 25 October 1880 [?], to Kimber.
3 See John Victor Singler, "Language in Liberia in the Nineteenth Century: The Settlers' Perspective," *Liberian Studies Journal* 7 (1977): 73-85. Discussing mission schools in Cape Palmas and Cape Mount, Bishop Penick writes: "... [I]t is easier to give them Christian ideas in the English language than in the heathen tongue. A heathen word conveys a heathen thought, with all the associations of a heathen life, and before we can make it carry the Christian idea we must divest it of its old associations, and then by throwing the life of JESUS behind it, cause life and immortality to shine through; while an English word comes now fitted to the new idea, and reflected from the Missionary's own life and surroundings." Penick continues: "If these heathen people were a mighty nation as the Chinese or Japanese, with a written language, of course every effort should be made to give them the Scriptures in their own tongue, and to elevate their literature by the richness of GOD'S own Word" (*Our Mission Work,* 9). As Penick well knew, the Vai had a written language.

is reflected in the Rev. John McNabb's report from November, 1880:

> With very few exceptions, the children that we have had came here knowing not one word of English, yet within three years many of them have learned to read their Testament fluently, spell in words of four and five syllables, and some of them cipher in fractions with comparative ease. Their progress in writing, and I might include grammar, has been correspondingly good.... Their thirst for knowledge is insatiable, and the rapidity with which they learn the English language is marvelous.[1]

These descriptions of the curriculum and of student progress mask the perpetual state of crisis in which the Mission operated in its early years. Illness defeated the missionaries, and none of them stayed long. The vagaries of the missionaries' health made for wide divergences in the school's enrolment. When the missionaries were healthy, they would admit as many students as they could. Then when the missionaries got sick, they would have to send students home. A remark that Penick made in an 1879 letter to church authorities in New York was to hold true for years to come: "We have certainly had 'unmerciful disaster following fast and following faster' in our work, it is next to impossible to keep things systematized when gaps in the ranks are so frequent and broad."[2]

We have discussed in some detail the circumstances surrounding the establishment and early years of the Cape Mount Mission because it was for Walters, as we have noted, "my *alma mater* where three years of my life was spent when a boy & where I received the first incentives to a higher & nobler life."[3] As a student, he would have been keenly aware of missionary attitudes toward the Vai and toward Vai society. If, as we suspect, he was the Bishop's houseboy, then he would have had even greater exposure to these views. These views tended to be negative, particularly the views of Penick himself, the man whom Walters called his "father in the Gospel":

---

1 Quoted in Foreign Committee, Episcopal Church, *An Historical Sketch of the African Mission of the Protestant Episcopal Church in the U.S.A.* (New York: Foreign Committee, 1884) 55.

2 AEC, RG 72 59, Charles C. Penick, 7 October 1879, to Kimber.

3 AEC, RG 72 69, Joseph Walters, Annual Report and Scholarship Record, 1894; see Appendix E9.

I do not find the widely circulated reports that the Veys are superior to other tribes, true. They are a more graceful, handsome people both in form and feature, but also more fickle, weaker, and more corrupt in their social life.[1]

As far as I can hear from the heathen, they appear still anxious to send us their children, but I am coming more and more to doubt everything here save what I see or know; for these heathen people will tell you anything they think is pleasing to you, without the slightest intention of ever doing it, or the faintest regard for the truth.[2]

... God has stowed a wealth here beyond computation if only the people can be taught to grasp it, but it is no easy matter to teach a heathen people, as low as these, to work.[3]

Most of the condemnations of the "heathen" that show up in the missionaries' letters back to the US are nebulous rather than specific. Occasionally, however, specific institutions or customs were singled out. On at least two occasions Bishop Penick condemned the "abominable system of domestic slavery among the aborigines here."[4]

For the author of *Guanya Pau*, the most critical issue would have been how the missionaries responded to the status and traditional education of Vai girls. To the extent that the early Episcopal mission-

---

1 Charles C. Penick, *Our Mission Work in Africa*, 9. Penick's lower opinion of the Vai may have been a consequence of the Mission's inability to get Vai children to remain in school. According to the 1883 scholarship list, which indicated students' ethnicity, while Vai children provided a majority of the students in the four lower grades (60%), they formed only 25% of the most advanced class. Rather, Bassa boys from down the coast—originally recruited by Penick—predominated.

2 Charles C. Penick, "Letter from Bishop Penick," *The Spirit of Missions* 43 (1878): 384.

3 Charles C. Penick, "Letter from Bishop Penick," *The Spirit of Missions* 43 (1878): 163.

4 Charles Charles C. Penick, "Letter from Bishop Penick," *The Spirit of Missions* 47 (1882): 298. The quotation comes from a lengthy account by Penick of three unrelated incidents involving enslaved people. At the end he comments, "Some twelve months ago, when I ventured to state in one of my published reports that domestic slavery was here among the aborigines, I was roundly called to task ..." (299).

aries in Cape Mount concerned themselves with proselytizing among adults, their focus was clearly on men. However, adults were secondary. The Mission's focus was on its school, which was for boys and girls alike. They discovered that boys were easy to recruit for the Mission school but girls were not. From an initial enrolment of 7 students in 1878 (all of them boys), the Mission had an enrolment of 108 boys in 1883 but only 14 girls.[1] The missionaries explained the unwillingness of parents to send their daughters to the Mission in economic terms, the combined effects of the customs of dowry and child betrothal and the perception that western education would diminish a girl's marriageability.

Walters in America: Storer College

Walters traveled to the US early in 1883 where Bishop Penick enrolled him at Storer College. Freewill Baptists had founded Storer in 1867. The Freewill Baptists were a small denomination, concentrated in New England. As Susan Bergeron and Gloria Gozdzik report in their history of Storer College, the "General Conference of the Freewill Baptists declared slavery a sin in 1835, and in 1837 they endorsed the methods and philosophies of the AAS [American Anti-Slavery Society]," a national abolitionist organization.[2] Immediately after the Civil War, the Freewill Baptists set up schools for African Americans in Harpers Ferry and other towns in the Shenandoah Valley. It was in order to provide African-American teachers for these schools that the Freewill Baptists founded Storer. The school was open to all regardless of race or sex; in practice, this meant that it was a school for African Americans, both male and female.

The Freewill Baptists met with great hostility in their efforts to establish Storer, but they persevered. By the time Walters arrived to study there, the school was not yet a college in that it did not award bachelor's degrees, but it had a State Normal Department, providing a three-year teacher training course, and a more advanced Academic Department, with a four-year course. In Walters's first year, there

---

1   Annual Reports: AEC, RG 72 58, Henry M. Parker, 30 June 1878; and RG 72 54, Harry C.N. Merriam, 30 June 1883.
2   Susan Bergeron and Gloria Gozdzik, *A Historical Resource Study for Storer College, Harpers Ferry, West Virginia* (Morgantown, WV: Horizon Research Consultants, 2001) 7.

were 211 students in the State Normal Department and 59 in the Academic.[1]

In all Walters attended Storer for five years. Presumably he entered as a second-year student in the State Normal program, for he graduated from that course in 1885. He then studied for three years in the Academic Department.

An indication of the State Normal curriculum that Walters would have addressed comes from the 1891 edition of the school's catalogue. The curriculum for the second and third years was as follows:

Second Year

Physical Geography	English Grammar
Science of Government	Penmanship
History of England	Natural Philosophy
Arithmetic	Scripture History

Third Year

Pedagogy	Algebra
Botany	Penmanship
English Literature	Book-keeping
Arithmetic	Reviews
Civil Government	

In addition, students studied "Reading and Spelling daily, and Declamations and Compositions regularly throughout."[2]

With regard to the Academic Department, Bergeron and Gozdzik comment that

... it represented the core of what Storer's founders and administration hoped that the school would become—a respected college for African Americans that could offer courses of the caliber of a traditional liberal arts education. Consequently, the curriculum of the Academic Department was centered on the reading and study of classical literature, as well as the study of Latin Grammar beginning in the first year. Students were required to read Caesar, Ovid, Cicero and Virgil, and study the history of Greece and Rome. By

---

1 Kate J. Anthony, *Storer College, Harper's Ferry: Brief Historical Sketch* (Boston: Morning Star Press, 1891) 8, 15, and Susan Bergeron and Gloria Gozdzik, *A Historical Resource Study for Storer College*, 54.

2 *Biennial Catalogue of the Officers and Students of Storer College, 1889-91* (Harper's Ferry, WV: The Board of Trustees, 1891) 18.

the third year, they were being taught Greek Grammar, as well as studying either German or French. In addition to studying classical literature and languages, students in the Academic Department at Storer were also taught other high school level subjects such as arithmetic, algebra, geology, botany, and astronomy. In the third and fourth years, students also studied Shakespeare and English literature, as well as rhetoric and logic.[1]

The final decades of the nineteenth century were marked by an increasingly heated debate as to the appropriate philosophy and policy for the education of African Americans. One approach was developed at the Hampton Institute in Virginia and later exported to Tuskegee Institute by Hampton graduate Booker T. Washington. It sought to produce students who were "instilled with good manual work habits, Christian morality, and an understanding of the subordinate role African Americans would play in the new Southern economy. Consequently, there was little emphasis on classical education at Hampton...." The competing approach was identified with Fisk University in Nashville and most vigorously advocated by W.E.B. DuBois, himself a Fisk graduate. Its goal was "to educate a new African American elite who would then be able to educate and lead their own people towards racial equality."[2] The classics were deemed the most suitable curriculum for effecting this. Essentially, Fisk students studied the same texts as students at the leading white liberal arts colleges of the day.

Bergeron and Gozdzik state that:

> ... the Freewill Baptists started Storer College in the true missionary education ideal, and their curriculum always included classical subjects like Latin, Greek, and History. In this sense, Storer remained true to the Fisk model of missionary liberal education, and through its Normal and Academic courses sought to train a corps of good Christian teachers who could go out and educate their people and help them earn their equal rights.[3]

---

1 Susan Bergeron and Gloria Gozdzik, *A Historical Resource Study for Storer College*, 55.

2 Susan Bergeron and Gloria Gozdzik, *A Historical Resource Study for Storer College*, 59, 61.

3 Susan Bergeron and Gloria Gozdzik, *A Historical Resource Study for Storer College*, 61. In the 1890s Storer—bowing to the pressures of the day—did introduce industrial training.

In Walters's case, the classical education at Storer led to a classical education at Oberlin and shaped his views as to what education should be. In 1894, back in Cape Mount as a teacher, the textbooks that he ordered for his students included a Latin Grammar, Caesar's *Gallic Wars*, and an algebra book.

Storer College closed in 1955, and the records that remain for individual students from Walters's era at Storer are scant. However, programs from the end-of-the-year graduation ceremonies do survive, and they attest to Walters's prowess as an orator. In 1885 he delivered an oration entitled "Outlook for Liberia," in 1886 an oration on "Africa," and in 1887 a "declamation" on "Foreign Aggressions in Africa." In 1888, when Walters graduated from the Academic Department, he entitled his oration "The Book of Books." (Additionally, at an "exhibition" program during the 1888 commencement season, Walters had a part in a short drama, "Wooing Under Difficulties.")[1]

From Storer, Walters transferred to Oberlin College in Ohio, entering the preparatory (pre-college) division in the fall of 1888. Oberlin was Congregational, a denomination that was—like Storer's Freewill Baptist Church—fundamentally a New England denomination. Founded in 1833, it is best known in American history for having been the first college to admit women. Two years later, it began admitting African-American students. Oberlin's Christianity concerned itself with the rights of all regardless of sex or race, and that was what Storer hoped to be. Bergeron and Gozdzik draw on letters exchanged among Storer's founders to comment: "Believing that their effort was on behalf of the Republic as well as the freed slaves, the Freewill Baptists worked diligently to raise the funds they would need for their school. They envisioned a place like Oberlin College in Ohio, the first school of higher education that was opened to students regardless of race."[2] While Storer's student body was exclusively black when Walters attended there and Oberlin's overwhelmingly white, the guiding principles at the two institutions (if not the day-to-day realities) were very similar.

---

1   Information on Walters's speeches comes from WVU, A & M 1322, Package 1, Scrapbook, 1870-1915.
2   Susan Bergeron and Gloria Gozdzik, *A Historical Resource Study for Storer College*, 30-31.

Walters in America: Oberlin College[1]

Walters spent his first year at Oberlin in the preparatory (pre-college) division. Beginning in January of that first year, he began receiving an Avery Scholarship, which furnished "free tuition ($3.00) for fifty 'indigent and worthy colored students.'"[2] When Walters entered the College itself in September, 1889, he took the "classical course," with its emphasis on Latin and Greek rather than the "philosophical course," which "substituted" modern languages for the classics.[3] Thus, Walters's college education conformed entirely to the "Fisk model" that had guided Storer's educational philosophy and, therefore, his education at Storer. American higher education deemed Greek, Latin, and the Bible the worthiest subjects of study for its finest young white men, and that is what Walters studied, first at Storer and then at Oberlin.

Nineteenth-century Oberlin had a "national reputation ... for piety and reform" such that "Oberlin and strict piety were nearly synonymous."[4] In his first letter from Oberlin back to the wife of Storer's principal, Walters expresses his happiness at Oberlin's religious atmosphere:

> The religious force is very good. There are class prayer meetings on Fridays, Bible classes Wednesdays and college prayers at 5 p.m. daily.
> I feel much assisted by the influence of the school—everything uplifting. Before commencing each recitation a prayer is offered or a hymn is sung....
> Mission spirit is very strong here; and the cause is held in high esteem.[5]

---

1 John Victor Singler, "The Day Will Come," provides further discussion of Walters's career at Oberlin. In particular, chapter 2.1 of that article examines the religious atmosphere at Oberlin in Walters's day.

2 *Oberlin College Catalogue 1892-93* (Oberlin: Oberlin College, 1892) 20.

3 The debate in African-American educational circles as to whether or not it was appropriate to teach the classics to African Americans paralleled a debate at Oberlin concerning the suitability of teaching the classics to women. Greek was held to be "the manly tongue" (Frances Juliette Hosford, *Father Shipherd's Magna Charta* [Boston: Marshall Jones, 1937] 57; see also John Victor Singler, "The Day Will Come," 132n).

4 John Barnard, *From Evangelicalism to Progressivism at Oberlin College, 1866-1917* (Columbus: The Ohio State UP, 1969) 16, 22.

5 WVU, A&M 2621, Box 1, FF2, Joseph Walters, 5 October 1888, to Louise Wood Brackett; see Appendix E1.

Oberlin Christianity had a strong commitment to social justice. The college was fiercely abolitionist from the 1830s onward and was heavily involved in the Underground Railroad. The Oberlin community considered the 1850 Fugitive Slave Law ungodly and invoked "higher law," i.e., Christian principles, in defying it. The theology that animated Oberlin's Christian militancy was known as "Oberlin perfectionism" and had at its core a belief in "the possibility of a sinless existence for the converted."[1] It was intrinsically optimistic: lead the heathen to the Gospel, and the Gospel will transform the newly converted soul.

At some point while Walters was in America, most likely while he was at Oberlin, he contracted tuberculosis. By the time he graduated, he was extremely ill. His classmate Hinman writes, "I remember how he lay for many weeks, during his Senior year, so ill that his life was for a long time despaired of."[2] However, he did recover sufficiently to graduate.

Walters Returns to Liberia

Walters and the Rev. Samuel D. Ferguson, Bishop Penick's successor as Bishop of Cape Palmas, had planned for Walters to continue his studies after he graduated from Oberlin, possibly at an Episcopal seminary in the US. However, Walters's health had so deteriorated by the time of his graduation from Oberlin that further schooling proved unfeasible. As *The Storer Record* reported in its Fall, 1893, issue: "J.J. Walters, '85, was graduated, last summer, from Oberlin College. He was obliged, on account of poor health, to give up, for the present, his intended Theological course, and he sailed, soon after his graduation, for his missionary field in Africa."[3]

When Walters arrived in Cape Mount, he discovered that the Vai were at war and facing widespread starvation. He wrote to the Rev. Kimber in New York to say that he had "written an article for publication in a few of the American papers" in an effort to raise funds to buy rice for famine relief.[4] (The "article" in question appears in the Oberlin *News* on November 30, 1893, and again in the *Baltimore American* in a larger article about Bishop Penick on January 21, 1894;

1 John Barnard, *From Evangelicalism to Progressivism*, 10.
2 George W. Hinman, "In Memoriam," 288; see Appendix F2.
3 *Storer Record* 11. 1 (Fall 1893): 1.
4 AEC, RG 72 69, Joseph Walters, 12 October 1893, to Kimber; see Appendix E5.

see Appendices E6 and 7.) In his letter to the Rev. Kimber Walters makes no reference to his own health. However, in January, 1894, Bishop Ferguson wrote to the Rev. Langford: "Mr. Joseph Walters is residing with a relative of his a little distance from the station. Consumption seems to have taken fast hold of his lungs, and I fear he will not be able to render much service to the Mission. He says he is much better than when he arrived, and seems hopeful."[1] The Bishop appointed Walters to be teacher of the advanced class; he also licensed him to be a lay reader.[2]

When the school year began early in 1894, the sole missionary on the Mission staff was Mrs. M.R. Brierley, who had been there since 1882. However, Mrs. Brierley had gone on leave in April, 1893, and did not arrive back at the Mission until October, 1894. The head of the mission for several years had been the Rev. O.E. Himie Shannon, a Grebo priest from the Cape Palmas region. The mission's school was divided into two "departments," an upper school, St. John's, and a lower school, St. George's. Mrs. Brierley and two African women teachers handled the lower school, and they had succeeded in attracting a larger number of girls. The 1894 report lists 83 girls and 60 boys among the boarding students.

Mrs. Brierley had long been critical of the Rev. Shannon, and she had earlier clashed with Bishop Ferguson about Shannon's behavior. In May, 1894, Shannon ran afoul of the Bishop himself and was dismissed, accused of insulting behavior toward the African women teachers and—it was suggested—embezzlement of rice intended for the St. John's boys. Walters, too, disapproved of Shannon, as the comments in his annual report of the Cape Mount Mission make clear:

St. John's needs one or two good teachers & the need is *imperative & paramount.* Men who will give their whole time to the work, whose hearts throb with a genuine love for & interest in these heathen children, but especially, men who are pronounced foes to tobacco & intoxicating liquors. It is high time that we learn to discriminate in the selection of those who are to train the young— especially the young of our heathens. The Bible incarnated in the teacher is worth more to them than sermons, precepts or creed. As is the teacher, so is the pupil—character begets character. But

---

1 AEC, RG 72 45, Samuel D. Ferguson, 20 April 1893, to Langford.
2 AEC, RG 72 45, Samuel D. Ferguson, Bishop's Annual Report, 30 June 1894.

yet, the late incumbent of this station in an address some time since—the two departments being at variance, or rather, the incumbent being at variance with the other department—said, "Children, you must not do as we teachers do; but do as we tell you to do."[1]

When Ferguson dismissed Shannon, he made Walters the superintendent *pro tem* of the Cape Mount Mission. In his annual report at the end of June, 1894, Ferguson wrote of Walters:

> Mr. Joseph J. Walters, fresh from first class intellectual advantages in the United States, and who had arrived in August, has been appointed superintendent *pro tem*. He is unfortunately in bad health—the victim of a lung trouble which seized him abroad. Our warm climate and especially the favorable location of that station for sanitary purposes have improved his health; and I trust that, through God's mercy, he will be quite restored to render much valuable assistance in the work for which he is evidently well qualified.[2]

Walters was enthusiastic about improving the Mission and training Mission youth. In writing the Mission's Annual Report to the Board of Missions in New York, he made a fervent plea to the Board for funds to enable the Cape Mount students to get the finest Christian training so that they might carry the Gospel to the world. Soon, however, Walters's ardor was undone by his illness.

On October 23, Mrs. Brierley returned to Cape Mount, accompanied by Sarah Walrath, an American missionary physician. Writing to Kimber to announce her safe arrival, Mrs. Brierley stated, "Poor Mr. Walters is suffering greatly, humanly speaking it will not be long before he is called to his Home on High."[3] A few weeks later, Bishop Ferguson visited the Mission. Writing from Monrovia, he told the Rev. Langford on November 16, "Mr. Walters had not improved in health but was rather getting worse. Dr. Walrath thinks his end might come at any time."[4] In fact, the end had already come, as a

---

1 AEC, RG 72 69, Joseph Walters, Annual Report and Scholarship Record, 1894. See Appendix E9.
2 AEC, RG 72 45, Samuel D. Ferguson, Bishop's Annual Report, 30 June 1894.
3 AEC, RG 72 34, Mrs. M.R. Brierley, 31 October 1894, to Kimber.
4 AEC, RG 72 45, Samuel D. Ferguson, 16 November 1894, to Langford.

letter from Sarah Walrath to Kimber, written three days earlier, sets out.

> We [she and Mrs. Brierley] reached Cape M. October 23. 94 after a journey of over three weeks....
>   On arriving at the station I found Mr. Walters (Supt pro tem) in a dying condition. And the (45) boys in the boys dept. of St John's Mission going wild no one to look after them. Mr W requested Mrs B to let me help him. This I have been doing since I arrived.
>   There is a wonderful work to be done within this boys department.
>   The bishop arrived here a few days ago leaving after a visit of 3 days, only leaving yesterday a.m.
>   ...
>   This P.M. at 11.30, I was over in the house where Mr. Walters was sick. He called loud for a boy and the exertion caused the bursting of an artery. or B. vessel. And he expired in a very few moments. So we have had the funeral to day.[1]

Walrath also wrote to Bishop Ferguson, who replied, "Yours of the 13th inst. has just reached me, bearing the sad tidings of the death of Mr. Walters. Though I knew him to have been in a critical condition, I did not think the end was so near. But if all was well with his soul, he could not get to rest too soon."[2]

Presumably Walters was buried in the Mission graveyard.[3] Mrs. Brierley wrote to Kimber in New York, "Mr. Walters did a great work & it was a mysterious dispensation that he should be removed, when workers are so needed."[4] Bishop Penick wrote to Kimber,

> We have just had a letter from Mrs. Brierley, saying Joe Walters at C. Mt. is dead. He was in my judgment one of the brightest, bravest, truest men we ever had from the Negro race. But God knows where such spirits can do the best work for Him & it is all

---

1 AEC, RG 72 68, Sarah Lane Walrath, 13 November 1894, to Kimber. Dr. Walrath's letter seems to have been composed at more than one sitting.
2 AEC, RG 72 45, Samuel D. Ferguson, 24 November 1894, to Walrath.
3 In June, 2000, Singler and Boakai Zoludua searched the St. John's Mission graveyard to see if a stone existed for Walters there. They examined every tombstone in the small cemetery, but did not find a marker for him.
4 AEC, RG 72 34, Mrs. M.R. Brierley, 8 March 1895, to Kimber.

well. We don't know how many thousand fold one's power is multiplied by passing on up nearer the "King" & the "Great White Throne." Amen.[1]

Years later, in mourning the loss of the Grebo priest the Rev. M.P. Keda Valentine, Bishop Penick commented: "Now he is gone to join the other brave cultured, true spirits—Montgomery and Walters—three bright stars in that dark land's firmament."[2] The most detailed obituary of Walters that survives is one that appeared in the *Oberlin Review*. (It is presented in full in Appendix F2.)

> Perhaps no one of the many students who have come from heathen countries ... has come into closer and more intimate association with the general life of the College than Mr. Walters. Perhaps no one of them has so influenced the life and thought of his classmates toward the development of truth, not only in regard to the condition and needs of Africa, though that was a subject very dear to his heart, but as well toward all noble conceptions of justice and religion.... To have known Mr. Walters well was to have obtained a stronger and clearer faith in the practicability of Christianity and civilization for the world, and especially a keener sense of sympathy in the great work of redeeming Africa.[3]

In 1985, after learning of *Guanya Pau's* existence and determining Walters's connection to the Cape Mount Mission, Singler traveled to Robertsport. He spoke with Mr. Isaac Perry, who had been a St. John's boy in the first decade of the twentieth century. Mr. Perry was an elder widely admired for his command of local history, especially as it pertained to the Mission. In 1954, Rebecca Ware had interviewed three different Vai men on the history of the Episcopal schools of Grand Cape Mount, including Mr. Perry. At least one of them remembered Walters and told Ware about him. But by 1985, neither Mr. Perry nor anyone else Singler spoke with had heard of him. At the Mission too long ago and for too short a time, Walters had ceased to be a part of its lore.

---

1 AEC, RG 72 59, Charles C. Penick, 9 January 1895, to Kimber.
2 Quoted in *Liberia: Handbooks of the Mission of the Episcopal Church, No. 4* (New York: National Council, 1928) 58. "Montgomery" was the Rev. L.L. Montgomery, a Settler priest who was stationed in Grand Bassa and Sinoe Counties.
3 George W. Hinman, "In Memoriam," *Oberlin Review* (6 February 1895): 288. See Appendix F2.

Joseph Jeffrey Walters: A Brief Chronology

1860s   Joseph Jeffrey Walters is born to Vai parents on or near the Cape Mount peninsula, Liberia.

1878   Bishop Charles C. Penick of the Episcopal Church of the US founds the Cape Mount Mission.

1878-82   Walters attends the Cape Mount Mission for three years; may have worked as Penick's houseboy.

1883   Penick brings Walters to the US for further schooling; Walters arrives in the spring; in the fall enrolls at Storer College, Harpers Ferry, West Virginia.

1885   Completes the State Normal Course for teachers, enrolls in Storer's Academic Department.

1888   Transfers to the pre-collegiate division of Oberlin College, Oberlin, Ohio.

1889   Begins the degree course at Oberlin in the fall; elects the Classical curriculum.

Late 1880s–Early 1890s
    While in the US, presumably while at Oberlin, contracts tuberculosis.

1891   *Guanya Pau: A Story of an African Princess* published in Cleveland, Ohio.

1893   Completes his studies at Oberlin and receives his bachelor's degree; too ill to remain in the US for further study he returns to Robertsport, Cape Mount, Liberia, in August.

1894   Begins teaching at the Cape Mount Mission; Episcopal Bishop Ferguson appoints him superintendent *pro tem* of the Mission in May; his illness worsens, and he dies on November 12.

A Note on the Text

Guanya Pau: A Story of an African Princess was published in 1891 in Cleveland, Ohio, USA. We have reproduced that edition here exactly as then printed. The only other edition was that reissued in serial form in *The Liberian Recorder*, a Monrovian newspaper in 1905-6. Chapter 1 and part of Chapter 2 appeared on 11 November 1905. Copies of the editions in which the rest of Chapter 2 may have appeared have not been found. In the later editions which survive, Chapter 3 and Chapter 4 appeared on 9 December 1905; Chapter 5 appeared on 23 December 1905; and the whole of Chapter 6 appeared on 10 March 1906. No later issues survive in the runs of the newspaper we have found. What survives of this reissue is identical with the 1891 edition except for the omission of the footnote referencing Niebuhr in Chapter 5.

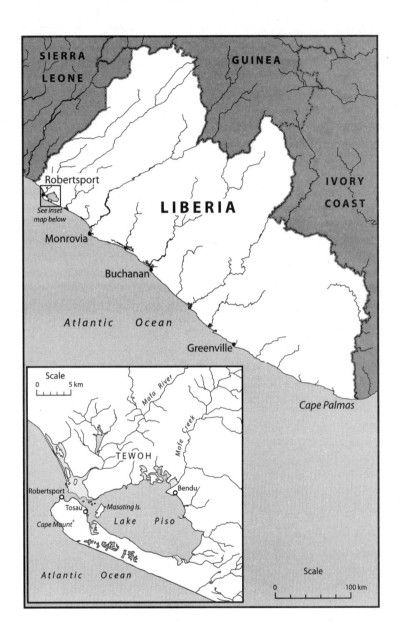

Introductory Notes to Guanya Pau

A note on flora and fauna
In Liberia names for European and North American plants and animals have often been applied to local species even when there is little taxonomic connection. However, Walters goes beyond that in his use of names for flora and fauna, presenting not so much a real world as an idealized one, specifically a late Victorian world of romantic hue. Even though there would have been nothing in the Vai region at the time to correspond to a "rose" or a "lark" or a "squirrel" and even though these were not words that had entered Liberian nomenclature, they show up in *Guanya Pau*. Rather than pointing out each such instance, we have instead limited our notes about flora and fauna to instances where Walters is making reference to a specific entity known to exist in West Africa.

A note on topography and toponyms
Walters makes crucial reference to the Marphar River and Lake Pisu. As a map of the Vai region indicates, these exist and are central elements of Vai geography. (On the map, in the Introduction, and in the notes modern spellings are used, i.e., "Mafa" and "Piso.") In giving names to villages, Walters has generally used the names of real places, but he has used them in ways that neither correspond to their location nor their history. "Tosau Island" (149ff.) is a case in point. There is a village named Tosau on the banks of Lake Piso, a few miles away from Robertsport. It is not on an island. There is an island, Masating, in Lake Piso not far from Tosau. It is uninhabited. In the book, while Guanya is on Tosau Island, a woman there tells her that "[d]own the Beach ... is an American (Liberian) settlement," i.e., Robertsport. Guanya tells Jassah that the woman "then advised me to accept a passage in the king's big canoe, which leaves for Bendoo, where we can get an easy opportunity to go to the Beach" (150). Accordingly, Guanya and Jassah travel by canoe to Bendoo, arriving there in "a few hours" (152). They then set out on their own in a canoe for the twelve-hour journey from Bendoo to the "American (Liberian) settlement." In fact, if Guanya and Jassah had been in the factual Tosau, they would have walked to Robertsport, as it is less than an hour's walk away. If they had been on Masating Island, they would have taken a short canoe ride to the mainland, i.e., to the peninsula, to a point between Tosau and Robertsport and then walked to the settlement.

A note on the credibility and realism of Guanya Pau

In the course of *Guanya Pau*, certain events occur that are improbable and are not consonant with known facts. These are generally of two types. In the first, Walters overstates particular instances of the mistreatment of women. For example, a man who beats his wife to death, Kai Jalley, successfully defends himself from a charge of murder on the grounds that his wife was his personal property that he was free to use or abuse as he chose (110). In fact, a Vai person who killed another freeborn person of either sex would have been considered guilty of murder. The second type involves implausible events introduced simply to advance the plot, e.g., when Guanya and Jassah crawl into the *bugbug* hill to hide. As indicated in p. 95, note 2, it is not physically possible for two adults to hide in a *bugbug* hill.

A note on personal names

A few names in *Guanya Pau* carry meaning, notably *Kai Kundu (kàì* "man" + *kúndú* "short")–"his name was Kai Kundu, because of his short, stumpy form" (Chapter IV)–but also *Kai Jalley (kàí* "man" + *jààlè* "red"). Ordinarily, a *Kai Jalley* would be a European or, as in the case of the man in Chapter VIII, an African with reddish skin. More commonly, the names in *Guanya Pau* are simply common names and do not carry special meaning. These include the women's name *Jassah (jàsá)* and the men's names *Momo (mɔ́mɔ́), Musah (músâ), Jallah (jàlá), Ballah (bàlá),* and *Varney (vàànìí)*. (Some Vai names, e.g., *Momo* and *Musah,* are Arabic in origin.) A name like *Guanya (gwànyà)* occurs in Vai but is not common. A further point about Vai names is that terms of respect sometimes get incorporated into people's names. This is the case with *Mànjá* "chief," *Màmá* "a distinguished elderly woman" (also the Vai word for "grandmother"), and *Pápá* "a distinguished elderly man." Sometimes a man's name begins with *Kàí* "man." Some of the names look as if they *should* mean something, most conspicuously *Pandama-Pluzhaway, the Devil's brother-in-law* (Chapter III), *Gandanya the Witch* (Chapter VIII) and *Dr. Papa-Guy-a-Gey, the famous physician of the Marphar* (Chapter VIII), but they are unrecognizable to the Vai speakers whom we consulted.

A note on orthography and on the transcription of Vai words

In spelling Vai, Walters uses <au> for [ɔ]. (This is the vowel in *caught* in British English.) Thus, "Guanya Pau" is pronounced *gwà-nyà pɔ*. Vai uses lexical tone; thus, each syllable has a characteristic pitch assigned to it, either high, low, high–low, or low–high. When we have been able to determine the Vai words that Walters is using, we have provided the word's tone melody in the notes. <´> marks a high pitch, <`> a low one, <^> a falling pitch, and <˅> a rising pitch. The transcription of Vai words makes use of Welmers and Kandakai's 1974 dictionary and Welmers's 1976 grammar where possible; we have supplemented that source by working with native speakers of Vai. The tone melody of a word often changes when it is part of a compound; when we present a compound, we present the adjusted tone melody. (Thus, kàí "man" appears in the notes at different points not only as kàí but also as káí, kàì, and káì.) When Walters writes a Vai word as beginning with a <d>, we have transcribed it with an <l>; there is variation in the sound's pronunciation, and we follow Welmers and Kandakai in representing the more common modern pronunciation. When a Vai word has an /l/ in the middle, its pronunciation is optional; this sound in this position appears to be in the process of slowly disappearing from the language. When Walters writes a word with an <l> internally, we have written it with an <l>. When he leaves it out, we have left it out.

GUANYA PAU:
A Story of an African Princess.
BY
JOSEPH J. WALTERS,
NATIVE OF LIBERIA, WEST AFRICA.

Cleveland, O.
Printed by Lauer & Mattill.
1891.

"It seems needful that something should be said specially about the education of women. As regards their interests they have been unkindly treated— too much flattered, too little respected. They are shut up in the world of conventionalities, and naturally believe that to be the only world. The theory of their education seems to be that they should not be made companions of men, and some would say they certainly are not."

Friends in Council, B. I. ch. VIII

QUEEN RANAVALONA III.,
OF MADAGASCAR.

CONTENTS.

INTRODUCTION.

This little book I give to the public, conscious of its defects and lack of literary finish. The author is an undergraduate and cannot hope to be able to make a valuable contribution to Literature. But this book, incorrect as it is, with its many errors of grammar and composition, has its MESSAGE. I feel assured that it will not fail to arouse the sympathy of those who read it, the women especially, in behalf of their unfortunate sisters in that dark land.

The facts herein given, though perhaps in some places misstated, are nevertheless a fair picture of woman's life in Africa, coming from one who has had ample opportunity to learn whereof he writes, and who has coursing through his veins the same blood as those for whom this book pleads, and who has consecrated his life to the evangelization of his people.

This is the author's first plea in behalf of his native land, and how appropriate that it should be for those who constitute the prop and stay of the national fabric; for no country can become great until it has pure, true, virtuous women, and Africa will take her place abreast of her sister continents only when her women are saved.

In short, our women must be educated. The infamous system of betrothing girls when three and four years old must be obliterated. *Polygamy must be wiped out of the land.* There are women in that country who would be as pure and good, who would make as blessed wives and noble mothers, as those of any land were it not for the incestuous pandemonium[1] in which they are incarcerated.

I beseech you, my lady readers, to take this matter to heart,[2] and to help us in this great work for God and humanity. Remember, they will be educated and saved only when you will help us with the three means necessary for the work:

First, *Human forces*—"How shall they hear without a preacher?"

---

1 At no point in *Guanya Pau* does Walters elaborate, nor does he attempt to justify this phrase. According to Svend E. Holsoe, "The Vai have few limitations on marriage. Any woman who is not related to [a] man closer than two generations on the patrilineal side ... is eligible for marriage" (*The Cassava-Leaf People*, 11). It is a considerable leap from this description of Vai marriage restrictions to Walters's "incestuous pandemonium."

2 This clearly indicates that Walters had an audience of women in mind, and that as he says elsewhere his main reason for writing the book is to raise money to facilitate the work of educating Liberian women.

Second, *Prayer*—"The effectual, fervent prayer of a righteous man availeth much."

Third, *Giving*—"Give ye them to eat."[1]

And God will reward you richly for doing this for His Name's sake.

JOSEPH J. WALTERS,
Oberlin, Ohio.

---

1   Matthew 6:37.

GUANYA PAU.
A Story of an African Princess.

CHAPTER I.

GUANYA PAU'S FATHER.

Among the many tribes living about Liberia, is the Vey,[1] the most intelligent, the Kru[2] excepted, and promising of all the natives of the west coast. They live on both banks of the Cape Mount[3] and Marphar Rivers[4] and Pisu Lake.[5] Neat little towns and villages at intervals of five and ten miles dot the banks making a chain of stations as far as the streams are navigable by the smallest canoe. The Veys are a comparatively industrious people. They cultivate the cassada,[6]

---

1   Modern "Vai." An ethnolinguistic group in modern Liberia and Sierra Leone. The Vai language falls within the Northern branch of the Mande branch of the Niger-Congo family. See David J. Dwyer, "Mande," *The Niger-Congo Languages*, ed. John Bendor-Samuel (Lanham, MD: UP of America, 1989) 50.

2   An ethnolinguistic grouping in modern Liberia. While it can refer narrowly to the Klao (Liberian English "Kru"), it often extends to the Bassa and the Grebo as well. Klao, Bassa, and Grebo languages fall within the Western branch of the Kru branch of Niger-Congo. See Lynell Marchese, "Kru," *The Niger-Congo Languages*, ed. John Bendor-Samuel (Lanham, MD: UP of America, 1989) 125. From at least the beginning of the nineteenth century, "Kru mariners" worked on board European ships when they reached the African coast; they also served as middlemen in trade between European ships and Africans. See George E. Brooks, Jr., *The Kru Mariner in the Nineteenth Century: An Historical Compendium.* (Newark, DL: University of Delaware, Department of Anthropology, 1972), and Jane J. Martin, *Krumen "Down the Coast": Liberian Migrants on the West African Coast in the 19th Century* (Boston: Boston University, 1982).

3   A peninsula that stretches between the Atlantic Ocean and Lake Piso. The term usually refers either to the communities at the tip of the peninsula or to the region more generally that extends from the coast inland. (See "The Vai country" in the Introduction.) There is no "Cape Mount River."

4   Modern spelling *Màfà*. A river that flows through the interior of the Vai region before emptying into Lake Piso near the "bar mouth," i.e., the place where Lake Piso meets the Atlantic Ocean.

5   Modern spelling, *Pìsò*. A lake of brackish water that borders Cape Mount on one side. Various rivers, most significantly the Mafa, enter into it. The Piso connects to the Atlantic via a narrow inlet.

6   Cassava, manioc. "the tuber of the sweet manioc (*Manihot palmata*)." See Warren d'Azevedo, *Some Liberian English Usages* (Monrovia: The United States Peace Corps, 1971) C-1.

yam, edo,[1] rice, maize, millet, and most of the fruits common to the country. They have a dialect peculiar to themselves, and withal are very conservative, and are extremely superstitious.

Each town and village has its own chief, with a king at the head of the whole tribe.

The chief of the town of Gallenah[2]—which was a marvel of beauty for a heathen town and the idol of the Gallenians, admirably situated on the left bank of the Marphar, on an eminence overlooking the most beautiful views of the Marphar. The chief of this town was Manja (king) Kai Popo, the father of our Princess. Here Guanya Pau was born, and among the jagged hills and villages and the rural scenes of this lovely spot she spent her earliest days of girlhood.

Guanya Pau was proud of her ancestry, and well she might; for hers was a worthy one. They were all men of war, who had battled for their country's freedom, and fallen heroically in the front ranks. Those men who could show scars on their person, or other indications acquired in their country's defense, used to constitute among them the true nobility. "Martial prowess"; "war-like stamina"; "ready to respond to the peal of the clarion"; these were the watchwords of the once patriotic Veys.

The Veys of to-day are but pigmies to what they once were. The martial spirit has waned. The patriotic sentiments, the undaunted heroism, the give-me-liberty-or-give-me-death principle, the contempt for the coward and praise for the brave, have dwindled to an alarming degree. It has been truly said that a nation is great in proportion as it has great men.

The Veys were at their zenith in the days of princes Mannah, Ballah, Hole-in-the-Head, and kings Sandfish and Kai Popo.[3] These

---

1 Edo, later edoe, is "the tuber of the *Colocasia escalenta* or *Xanthosoma sagittifolium*. Known elsewhere as coco-yam, or taro." Warren d'Azevedo, *Some Liberian English Usages*, E-1.

2 According to Walters, Gallenah was "situated on the left bank of the Marphar." In fact, *Gallinas* is a Vai region on the Atlantic in what is today Sierra Leone; it is not at all near the Mafa. (For a discussion of Walters's adaptation of place names, see the note on p. 65.)

3 The two persons in this list who represent known historical personages, Mannah and Sandfish, were not the champions of liberty and statesmanship that Walters would have them be, particularly not Prince Mannah, who was a powerful and bellicose Vai leader from Gallinas in the

were men of superior fibre. In strength, herculean; in statesmanship, brilliant; in principle, uncompromising. With them liberty was man's supreme and divine right, and he had no reason to live except in the full, untrammeled exercise of it. No threat could baffle them, no sudden appearance of the enemy on the frontier could intimidate them, no amount of money could bribe them. But one reason for the present degeneration of the Veys is due to their alliance with the Liberians who fight their battles for them.[1]

Guanya Pau could trace her ancestry back four generations. Her father was the last of the long line of mighty warriors—the last prop of the Vey national fabric. Prince Mannah, her great-grandfather, was he who led the victorious legions through the turbulent struggles of Bessie and Cabah (the most famous battles of the Veys);[2] her grandfather, Prince Ballah Kai Palley, met the combined forces of the Cor-

---

mid-nineteenth century. When Mannah's father died in the early 1840s, Mannah resumed a war that his father had commenced in the 1820s. The war dragged on through the 1840s and into the 1850s. Then, at a peace conference to end the war, Mannah and his allies killed large numbers of the enemy chiefs and elders. The survivors fled southeast into the Tewoh chiefdom, on the banks of the Mafa River. Late in the 1860s, Mannah waged new wars against fellow Vai and was still at war with them and their Settler allies when he died in 1872. King Sandfish (Vai name, *Gafe*) governed a region on the coast between the Mafa and Mano Rivers. Early in his life, he was an important slave dealer. In 1848, however, he signed a treaty with the British Navy by which he agreed to prohibit slave trading in the territory that he governed. He was estimated to be in his eighties in the 1850s. See Svend E. Holsoe, *The Cassava-Leaf People* (Boston University PhD dissertation, 1967) 121, 138, 154, 164, 182-83.

1   In the late 1860s, the Settlers dominated the joint Settler-Vai armies that drove Prince Mannah—also Vai—out of the Manna chiefdom (north of the Mano River) and then defeated him at Gbehseh [Walters's *Bessie*] (see the next note). Walters's loyalties are clearly to the Vai of his home area, i.e., the Lake Piso and Mafa River region, and these are the Vai who were the Settlers' allies.

2   While Prince Mannah did participate in the battle at *Bessie* (*gbὲsὲ*) in Tewoh chiefdom, it was as the leader of the other side, the foe whom the local Vai and their Settler allies were fighting.

sau, Hurraw and Pahn[1] near the Pisu Lake, and gained a triumphant victory, which made the Marphar free. Her own father, Manja, Kai Popo, excelled his father and grandfather by having in addition to his martial prowess the ability of a statesman. Had this man been born under the benign heaven of Europe or America, his name would stand in history beside the immortal Napoleon and Washington. How true the lines of Grey's elegy:

"Full many a gem of purest ray serene
The dark unfathomed caves of ocean bear;
Full many a flower is born to blush unseen,
And waste its sweetness on the desert air."

He could martial his phalanx against the fort of the enemy, carry it by storm, and found on its very ruins an emporium which would soon take its place in agricultural and commercial importance. Like the Roman Cincinnatus,[2] many a time did the messenger, who brought the summons for him to go to war, find him cultivating the yam or edoe. In this respect their dignitaries of yore differed from those of to-day; and I may say that this is the supreme cause of their decline. They did not look upon work as something beneath the dignity of a gentleman. One would often see the chief with hoe in hand working side by side with his servants. The Vey gentleman of

---

1   *Corsau* refers to the *Kɔɔ* Mende, i.e., those in the eastern part of Mendeland. *Pahn* refers to mercenaries from the Kpa or western Mende region (Vai *kpaŋ*). Indirect evidence suggests that *Hurraw* is another term for *Corsau*. (Bishop Penick refers to Pela Penick as "Cossa"/"Cossar," while records at the Cape Mount Mission designate him and certain other boys as "Hurrah." Also, the Vai word for the Mende is *hùɔ́wɛ̀*.) Thus, all three terms refer to the Mende. The Mende are an ethnolinguistic group in much of modern Sierra Leone and a small part of Liberia; they are customarily divided into Kɔɔ (*Corsau*) in the east, Sewa in the center, and Kpa in the west. The language falls within the Southwestern branch of the Mande branch of Niger-Congo (David J. Dwyer, "Mande," 50). A war among the Vai, Gola, and Mende that lasted from 1878 to 1882 is referred to by the Vai as "Pahn war," a reference to the *kpaŋ* mercenaries; presumably that is what Walters is referring to here.

2   Lucius Quinctius Cincinnatus, who in the year 458 BC was called upon by a delegation from the Roman senate to defend Rome from attacking forces. The delegation found him plowing his small farm.

to-day, on the other hand, has many *jonkais* (servants)[1] and *musus* (wives)[2] who do the work, while he lounges around chatting and smoking, and flirting with the pretty Borneys.[3]

It is said of Manja Kai Popo that one day while he was engaged in digging a furrow in which to plant yams, he was asked by a gentleman, who came up dressed as if for a monkey banquet, whether he would not feel ashamed if some distinguished visitor from afar, who had heard of his fame and had made the journey thither with the expressed purpose of seeing him, to be found with nothing on but his "*bellay*"[4] in the hot sun working like a slave.[5] When Kai Popo curtly replied: "No; but I *would* be ashamed if such a one would find me in your condition, always dressed up strutting around like a peacock, interrupting those who are at their work, both by my appearance and my unseasonable conversation. It is not always, my dear man, that the 'apparel proclaims the man.' Men know me by *what I have done and am, not by what I have on.*"

Kai Popo's chief pride was in laying bare his breast to show a stranger the multitudinous scars which adorned his person. "These," said he, "are my greatest possessions; by them I show to the world that I love my country and would die for her welfare."

But Kai Popo's greatest achievement was the bringing the two sections of the Marphar, which had long stood apart and constantly wrangled with each other, into friendly and harmonious relations.[6] He saw

---

1 *jɔŋ* "slave" + *kái* "man" + -*s*. Though Walters translates the term as "servant," "slave" is more accurate. See the discussion of Vai servitude in "Domestic slavery among the Vai" in the Introduction.

2 *mùsú* "woman, wife" + -*s*.

3 *bɔ́nê* + -*s*. A stage in a Sande student's training. While a Borney, a girl is permitted to go outside the bush school fence under certain circumstances. See "Bush Schools and Traditional Education" in the Introduction.

4 A single strip of cloth that is wrapped around the waist and then between the legs, it is sometimes worn as the sole object of clothing by men engaged in farming. The term is no longer used in Vai. See S.W. Koelle, *Outlines of a Grammar of the Vei Language* (London: Church Missionary Society, 1854) 147.

5 For a discussion of Walters's use of the word *slave* in *Guanya Pau*, see the "The Treatment of Slavery in *Guanya Pau*" in the Introduction.

6 The "left bank of the Marphar," where Kai Popo lived, is part of the Tewoh chiefdom. If Kai Popo's unification of "the two sections of the Marphar" is meant to have a factual basis in Vai affairs in the second half of the nineteenth century, then it would presumably refer to the cessation of hostilities between Luambo Combo, the head of the Fahnbulleh clan (and an ally of Prince Mannah), and his nominal overlord, Mwana Sando, the chief of Tewoh.

that that state of things rendered them an easy prey to the Bush Tribes,[1] and would eventually bring upon them serious calamities. "In union alone," he argued, "there is strength." Out of which alliance grew several institutions, the most noteworthy among them are the Sembey[2] and the Boys' Gregree-Bush; the Girls' Gregree-Bush,[3] which was weak and threatening, he placed on a more permanent basis.

Like all the heathen worthies, Kai Popo was a polygamist—he had ten wives, to whom he was very kind, and it was a question with his friends how such a warrior as he was, could be so indulgent to his wives; for such nature in a man is considered among them to be indicative of effeminacy. This man showed by his life that a man can be great and at the same time be kind and amiable, and that too to his wives. His head-wife was Mama Kendidia, the mother of our Princess. She was a woman, imperious in her bearing, of remarkable self-will, with a temper that would catch fire on the touch of the smallest spark, and withal she was pretty, characteristics which were diametrically opposite to those of Kai Popo, who was of amiable and pleasing disposition, always ready for a good joke and laugh, endowed with the face that could not at all lay claim to comeliness. But this last we could judge from the description of his wife, as it is a common experience that homely men for the most part secure pretty wives.

---

1   It is not clear whether this refers to the Vai's Gola and Mende neighbors or, rather, to groups further into the interior.

2   The term "sembey" is unknown in modern Vai. Presumably, Walters's source is Mende *sɛmɛ́*, an "open-sided building for public meetings, court-house." See Gordon Innes, *A Mende-English Dictionary* (Cambridge: Cambridge UP, 1969) 132.

3   The Poro and Sande secret associations, respectively. (See the discussion of "The Poro and Sande" in the Introduction.) They appear to antedate the Vai arrival in the region in the sixteenth century; thus, attributing the founding of the "Boys' Gregree-Bush" to a mid-nineteenth-century Vai chief is ahistorical, as Walters would have known. The term *gregree* appears to have its origin elsewhere in Africa and then to have been brought to the Vai region by Europeans. Webster's defines *gris-gris*, i.e., *gregree*, as "an amulet or incantation used chiefly by people of African Negro ancestry." Amulets are centrally associated with the Poro and Sande and embody each society's authority and spiritual power. "Poro" itself can refer to an amulet: Holsoe reports that the British, in an 1878 effort to end a war among Vai chiefs, asked Mwana Sando, the chief of Tewoh, "to send a *poro* to all the chiefs involved, asking them to swear upon it to cease fighting" (Svend E. Holsoe, *The Cassava-Leaf People*, 191).

CHAPTER II.
GUANYA PAU'S EARLY LIFE.

Guanya Pau was denied the pleasure of her father's genial society through girlhood, as he died when she was scarcely four years old. She had a faint recollection of him coming in from the chase or farm and taking up her baby brother, who was greased over with palm oil, lying out in the sun (a precaution used with children to make them supple and strong); and of his once administering a reprimand to one of his refractory wives.

She was the second edition of her mother. The same independent bearing, the queenly carriage, the scornful air, the careless attitude, the cleanly-cut, well-made features, large expressive eyes, the reckless abandon which characterized the toss of her pretty little head, dimpled cheeks, pearly teeth, mouth and lips a decided improvement on the typical African's, lithe, elastic, a little graceful, straight-forward, practical, a matter-of-fact kind of girl, somewhat headstrong, with the air of one who was born to rule and not to be ruled.*

Guanya Pau was, of course, a Gregree-Bush girl, consequently her name was changed to "Borney," the common name of the Gregree-Bush girls; by which name we shall occasionally call her.

On her father's death, she, scarcely four years old, was betrothed to a "gentleman" of the Pisu; not one of the royalty as her father had wished.[1] Her mother, who understood her disposition, knew well that she would incur bitter experiences should she be clothed with power in a land where woman is not considered man's equal.

The man to whom she was betrothed, though of lower rank, was comparatively wealthy, according to their standard of wealth, and was therefore able to pay a handsome dowry for her of about $300 in

---

* It is nothing strange that in Africa, and that too in the parts called "Negro land," we find women with features as fair and delicate as the Caucasian; small hands and feet, oval cheeks, teeth of marvelous whiteness, and many exceedingly beautiful. The writer in his travels accidentally met a "Borney" whose superior he has not seen in the United States. Not only had she a beautiful face, but possessed a symmetrical and well-proportioned figure, and withal she was superlatively modest. [Despite his frequent support for Africa and Africans, Walters is not immune from the general prejudices which missionaries and others frequently expressed concerning the superiority of European to African "features."]

---

1 Among the Vai, chieftaincies were inherited.

wood and ivory.[1] The average dowry is between fifty and one hundred dollars; and after you have gotten the woman, if you find that she is not a whole hundred per cent., like any other transaction, she can be restored and the money refunded. The custom in some sections is that when a man takes unto himself a wife, a report of several guns testifies that he is pleased with her,[2] and no salute signifies displeasure, and to-morrow morning she may be seen with her little bundle making her way back to her mother's house, to await another chance for disposal.

But no sooner did our Borney come to years of discretion than she expressed extreme dissatisfaction with the system in vogue, and positively declared more than once that she would never submit to it.

Just at this time a new star crossed the orbit of her life. My gentlemen readers would think from the description I have given of Guanya Pau that she was unamenable to masculine influences; but Guanya Pau was *genus homo* after all. A bold youth of her own age *did* succeed in capturing her affections, and they both vowed eternal love.

But the crisis came. The man to whom she was betrothed when a child, who was her senior by nearly twenty years, and who had already six wives, with bright prospects for six more, put in his claim; but after recovering from the shock, which it caused her, she told her comrades with all the emphasis of her positive nature, that *sooner than marry him she would drown herself in the lake.* Her fellow Borneys, and especially her bosom friend, Jassah Guey, remonstrated with her, telling her that it was useless, that the system was an old, established one, that other maidens of her spirit, they learned, had been brutally forced into submission, that the wisest thing was to submit cheerfully.

One day when Guanya and her friend had gone to their room, after a lecture from their matron to the former for some alleged act of misdemeanor, Guanya took her seat on the mat beside Jassah, and holding her hand, said: "Jassah, can I trust you?" "O Guanya Pau!" replied Jassah, "what a question! Have I ever deceived you before?" "No, my dearest, sweetest, little friend; no, no, you have never deceived me; but you know you have had no special occasion to do so, nor do I believe if there were would you have done so. But I ask it because I have a secret to disclose to you, and I want to know if you can keep it all to yourself. Jassah, will you promise me that you will be my second-self, and keep my secrets as you would your own?" "Guanya,"

---

1 A fancifully large sum for a dowry in Walters's time. (See "Child Betrothal, Women's Agency, and Vai Marriage Practices" in the Introduction.)
2 This discussion refers specifically—and only—to the bride's virginity.

rejoined Jassah, "I am surprised at the seeming doubtfulness you have of my sincerity and love, which your question implies. But perhaps I am mistaken, this may be something serious, and therefore you want me to feel its importance, so then I promise you that sooner than betray you, my darling Guanya," putting her arms affectionately around her neck and pressing her to her heart, "may the Gregrees curse me."[1] "Well," continued Guanya, "my mother has brought me word that within two moons (two months of eight weeks) some kind of a man is coming to take me to his home. She tells me that the money was paid for me when I was a little girl. Dreadful! That the dislike I then manifested for him she hoped had vanished with my increased age and experience. She added further, that if I still have repugnance toward him I might as well dissipate it as soon as possible, or she would see that I was severely punished. Saying that I was always too proud, thinking more of myself than was right for a girl, that she and thousands of other women are content with the condition of things, and what am I more than they. She would hear nothing about my loving Momo or anybody else except that somebody of whom she spoke. Indeed, Jassah, she said many bitter things which I must not take time now to recount. The truth is, my friend, my mother and the other women to whom she alluded are satisfied with this state of things, because *they know of no better. They accept them as being absolutely necessary to the life of society.* If they could see things as they really are, that they were never destined in this world to be servants—sold and treated like slaves, but on the contrary, that woman is as good and great as man, and intended to be his equal, and that the realization of this is *possible*, they would soon change their minds, and be as hostile to the present deception as I am. *But the day will come.* My mother may call me 'hot-headed,' 'headstrong,' 'wilful,' and what not: but, Jassah, I am inexorable and mean to swerve not a hair-breadth from my purpose.

"Now, Jassah, my secret is this, that baboon, I hear, is coming to see me tomorrow. I shall await him, and as soon as possible after his departure I shall run away and search for some other land, or if the Gregrees will, perish in the attempt. Now you have my secret, and my safety is in your hand. When I am gone you will pray to the Gregrees for me, won't you?"

Jassah heaved a deep sigh, then embracing her more affectionately, answered determinedly: "Guanya Pau, I shall never leave you."

---

1   Even in modern times, Vai women who are initiates of the Sande may say, "Let my Sande catch me," i.e., "If I break my promise, may the spiritual powers of the Sande doom me." Jassah's oath is arguably the strongest one available to her.

CHAPTER III.
THE GREGREE BUSH.

The Gregree Bush is an institution in some respects similar to the "White Cross Society" of America.[1]

The Girls' Gregree Bush is of time immemorial. Said to be as old as the Vey tribe itself and founded by the old wizard, Pandama-Pluzhaway, the Devil's brother-in-law. The story runs like this: This man died. Of course, he went to the Devil; for he was a devil in this world and what will hinder him from being the same in the next? When he arrived at the Devil's Palace he was asked on what business he had come. He replied he would make a contract with the Devil. Thereupon the Devil challenged him to a combat, which was the means of testing his ability to make a contract with him. But the Devil found him his match and granted him whatever favor he desired.

Upon Pandama-Pluzhaway's return to earth he instituted the Gregree Bush and appointed certain old women at its head. This is the Girls', the Boys' are of later origin and is said to owe its founding to Guanya Pau's eminent father.[2]

The Zobah,[3] as the leaders of these institutions are called, are those who lecture to the young women on matters of practical importance, and some of the instructions given by them are beneficial and wholesome. In their dress they approximate as near as possible the image of the Devil. Hence foreigners call them "Country

---

1   The White Cross Society was concerned with changing the attitudes of men towards women. The "women of many countries combined in the work of man's reformation in an organization known as the 'White Cross Society' founded in 1886, by Miss Ellice Hopkins of England, and now possessing branches in every part of the civilized world. To this society, men alone belong; its work is of a still broader character than mere reformation of the vicious; it seeks to train young men and boys to a proper respect for woman and for themselves." See Matilda Joslyn Gage, *Woman, Church and State: A Historical Account of the Status of Woman Through the Christian Ages; with Reminiscences of the Matriarchate* (New York: Truth Seeker, 1893) 212-13. Walters's comparison of the Poro and Sande societies to the White Cross Society seems odd if not misguided.

2   As indicated on p. 84, note 3, the Boys' Gregree Bush, i.e., the Poro, had been established several centuries earlier.

3   A masked figure who embodies the authority of the Sande; see "*Zobahs* and the *Gregree Bush*" in the Introduction.

Devil."[1] Their attire consists of a black gown, reaching to the ground, a false-face, a head-dress two feet long, carrying in their hand a plaited brush. They are present at all weddings and deaths of great men to lead in the song and dance.

The natives try to persuade foreigners that the Zobah are not human, but real devils. An amusing story is told of how an American was affected on meeting a Zobah. There was some celebration at a certain town when he was eager to see the whole. But in his curiosity he ventured outside of the prescribed limits[2] and, of course, one of the Zobah started at him. Fortunately the American had his gun with him, and after retreating a few steps stopped and with one of those "d—— you", for which the average American is famous, made the Devil halt, turn around, and march back to her quarters. The bully American, of course, had to pay five dollars for his imprudent act.

The Gregree Bush girls are under some strict rules. For instance, they seldom dance with men.[3] Men dance by themselves and maidens by themselves.

For unchastity the punishment is so severe that very few ever recover from it.[4]

On entering the Gregree Bush they are given a peculiar kind of beads and a small horn for the neck, which they are required always to wear.[5] As a rule these girls are respected and cases of unchastity are comparatively few.

I believe I can truly say that cases of mortal turpitude are more frequent in America than it is among these heathen people.

---

1 The term used in English in Liberia to refer to masked figures like the *Zobah*.

2 When a masked figure associated with the Poro or Sande enters a town, there are restrictions as to where anyone not associated with that Society may go and, indeed, whether non-initiates are permitted to view the masked figure at all.

3 Traditionally, a given Vai dance involves only members of one sex and is not partnered. This represents custom rather than a restriction specific to Borneys. In modern times there is one dance in which both men and women participate, the *ŋé*.

4 Vai people today say that formerly, if it was discovered that a Borney was no longer a virgin, she would be compelled to identify the man with whom she had had sex. Both parties were then stripped, tortured, and beaten by all the women of the Sande. The punishment was often fatal.

5 For a discussion of the significance of the small horn, see "Bush Schools and Traditional Education" in the Introduction.

CHAPTER IV.
KAI KUNDU'S VISIT.

On the following day, Guanya Pau being now near her sixteenth birthday,[1] within a few weeks of the time when her master would come to take her to his home, he came to the Gregree-Bush to visit her. His name was Kai Kundu, because of his short, stumpy form; he was homely beyond description, with nose and lips twenty-five per cent. in excess of the average African, with a face perpetually bearing the expression "I-don't-care-which-way-the-wind-blows, I am Kai Kundu, the short, the ugly, the clumsy, Kai Kundu."

He made an attempt to seat himself on the mat beside Guanya Pau, who immediately rose, went into the adjoining room, brought a bamboo chair, which she set at a more than respectable distance from the mat, thus avoiding all possible means of proximity between herself and his lordship. Looking up into her face with one of his characteristic grins, which made him look like a full-grown chimpanzee, he said: "Guanya Pau, I understand it all, you are yet young and inexperienced; your fair complexion has not yet been burnt by the sun's heat, nor your hands hardened by work. Your action is like that of many other maidens." Then thinking that she was persuaded of the truth of his assertion, because she made no reply, he again made an effort to bring his chair near, only to be told peremptorily that if he didn't keep to the distance she had assigned him, she would report him to the authorities for indecorum.

Finding argument useless, Kai Kundu made himself comfortable, and grinned more than ever.

The two together certainly resembled Dr. Talmage's "hawk courting a dove."[2] Finally, he mustered up enough courage to tell her his purpose for coming to see her, winding up with "I have watched and cared for you, Guanya, since you were a baby; O, my joy, when a very small girl, your mother consented to my having you, and fixed the dowry. I was so elated that I paid her more than

---

1 Since her fiancé was "her senior by nearly twenty years," he would have been approximately 35.
2 This is presumably a reference to one of the innumerable sermons of Thomas de Witt Talmage (1832-1902). He was an extremely prolific writer and preacher in America before and during the time of Walters's education there. Here it refers to the discrepancy between the ugly Kai Kundu and the young and beautiful Guanya, with a strong suggestion that he is preying on her.

what she asked. I shall make you my head wife.[1] I have cassada and rice farms all along the Marphar, have men and women gathering my nuts and making my oil.[2] I have several large canoes which carry my produce weekly to the Beach[3]—oil, kernel,[4] wood, ivory, cloth, hides, rice, etc. Now, Borney, my child," this time grinning with his whole face, "tell me what you think of me."

"When the blood burns, how prodigal the soul
Lends the tongue vows: these blazes, daughter,
Giving more light than heat,—extinct in both,
Even in their promise, as it is a-making,—
You must not take for fire."[5]

Guanya Pau with all the contempt of which her full, strong voice was capable, replied: "*Elombey,*" *etc.*[6] "What do you mean? Believe me if I tell you the truth from my heart, will you? I have not cared to think about you in any way except to hate you. As to loving you, I'd just as soon love a monkey. I shall never be your head wife, I don't care if you own all Marphar and Pisu put together, and you may convey this intelligence, if you choose, to my mother."

Kai Kundu, contracting his grin into a small compass, assured her that she would rue such expressions when she was in better spirits; but finding all attempts to make her believe this futile, he took up

---

1 Holsoe reports that, for a Vai man, "[t]he first wife he marries will remain his head wife during his and her lifetime" (*The Cassava-Leaf People*, 13). However, while exceptions to this occur only infrequently, it is possible for a man to bestow that position on a subsequent wife even if he is still married to the original head wife. As the name implies, the head wife has greater stature than other wives and authority over them. (See the discussion of "Child Betrothal, Women's Agency, and Vai Marriage Practices" in the Introduction.) A man convicted of adultery with another man's head wife has to pay a larger fine than if the adultery involves a junior wife.

2 This is a reference to palm nuts and to palm oil. Palm oil is produced by skimming the pounded pulp of the palm nut.

3 A reference to trading stations on the coast, where such items would be exported.

4 The kernel of the palm nut. Palm kernel oil, distinct from palm oil, is produced by cracking palm kernels.

5 Polonius in *Hamlet*, I.iii.116-20.

6 *í* "you" + *lɔ* "say" + *mbê* "what"? "What do you mean?"

his ungainly body, grinned like a chess-cat,[1] and stalked out of the room.

---

1   "'Please would you tell me,' said Alice, a little timidly, for she was not quite sure whether it was good manners for her to speak first, 'why your cat grins like that?' 'It's a Cheshire cat,' said the Duchess, 'and that's why'" (Lewis Carroll, *Alice in Wonderland*, Ch. 6).

CHAPTER V.

GUANYA PAU RUNS AWAY.

Immediately upon Kai Kundu's departure, Guanya Pau looked up Jassah, and told her all that had happened, assuring her that the time was ripe for their departure, and that they should use all possible precaution so as to leave behind no clue as to where they had gone.

The girls were wholly inexperienced to traveling and to the country around, not having gone ten miles from their home in all their life. After debating the question of the road, they finally concluded to take the country highway, going north, and making for the woods, several miles beyond, trusting in the Gregrees to make whatever disposition of them they will. Soon all was settled, and the two made hasty and secret preparations to run away.

That night, when it was quite dark, and the little village was buried in deep sleep, the two spirited maidens, after arranging their beads, disrobing themselves of those which would give a clue to their identity, and after invoking the Gregrees to protect them from harm, came out into the open air, with uplifted hands, looked up into the sky and made a deep, prolonged sigh. Was it our God they thus invoked in the silent recesses of their souls? Was it to Him who has said, "Come unto me all ye that labor and are heavy laden, and I will give you rest,"[1] that these poor girls in the solemn hush of that midnight hour, their souls tossed heavily by fears and apprehensions because of the risk they were about to take, leaving home and friends to go they knew not where, and that too when their whole country was pervaded with the same sentiments respecting woman; was it to Him that they went for help? Did they lift up their eyes unto the hills from whence cometh *our* help? I trow not. They had never heard the sweet call of the church-bell, nor soul-stirring words fall from the lips of some Kanabah-Kai (God man),[2] nor the inspiring strains of the Sabbath-school. No one with heart full of love for God, and with deep solicitude for souls had come among them and told the old, old story of Jesus and His love. Never had a missionary, the herald of good tidings, trod this part of the world; and oh, how true is this the case of many of the tribes of West Africa, yea, of all that continent!

---

1 Matthew 11:28-30.

2 *kàmbá* "God" + *káì* "man," i.e., "preacher." Holsoe identifies *kàmbá* as the word that the Vai use when referring to "the highest spiritual authority they know" (*The Cassava-Leaf People*, 37).

Jesus Christ died to save them nearly nineteen hundred years ago, and yet there are millions in that dark land dying ignorant of His great sacrifice and love. Dying without hope, without Christ, within [sic] Heaven!

Truly, darkness covers the land, and gross darkness the people. Oh, Lord, how long? when will this gloom dissipate and the light from the Sun of Righteousness flood the land? When, blessed Saviour, will Thy promises concerning Ethiopia be verified?[1] No, her sad condition is not *organic*, and it *is* possible to turn the tide from the channel in which it has flown for ages.

"The night is long that never finds the day."[2]

"Though ye have lain among the pots, yet shall ye be as the wings of a dove covered with silver, and her feathers with yellow gold."[3]

"For your shame ye shall have double."[4]

"Shall drink at noon......

The palm's rich nectar; and lie down at eve

In the green pastures of remembered days;

And walk, to wander and to weep no more

On Congo's mountain-coast, or Guinea's golden shore."[5]

Hark! methinks I hear a voice from the clouds, which says: "*Give ye them to eat*," [6] implying that no angelic band will descend from the skies who, with one spark, will set that land aflame with the fire of the Gospel. But YE, men and women of flesh and blood, having but five loaves and two small fishes. Yes, yes, this stupendous work, the evangelization of Africa, must be done by human agencies. Another fact is worthy of note here, and that is, civilization is never indigenous, but *conditioned on the contact of races*. "There is not in history a

---

1   Compare "Princes shall come out of Egypt; Ethiopia shall soon stretch out her hands unto God" Psalm 68:31. As a result of this verse in the Bible, "Ethiopia" was often used to represent Africa in nineteenth-century missionary literature.

2   Malcolm in *Macbeth*, IV.iii.240.

3   Psalm 68:13.

4   Isaiah 61:7.

5   We have been unable to locate this quotation despite extensive searches in hymnals and in devotional and other verse collections of the period and earlier. It is clearly part of a general missionary devotional discourse, e.g., Reginald Heber's 1819 hymn: "From Greenland's icy mountains, from India's coral strand, where Afric's sunny fountains roll down their golden sand."

6   Matthew 6:37.

record of a single indigenous civilization; there is nowhere in any reliable document the report of any people lifting themselves out of barbarism. The historic civilizations are all exotic. The torches that blaze along the line of centuries were kindled each by the one behind."*[1]

Pardon, dear reader, these occasional digressions. They are impromptu outbursts of a soul that is full of enthusiasm for his native land.

After the Borneys had finished these invocations, they took their little bundles and struck out upon the country road for the distant woods, which they reached as the first streaks of the morning reddened the eastern sky.

Through fear of detection, they crept into one of those "bugbugs"[2] in which that country abounds, and after refreshment of

---

* Niebuhr.

---

1 It seems almost certain that the Niebuhr from whom this quotation was taken was Berthold Georg Niebuhr (1776-1831). There are eight of his books in the Oberlin Library, seven of them from the period when Walters studied there. Many of these have similar sentiments, e.g., *The History of Rome*, 3 vols. (London: Walton and Maberley, 1853). A strong focus of this text is the relationship between Rome and the pre-Roman civilizations: Etruscans, Umbrians, etc. Niebuhr wants to assert that Roman civilization arises from these, thus, the book is in the spirit of the quotation that Walters cites, as the following excerpt illustrates: "... [N]ot a single instance can be produced of a really savage people which has become civilized of its own accord ..." (*History of Rome*, Vol. 1, 83). The quotation in Walters is so close in spirit to B.G. Niebuhr's work that one wonders whether Walters was paraphrasing a remembered section or general sentiment. It may be significant that he does not give the title of his source as he does in the case of the quotation from *Friends in Council* used in the book's frontispiece.

2 Mounds created by the large white ant or termite, *Macrotermes natalensis*. Such mounds can reach a height of eight to ten feet and have the strength of hard clay or cement (Warren d'Azevedo, *Some Liberian English Usages*, B-8). If the mound is at the right stage of decay and a child is small enough, then the child could crawl inside it while playing. A mound that was big enough—and with an opening that was big enough—to allow not one but two adults to climb inside would be exceptional, at the very least. Further, a mound with a hole large enough to enable Guanya and Jassah to climb into it would not be a very good hiding place. (The Liberian English word *bugbug*, more often *bugabug*, comes from the word for "termites" in Northern Mande languages, e.g., Bambara *bágàbágà*.)

some of the cassadas and dried fish, with which they had provided themselves, they remained quiet.

When the sun had set, they crept out stealthily, made a brief and hasty survey of the woods, then went on, going they knew not where, but with the satisfaction that the distance between them and their home was becoming every minute greater.

But they had not proceeded far before they heard the fall of footsteps in the distance, and soon voices of men greeted their ear. They started, looked hither and thither, but there was no place for concealment. In their extremity, with their hearts in their mouths, they retreated double-quick to the place of "bugbugs," and were soon swallowed up in one of those hospitable caverns. How they blessed the little insects for building these strongholds.

"There is a special providence in the fall of a sparrow."[1]

The voices came nearer and nearer, ever increasing in volume, from which it was evident that they were disputing. As they approached the mound in which the girls were concealed, they stopped and took their bearing; then they came up to it, lay down their spears and other hunting outfit, took down from their shoulders bunches of country bread,[2] then set to making a voracious dispatch of its contents; when one went a few feet away, cut a peculiar kind of vine, which grew suspended from a limb of a tree, from which they got a supply of water. They then talked over their plans, and again tried to ascertain their whereabouts. They were two Vey men from a town several miles away on the chase of a wounded elephant. You may imagine what relief the Borneys felt when such discovery was made. But they soon became anxious, when one of the men intimated his intention to crawl inside the same hill and take a nap; he was on the point of suiting the action to the word, when his companion dissuaded him, saying that they had no time to lose, and that he could hear the horns of their comrades calling.

The two hunters had not gone ten minutes, when there was a loud peal of a horn, which was repeated again and again, in the

---

1 *Hamlet*, V.ii.208-09. The phrase would no doubt also invoke for a nineteenth-century reader the popular hymn by Maria Straub written in 1874 "God sees the little sparrow fall." Both reference texts in the Gospels, Matthew 10:29-30 and Luke 12:6-7.

2 A snack food, hence one used by travelers, created from rice. The rice is cleaned, then soaked, then dried over a low fire, and then pounded in a mortar, producing a powdery consistency. The *bunches* would be "handfuls."

direction they had gone; and presently there was a tearing, bellowing noise, as if the trees of the forest had been uprooted, and the mountain was tumbling down. The roar, mingled with the yells and screams of men, made the solemn aisles of the wood echo, and re-echo. To the girls it brought unspeakable anxiety. Every moment the tumult increased in force and intensity, and seemed to be making straight for the ill-fated "bugbug." The ground beneath them literally trembled, the lofty beech and mango tossed to and fro, the pointed tops of the bugbugs were knocked off; a violent whirlwind swept the mountain, the air became charged with a mal-odor almost stifling, and surcharged with a fume as if from the crater of some volcano. Trees and shrubs were pulled up and hurled high into the air; the whole forest seemed in violent agitation; and oh, what must be the fate of the bugbug!—certainly it will not stand against the onrushing storm when such hardy trees were yielding. Another prolonged bellow, and a monstrous elephant, transfixed with a spear, tore out of the thicket with marvelous swiftness, followed by some twenty more than half-naked Veys, in full pursuit. He made straight for the bugbug, as if to hide from his pursuers. But no such intention had crossed his brain. The elephant is no coward. His aim was to get possession of this vantage ground where he could make a bold fight.

When in front of this, he halted. The men also halted. Each waited for the other to make the initiative attack. Finally, a youth of about nineteen years, with more daring than common sense, advanced nearer, and threw his dart. The elephant turned around, lifted his snout in the air, and the imprudent young brave went up in the air, and came down crashing against the unlucky bugbug. The elephant in his turn accidentally struck the mound, crushing in part of a side, making a hole large enough to expose the unfortunate girls. But this he did not do purposely; he had nothing against the maidens, and probably would have stopped and apologized, had his tormentors permitted him.

With a surprising maneuver, he turned about-face, going due north, carrying the eager huntsmen with him.

Then the winds hushed, the tempest subsided, the trees assumed their normal posture, terra firma became steady, the atmosphere received back her redolent and healthful elements; peace and order was everywhere restored, and the Borneys brought back to their right minds safe and unharmed.

CHAPTER VI.
PRINCE MARANNAH.[1]

When travel again was safe, the Borneys crept out of their hiding place, and continued their journey. At twilight of that day they came to a large rice farm. The people had ceased working for the day, and had gone to the village, at the farther end of the farm. The crackling notes of dumboy,[2] and the sweet odor of palaver-sauce and palm butter[3] (fine African dishes), reminded them of the good things they had left behind.

After it had grown dark, and they had disfigured their faces beyond recognition, they came into the village, and mingled with the crowd that had assembled before the king's house. The presence of Zobah with the particular cymbals, songs and dance, together with the peculiar attire of the participants, the disfigured and powdered faces, the manipulation of hair, so that it or its substitute stood perpendicular on the head a foot high, beads tastefully arranged around the neck and waist, and many other nameless appendages which baffle masculine vocabulary to find names for—these indicated that the celebration was that of a wedding.

The girls recoiled at the thought of another innocent damsel decoyed into the trapper's meshes. They were, therefore, anxious to learn something about the couple; for their breasts were heaving convulsively because of the injustice heaped upon their sex. They also startled at the idea of the women around manifesting such great

---

1   There is no further reference in this chapter to "Prince Marannah." Presumably, Walters changed his name to "Prince Musah" and forgot to change the chapter heading.

2   Dumboy is "boiled cassava pounded into a thick, viscous dough" (Warren d'Azevedo, *Some Liberian English Usages*, D-6). It is made by peeling the cassava, washing it thoroughly, and then boiling it. It is then placed in a mortar and pounded. As the pounding continues, the dough becomes stickier and stickier, and individual strokes of the pestle produce a sharp report, hence the crackling notes.

3   Palaver sauce is a stew made from a particular type of greens, while palm butter (French *sauce graine*) is the "thick, oily gravy strained from the pounded pulp of the palm nut" (d'Azevedo, *Some Liberian English Usages*, P-8). In each case, meat or fish and other ingredients are added, and the stew is then served with rice, cassava, or a form of prepared cassava such as dumboy or fufu.

enthusiasm over the same. It was true, as Guanya Pau had said, that they were both ignorant and blind.

Accordingly, when the chorus had sung, or rather had hallooed themselves hoarse, the door of the king's house was opened, revealing a large room, on whose hard dirt floor-mats of matchless whiteness were spread, on which were massive bowls of food. After dispatching the palatable dishes, then came the climax. The king, with his own hand, opened case after case of Holland gin,[1] until many were intoxicated. Would that I were allowed here to tell my readers something about the effect of rum and gin on the heathen. But my feelings would lead me too far off, and besides it is irrelevant to the story. Suffice it for me to say that the heathen, at his best, is little better than the beast, and can you contemplate his condition after imbibing this distillation of hell?

After the feast, reports of several guns were given, and the crowd dispersed. Guanya Pau then secured a conversation with certain women of the place, who told them the following story:

Young Prince Musah was traveling incognito, when he made a visit to his old home, where he was born and reared, a village, as he called it, "of lofty palms and pretty women."

When he had sauntered through the glens and dells of his boyish haunts, along the shady banks of streams where he used to listen to the sweet warble of the mocking-bird, and watch the squirrel prance and chirp, and had strolled around refreshing his spirits with reminiscences of by-gone sports, he decided to make the visit more remindful by taking back with him one of the pretty Borneys.

He had not long to make up his mind which of the many maidens he should choose, as the only satisfaction he required was a face fair to look upon, and one pleasing to the eyes (a fault common with African youths). Musah made his choice, and found out her guardian, who told him that the girl was sold, intimating at the same time that the whereabouts of her lover was unknown to him, he having left the country when she was quite small. But the possibility of the Prince losing this sweet girl, made him exert himself to the utmost to get her. He therefore doubled the dowry, and promised to make her his head wife, arguing withal the absurdity of hoping against hope the return of the vagabond

---

1 Presumably Dutch or Genevere gin, sometimes known as Hollands Gin. Gin was a staple of trade all along the West African coast.

lover.[1] Adding that such action on the part of the lover indicated that he was not concerned about her; "for men are generally," said he, "anxious about those to whom they are attached, and show this by their frequent presence and their attempt to cultivate acquaintance." "I can testify to this," continued he, "from personal experience." Then the Prince dwelt largely upon his worth, becoming ever eloquent, giving true examples of persuasive oratory. He was a natural orator, and he knew it, and he knew besides that with his voice he had influenced the most fastidious maiden.

The guardian, overcome by the Prince's offer and logic, sat still for a while plunged in deep meditation; then he looked up into Musah's face, as if to study his physiognomy, looked off into space, scratched his head, and drew a deep breath. His eyes then fell upon the timid Borney, who was standing behind the mat, pretending to be engaged in the arrangement of her beads.

"Borney, child of the patient heart, and idol of my house," said he, "are you willing to forego your husband who is lost to you and me, of whom during these many moons the sun has run his course, no wind has brought us intelligence? Surely such ill becomes a lover. I fear he does not care anything for you. But he may be dead, my child, and in his grave, who knows; for though we feed and nourish our dead, yet you know that no correct tidings do they send us. But, Borney, be not persuaded. In this matter I want you to be alone in your decision. Would you not though prefer this stranger, a Prince from the Pisu,[2] of noble mien and warlike appearance? Let your heart answer, Borney; but for my part, I would prefer this gentleman, though I shall not influence you." Whereupon he swung the mat back, revealing a shy maiden of "sweet sixteen," of pretty face and figure, in a profusion of blushes.

---

1 A dowry is a contract. By accepting a man's payment of a dowry, the young girl's guardian was obligated to uphold his contract with him. It would be rare for a parent to accept a second dowry like Prince Musah's. On the other hand, the protracted absence of the first suitor increased the likelihood that he would not be returning, hence that the guardian could safely enter into negotiations with somebody else. As for the Prince's promise to make the young woman his head wife, see p. 91, note 1 and "Child Betrothal, Women's Agency, and Vai Marriage Practices" in the Introduction.

2 A rhetorical flourish—this episode could not have taken place very far from the Piso.

The truth is, the girl had no decision to make, as her guardian had implied in his questions what course she should pursue. So she, without further ceremony, took her stand beside the noble young prince, and whispered, amid sobs and blushes: "I shall be your head wife, Prince Musah."

CHAPTER VII.
THE WAYSIDE WOMAN.

The next morning, as they proceeded, they met a woman who was plodding along with a child on her back, and a basket on her head. The customary greeting "*Ya ku neh*"[1] having been exchanged, Guanya Pau asked her why she looked so jaded and worn out. Taking down her basket, giving the little fellow a gentle tug, and asking them to sit down with her on a log near by, she replied: "Ah, child, my lot has been and is a hard one. May you never have to suffer what I have suffered. I was born a child of ill-luck. The Gregrees must have frowned upon me ere I saw the first light of day. Words cannot describe what sorrows and heartaches I have endured. When a little girl, I was sent to the Gregree-Bush, where I met a youth, who performed some menial services for the Zobah, and who would occasionally assist me with my work. In course of time, as we grew up, our little friendship ripened into strong attachment. I told him that if he would promise me that he would think of no other woman, I would consent to have him, and that probably I could influence my mother to reduce the dowry. He swore, adding that there was not room in his heart for another woman, and said that he had always since a boy looked upon the polygamous system with extreme disgust. He further promised that he would work hard from henceforth, and save money to buy me. In a few days he left for Solama (an English trading station on the coast),[2] where he hired himself for wages. After six moons, he came to visit me. He had improved so much, he could speak another language, called Englishee (English), and said that after six moons more he would be able to buy me. O what anticipations I allowed to flit through my young brain. To be the sole possessor of that worthy young man I thought would be something enviable. I laughed and cried, and cried and laughed. How I wished those six moons would come and go. One passed, then two, then three, then four, then five passed. I began then to count the days.

"Within two weeks of the time, I got communication from him that I must be patient and wait an additional moon longer. I was disappointed, but I knew it was all right, so I waited patiently. I was sure

---

1 *yá kùnè éé*? The greeting used upon seeing someone for the first time on a given day; literally, "have you awakened?"

2 Presumably, this is *Sùlèimà*, a trading post near the mouth of the Moa River in the Gallinas region.

Jallah, for that was his name, was true as the sunlight. But alas for me! I had in my youthful enthusiasm inadvertently disclosed the delightful secret to my fellow Borney, who told it to another, and she to her friend, and so on it went until it came to the ears of my mother. But I was not anxious even then, for I was sure that Jallah would have means sufficient to buy me. Now judge of my surprise when my mother visited me, and told me that I had been betrothed to another when a little girl.[1] I protested, told her that I loved Jallah, and would have nobody but him. She laughed saying that I had no say so in the matter, that she would dispose of me as she saw fit. But I was obstinate, and told her that she had no control over my affections, and therefore had no right to determine whom I should have. She laughed again, saying that 'affection' and 'love' had no place in this transaction, and that I would learn the same sooner or later; adding that she would have me punished if I should mention again what I was going to do. Perhaps I was impudent, for I protested to the last that I did not think it was right for her to sell me to one whom I didn't remember to have seen, and whom I was not sure whether I could love; becoming warm, I swore, yes, I became vehement; and, my child, was I not right?" Here the woman stopped short, wiped the tears which were coursing down her cheeks, gave the baby behind a touchup, then resumed her story: "They act as though we are no better than the dumb brute, *wholly destitute of womanly affections, and have no preference whatever.* If they want a reward for their care over us, why not wait until we are of sufficient age to make our own bargain? Why betroth us when we are so young, and that too to those brutal men who have already many women whom they abuse. I repeat it, *it is unjust!*"

At this point she broke completely down, and gave way to a flood of tears. The two girls were naturally similarly affected, and contributed their share of water to the already copious stream.

For a few moments silence prevailed. Finally the woman continued: "But the worst I have yet to tell. My mother left me, and I was about to congratulate myself that I had carried my point. Of course, I regretted very much that I had had occasion to express myself so positively to my mother. My passion got control of my better judgment. I know now that my mother was so hard with me, because she had spent her whole life amidst such experiences and thought nothing else could possibly be right. These were warped and woofed in her very life; consequently my poor mother could do no better. My views of life seemed a deliberate attempt on the order of things—*a revolution on society.*

---

1 It would be extremely odd for a young girl not to be aware of her betrothal.

"But I must hasten with my story, no doubt you are anxious to continue your journey." When Guanya Pau assured her that they had the whole day at their disposal, she went on: "The worst of it is, my friends, that night when I had lain for a few hours on my bed, tossing from one side to the other, unable to go to sleep from thinking of Jallah and the incidents of the past day, I heard the mat at my door rustle, then a head peeped in, soon followed by a stalwart body. I jumped from the bed, and was on the point of screaming, when a coarse voice said sternly: 'Jassah, if you make any racket this time of night Zobah will punish you most severely.' 'What in the name of the Devil-bush do you want here this time of night?' I cried. 'I have,' said he, 'an order from your mother, signed by Zobah, to take you with me.' 'Who, me?' I screamed, 'Where to, what for, who are you, who is my mother, and who is Zobah, where do they live, where did you come from, who has any right to give you commission to come and take me, who in the name of your head are you, any how, who——?' I had not finished my interrogations, when I felt a strong arm clasp me around the waist, and a hand pressed against my mouth. I struggled and fought until exhausted, when I fell motionless at his feet.

"The next morning when I awoke, I was under a shady colanut tree. The sunlight was streaming through its leafy boughs. An old woman was sitting by me with a bowl of chicken-broth, and bade me drink. I asked her where I was, how I had come there, and who she was. She promised to answer my queries if I would drink the soup. Being weak and hungry, I considered it to my interest to comply with her request. After the refreshment, I felt strengthened, and inclined to follow up my questions.

"She told me that on the previous night I had been brought there while in a swoon, that my life for a while was despaired of, (oh, would that I had died!) but that the Gregrees had been invoked, the medicine-man summoned, who performed many rites over me, and who received propitious response to his prayers. I felt something heavy around my ankle, and asked who tied it there, and for what cause. She said the medicine-man; that he had been advised to use such precaution. Then she told me that I was in the home of the man who had bought me when I was a little girl, that she was his mother, and noticing that I had became alarmed at this disclosure, she prayed me to keep still, or else I would aggravate my trouble, and fall into more serious dilemma. But her gentle words had no influence over me. Far from it for me to 'keep still.' Like one in an agony of despair, I screamed with all the strength I could command. Soon a crowd was around me, and him who had the audacity to call me 'Na *musu'* (my woman),[1] I recognized to be the same man who attacked me at my room. I screamed then the louder." She had to stop again to take breath, wipe the tears from her eyes, heaved a deep sigh, then continued: "My dear young women, may you never suffer the like. How I am living to-day, is more than I can tell. You said that I look jaded and worn out. Age is not the cause. No, it is not age. I have not yet reached my thirty-fifth year, and could easily pass for sixty. No, it is not age, *it is not age*; but something else that has made me old." "But," interrupted Guanya Pau, "did you ever hear of Jallah again?" "Wait," said she, "let me tell you. When they saw that no amount of coaxing would do, I was subjected to the severest treatment,[2] confined and fed upon rice and water for a week. After this I was somewhat cowed, and concluded to yield to my fate, thinking that perhaps some day Jallah would find me, and we would run away.

"Well, the first opportunity I got, after having been there a few weeks, I ran away; but before I had gone far, I was caught, for they suspected that I would do such a thing, and unknown to me had always watched me. I was caught, shamefully whipped, confined, and treated more cruelly than before. I was then sent along with some others of his women to work, who were instructed to lay to my share the hardest part. Suffice it for me to say that they more than obeyed the injunction; as no doubt you have observed that women can become toward their own sex even more cruel than men.

"After a few moons, that man concluded that I would never do for him, that I was more fit for a slave than for a gentleman's wife, so he sent me here to his uncle[3]—a man than whom the Devil could not be meaner; and so I am here, where I expect to spend my remaining days, which cannot be many more." "But in all this time," Guanya Pau asked again, "have you not heard anything from Jallah?" "No, child," replied the woman, "I have never heard a single word from him. We shall never meet again."

---

1 *ná* "my" + *mùsú* "woman" "my woman/my wife."
2 While it is not possible to know what that treatment would have been in the late nineteenth century, in living memory the leaders of the Sande would have punished a recalcitrant wife even more harshly than her husband would have.
3 In Vai society, there is a special relationship between a person and his or her maternal uncle (Svend E. Holsoe, "Slavery and Economic Response Among the Vai," 289). A nephew unhappy with his wife might send her to his uncle in the way Walters describes, where her status would have been largely indistinguishable from that of a slave. See the discussion of "Domestic Slavery among the Vai" in the Introduction.

CHAPTER VIII.
THE SEMBEY COURT.[1]

After the above conversation the woman arose, adjusted the little fellow behind who had began to squall, replaced her basket, pressed the hands of the Borneys, exchanged the "*Jemah weh*"[2] and they parted.

Toward the cool of the day the Borneys came to a house located at the farther end of a large cassada farm, where they stopped and rested.

Here again their indignation was intensified when they saw the wife wait upon her lord in the capacity of a servant, placing the best of everything before him, and satisfying herself with the remnant that escaped his gastronomic appetite.

After he had eaten, another brought him his pipe, and still another was preparing the mat under a shady cola, where his majesty could recline and sleep and smoke.

Then they scattered, the one with her fishing nets to the river, the other with her bill-hook[3] to the cassada farm, and the third to her mortar to beat out rice.

If reproachful frowns and glances could have inflicted injury, this distinguished personage lying out there under the shade would certainly have been seriously harmed by these girls as they passed by him on their way out.

---

1 As indicated in note 2 on p. 84, the term *Sembey* seems to be based on a Mende word. Jones cites two historical sources describing council meetings of senior officials in Gallinas that bear a direct resemblance to Walters's *Sembey Court*. Both of the historical sources identify the meetings as being Poro events. If the *Sembey Court* was likewise held within the framework of the Poro (and aspects of the description certainly point to this), even two people so dedicated to resisting the established order as Guanya and Jassah would not have dared to spy upon it, especially to spy upon it without commenting on either the risk or the defiance such an act entailed (Adam Jones, *From Slaves to Palm Kernels: A History of the Galinhas Country (West Africa) 1730-1890* (Wiesbaden: Franz Steiner, 1983); Olfert Dapper, Olfert Dapper, *Naukeurige beschrijvinge der afrikaensche gewesten* (Amsterdam, 1688); and John M. Harris, "Some Remarks on the Origin, Manners, Customs and Superstitions of the Gallinas People of Sierra Leone" (*Memoirs read before the Anthropological Society of London* 2 (1865-66)).

2 *jèmà* "evening" + *wóé* "marker of personal involvement," i.e., "good night" or "good bye."

3 A cutting tool consisting of a blade with a hooked point and fitted with a handle.

They went on talking together over what they had seen and heard, dwelling for a long time on the sad fate of the woman whom they had met, and resolving that they would never yield to such treatment.

Suddenly their attention was arrested by the site of a beautiful grove not far away, shaded by stately palms and lofty mangos, surrounded by a rustic fence with here and there curiously twisted bunches of Gregree; the same also hanging from the branches of every tree on the inside, while at the gate there was an arch of rush and reeds coarsely interwoven, and just inside the gate standing on a broad stump was a hideous representation of *Jehama* the devil;[1] standing by his side was Zingbatutu,[2] the medicine man.

In the center of the grove were several graves of kings at whose heads were basins of food, and at the foot jugs and bottles of water.[3]

In the midst of this sacred spot, sitting on a low wooden stool, was Gandanya the witch, holding in her hand a short brush to prevent any unhallowed feet from desecrating this holy ground. By her side stood a lad of some nine years, who did her biddings.

At the farther end of the grove was the sanctum sanctorum, an elevation of a few feet, made of bamboo and rattan, walled in by a neat fence of saplings and rattan; in the center, hanging from a column standing upright in the ground, was an image of the devil, a little more artistic than the one at the gate.

Beads of all descriptions hung from the wall on the inside, and the low, narrow door was decorated with bones and skulls of animals, with two beautiful ivories overlapping each other; four rows of elaborately wrought chairs of bamboo and rattan made up the furniture of the room, upon which were sitting Vey gentlemen who wore red caps and muslin breeches.

In the center, on a chair more tasteful than the rest and more elevated, sat the chairman, likewise more gaudily dressed.

His breeches were of black silk, reaching about two inches below the knees, each leg large enough to hold a bushel; over this a leopard skin coat, which gave him a shaggy and savage appearance; about his ankles were several kinds of Gregrees, his feet were adorned with

---

1   *Jàhámá* (from Arabic) is the Vai word for "hell," not "devil."
2   Most likely it is *zèŋbétùùtùù*, the Vai word for "owl."
3   At certain times after a person dies, especially a person of rank, food and water are placed on the person's grave. Vai belief has it that a living person who eats this food or drinks this water will not assuage hunger or thirst thereby.

tastefully carved sandals, on which were several small bells which jingled every time he turned; on his shoulders hung three kinds of beads, upon his head a cap of leopard skin, about three feet long, tapering to a point.

This august personage, one could judge from his face, had a disposition which comported uniformly with his dress.

This was the Sembey, which was now in session and which at this moment was about to consider the latest medical discoveries of Dr. Papa-Guy-a-gey, the famous physician of the Marphar.

The Borneys reached the place just as the Doctor rose to make his speech, which, after a few flattering remarks addressed to the chairman and the members in general, was as follows:

"A week ago, Kai Denu (fellow citizens),[1] with gun under my arm, and knapsack across my shoulders, I struck out for the woods in quest of game.

"I had not proceeded far into the forest when I heard a coughing, like that of a child. I stopped and concealed myself behind a bugbug. Soon a monstrous female baboon came out of the thicket, went to a certain hill, got a peculiar kind of dirt, plucked the bud from a certain bush, mixed these to the consistency of jelly, and gave it to her coughing child.

"On my return home, I tried the same on some of my servants, who had dreadful colds, and find it an unexcelled cough syrup.

"Farther in the woods, the next day. I ran across a limping chimpanzee, and watched him go to a certain shrubbery and apply its tender leaves to his wounds. I shot him, in the interest of the medical science, and found he had been snake-bitten.

"I marked the shrubbery, had one of my good-for-nothing female servants bitten by a snake, applied the leaves, and found a wonderful liniment for snake-bite."

Whereupon the Council unanimously voted that Dr. Papa Guyagey should be considered in all lands as a nobleman and a benefactor of mankind, and to further attest their appreciation and gratitude, by giving him for a paramour the prettiest woman in the village.[2]

---

1 *kài* "man" + *lèŋ-nù* "child-plural," literally, "men's children," i.e., "citizens."
2 This gift is puzzling, specifically that the elders gave Dr. Papa-Guy-a-Gey a paramour rather than a wife. To the Vai, the gift of a slave—no matter how beautiful she was—would have shown scant gratitude. On the other hand, the elders would not (indeed, could not) have assigned a relationship other than marriage to a freeborn Vai woman. The appropriate gift to the doctor would have been to give him a wife without requiring him to pay a dowry.

Next the case of Manja Ballah was brought before the Council. His charge was that he had assumed the chiefship of the Dateah[1] town, not having the required number of wives and servants.

Whereupon Ballah arose, and defended himself as follows: "Kai Denu, I wish to show you as briefly as possible the fallacy of the accusation.

"Before I was twelve years old, my mother had bought for me seven wives, Borneys of the first order and rank.

"By cunning and sweet talk, I myself secured two at half price, women just as first-class as any who would have been willing to have given themselves to me for nothing, so great was their regard for me.

"As a reward for the kind services I recently rendered our neighbors, the Corsaw,[2] I was given a young girl, who is now in the Gregree-Bush—a girl of great beauty, and who is destined to become my head wife—ten in all—exceeding the number required of a chief."

Next the case of Kai Jalley was called up. This man was a notorious wife beater, and recently he had beaten one of his wives so severely that she died from the effects.[3] He stood there the very personification of brutality, and made his defense as follows:

"I am surprised, Kai Denu, to see you condescend to consider anything about *woman*. Isn't woman '*garna bale?*' (weak and effeminate,)[4] and '*mah tende koqua?*' (good for nothing?)[5] conditions which are beneath our dignity to consider for a moment.

"Now, you know, woman is nowhere among us recognized as man's equal, hence no redress can be demanded for her treatment.

---

1 *lààtìà, the* name of a village along the Cape Mount peninsula, on the shores of Lake Piso.

2 The Corsaw/Corsau are Mende; see p. 82, note 1.

3 See "A note on the credibility and realism of *Guanya Pau*," p. 66. For a position contrary to Walters's, see "The Devil Bush of West Africa," Appendix B, where Bishop Penick reports being told that, upon hearing that a man is "unusually cruel" to one of his wives, the leaders of the Sande will try him and, if the allegation proves to be true, will arrange for the man's death by poisoning, the death being "a long and painful or a quick one, according as they wish to inflict greater or less punishment" (Charles C. Penick, "The Devil Bush in West Africa," *Fetter's Southern Magazine* 2 [1893]: 229).

4 *gànàà* "strength" + *bélè* "not," literally, "without strength."

5 *má* "not" + *tìndì* "well-behaved" + *kòkwà* "nothing," i.e., "untrustworthy" rather than "good for nothing."

Furthermore, is she not in the same class with the mule or cow?[1] You would all answer yes. Well, if I should kill my cow, none of you would raise the least objection.

"I therefore argue that you have no right to raise an objection here. It is my loss, I paid seventy-five dollars in cloth and ivory for her, and if I choose to throw away this money it is nobody's business but my own.

"Manja Jallah (addressing the chairman), do I not speak the truth?"

Manja Jallah replied: "*Da hi ka, a be ke wah.*" (Yes, it is true.)[2]

After the chairman had exchanged a few words with his associates, it was announced that the Sembey had no business to interfere with a man's personal matters, that his wife was his property, and subject to whatever treatment he felt disposed to inflict.

---

1 A cow was often the central component of a dowry; in that way Vai men might see a woman as being "worth" a cow.

2 *làhííkà* "entirely, thoroughly" + *à* "it" + *bè* "is" + *ké* "true" + *wà* emphasis marker, "Yes, it's completely true."

Chapter IX.

SUNDRY EXPERIENCES.

So vehement did Guanya Pau become that she would have burst through the sacred precinct and collared old Ballah, had not her companion checked her.

After this they continued their journey for several days, sleeping often in the woods, when not favored with a lodge at some wayside inn.[1] For food, when their supply gave out, they ate palm nuts, which are abundant in that country, and other wild fruits, equally wholesome and plentiful. Africa is certainly a land flowing with milk and honey.

The traveler, away out in the forest, if his provision gives out, need not famish. Almost at any time of the year the woods have a liberal supply of fruits and nuts—walnuts, colanuts, hickory-nuts, troves, several kinds of plums, wild plantain, figs, monkey-apple and fruit, persimmon, lady-finger, alligator pear and pepper, etc., etc.;[2] if no brook is near, from which to quench his thirst, a large vine can frequently be found that has in its hollow abundant supply of cool, sweet water.

The Africans have not yet awakened to a full consciousness of their worth. It needs only the application of scientific and industrial principles to the illimitable resources of that wonderful land which are lying dormant, to make her rival the most affluent of her sister continents. Vegetation luxuriant. Climate miraculous. Already, with the veil but lifted, she is captivating the eye and intoxicating the brain of the daring lovers of mammon; and the cry-to-day is ringing throughout the length and breadth of civilization: "Go to, let us have a share

---

1 The entire notion of teenaged Vai girls traveling by themselves from town to town is implausible, a point that is addressed when the girls are "caught" in Chapter XII. Anyone who met Guanya and Jassah would have been suspicious, to say the least. As for where travelers slept: presumably, travelers arriving in a village at nightfall would have presented themselves to the chief, and he would have given them a place to stay. (At any rate, this has been Vai custom in more recent times.) There were no wayside inns.

2 There is an edible nut that is called "walnut" in Liberian English (Vai lóǎ). There is also a fruit called a "monkey apple." It is red and about the size of an apple. It is the white pulp of the inside, not the hard outer shell, that is edible. "Lady-finger" refers to "okra" (which does not grow wild), and "alligator-pear" to "avocado."

in the land." What stores of oil, kernel,[1] ivory, indigo, India rubber,[2] gutta percha,[3] copal,[4] skins, teak; wood enough to furnish the cabinet works of all nations; fruits sufficient to make pies and puddings for one-half the population of the world; cereals, waters abounding with all kinds of fish, etc., etc. May God soon open the door for the development of this great country, and preserve the whole land from Cape Bon[5] on the north to Cape of Good Hope on the south; from Cape Guardafui[6] on the east to Cape Verd on the west, for the black man, the African, whose exclusive, divine heritage it is.

To-day, being sultry and warm, the girls proceeded with almost snail-paces, bounding with new life, gay and jolly, oblivious to the trials of the past few days. But their gaiety is short-lived. A dark cloud covers the sun.

It is twilight; the first shades of evening are enshrouding the land. Hark! there is heard in the distance just ahead a rustle among the leaves, followed by heavy tramp of feet, accompanied with low, suppressed conversation. Can it be that the girls are seen? They have no time to test the truth of the inquiry; but creep as stealthily as possible behind a large fallen Mango and lie flat on their faces.

Like dogs on the scent of their game, the men come straight to the tree. But this is not surprising, since the huge log affords them an excellent seat on which they can sit and rest themselves. Fortunately they do not come to the lower part where the girls are hidden, nor on that side, but stop at the upper end.

They are two common-sized masculines, neither of whom can boast of a respectable beard; but supplied with well-developed muscles, hardy and able-bodied. Each carries a knife, fastened in a sailor's belt, and a rough cane of extraordinary weight and size, dressed in the free-and-easy style of the ordinary people, without the encumbrances which fashion and higher civilization impose.

---

1 References to palm oil and the kernel of the palm nut from which the oil is extracted; see the notes on p. 91.
2 An early term for rubber. The wild rubber collected in Africa was not from the rubber tree but from a long, spongy vine (*Landolpha*).
3 A tough plastic substance from the latex of several trees of the sapodilla family, imported from the Malay Peninsula to the UK beginning in 1843. There is no evidence that it was produced in Liberia.
4 A resin produced by various tropical trees.
5 Cape Bon is on the coast of Tunisia.
6 Cape Guardafui is the easternmost part of Africa on the coast of present-day Somalia.

Quiet everywhere prevails, so the Borneys easily hear the conversation which follows. "Varney," says one, "what do you think of our giving up the search, and going back home? It is my opinion that these devilish girls didn't take this road, but some other; or, what do you say about changing our course?" "Well," answers Varney, "for my part I want the reward which Kai Kunda offers for her capture, and therefore am willing to continue the search a few days longer. But I agree with you in the advisability of taking another route." "But, by the way, have you thought how we shall identify her?" asks the other. "Yes," says Varney, "her mother gave me a full description of her. She is of ordinary height and size, not what you would call pretty, but passable, rather dignified in her bearing, has a sharp voice, bright eyes, makes holes in her jaws when she laughs, walks as if she owned all Marphar. In short, her mother said that she is a girl that would attract the attention of any man."

"I tell you what," says the other, "I'd just like to catch her, if I wouldn't knock some of that pride out of her. The idea of a woman having such notions as to run away, because she doesn't want a man who has many wives. Ha! ha! ha! who has ever heard of such a thing? I tell you, Varney, I feel sore whenever I think of it, and unless I am in better humor when we catch her, I am afraid she will suffer something at my hands." "Yes," rejoins Varney, "it is outrageous. But haven't you observed that the girls nowadays are getting their heads full of sentimental nonsense? My brother, a few days ago, came near killing a foolish Borney he recently brought home,[1] because she didn't want to stay in the same house with his other wives."

After they exchanged a few words with reference to their route, they appropriated some korjally (country bread),[2] struck fire from a flint, lighted their pipes, and continued their journey.

The girls, who were half-dead with fright, lay still until they were well out of sight, breathed freely once more, and summoning all the strength they had, took a course diametrically opposite to that in which the men had gone; hastening as fast as their weakness would permit them, in order to find some place of lodging before it was quite dark. But darkness overtook them before they reached a settlement, so they made for themselves a bed of leaves under a branchy Mango.

---

1 A man would not be allowed to bring a Borney into his home, even his fiancée.
2 *kɔɔ* "rice" + *jéláé* "parched," "country bread"; see p. 96, note 2.

About midnight their feelings were again disturbed by ferocious growls of a hungry leopard, who made the forest echo with his cries.[1] But as he did not scent the girls or was indifferent to human flesh, the prince of beasts didn't further disturb the Borneys' peace of mind.

Before it was light the following morning, they continued in the same course, encountering a new kind of travellers. It was one of those typical December mornings—foggy and damp. Ever and anon they were greeted by a squad of merry, jolly-faced monkeys, who manifested as great surprise on seeing the young ladies as the young ladies did to see them. But, as they were on the monkeys' territory, the latter considered it their duty to take the initiatory step toward acquaintance and entertainment. They accordingly exhausted their catalogue of antic tricks and grimaces, for which their race is celebrated, often becoming too familiar in trying to see how near they could come to the anxious girls. In every squad there was here and there a "Dandy Jack,"[2] so called because he is the most beautiful species of the monkey family. He is somewhat more alert, and not as frisky as the ordinary monkey.

As they went on, they received further greetings from many lovely specimens of the winged tribes. The king-fisher upon the lofty oak struck up his carol, green pigeons whistled their stereotyped anthem, the mocking-bird gave his sweet trill, culminating with the owl, who sounded his trite hoot:

"Task done or no done, 'tis time to go home, go home;
I wear the shoe-boots, and chicken soup, so good, so good,
Big dinner at my house to-morrow,

---

1 Throughout Guanya and Jassah's journey, it is men they must fear, not animals. Earlier the elephant would have apologized to them (97), and in this chapter now the "ferocious" and "hungry" leopard is indifferent to them, the monkeys take "the initiatory step toward acquaintance and entertainment," and they receive "greetings from many lovely specimens of the winged tribes." Later, in Chapter XIV, wild ducks will "congratulate them" and a fresh-water turtle will lift his head "to tender his appreciation for their heroism."

2 Diana monkey. *Cercopitheous diana diana.* A small, white-bearded, black and red monkey.

John Bedab, Will Bedab, his wife,
And the Devil Knows who all, who all!"[1]

The sun soon made his appearance in the heaven, when the mist vanished, and nature's ten thousand voices became still.

---

1   This song, which is clearly meant to be the "song of an owl," is difficult to place effectively. Griffiths initially thought that it was a local Liberian song when he commented on it in a paper delivered in 1995 and subsequently published. (See Griffiths, 2001.) But an extensive inquiry subsequently in printed sources and from Liberian correspondents seems to suggest that it is not known there. It may be that Walters himself wrote the "song" or it may be from a different source that we have not yet been able to find. Although it is not Liberian in origin, as Griffiths argued in the article cited, it does offer a contrasting and colloquial form of English to the rather stilted and formal descriptive sections in the book and this contrast is still worth noting.

At the cool of the following day the Borneys, after many turns and windings, caught sight at last of smoke curling up above what seemed to be a little village. But no sooner had they come within hearing distance than a sound of weeping was heard. A nobleman had lately died, and according to custom, mourners were stationed in his house, who made the village echo with their lamentations.[1] But the saddest sight was to be seen in the house adjacent to the king's court.

The deceased during his lifetime had been a terror to his wives, so that when he died they were not disposed to shed tears over him; wherefore it was inferred that they had witched him.[2] The witch was called in, who confirmed the decision, after counting her beads and muttering something to the unknown, imprecating upon the beads of the criminals the condign punishment and going through with the hackneyed formula:[3]

"Yáng-Kate Yáng-Kate
Zum bu yu vah, zum bu zhé!" etc.[4]

She then advised that a large tank of pepper be prepared, and the women be made to kneel down in it, pending the further advice of the Medicine-man; forbidding any one to render them the least aid. Even the women railed upon the unfortunates for their lack of respect for their husbands.

But one of the women, more heroic than the rest, protested her innocence, lifted her knees from the tank, declaring that she would sooner die than submit. She was right. No sooner said than done— the action was suited to the word, and she lay weltering in her blood.

The Medicine-man then passed into the adjoining room, attended by two little boys, who carried his portmanteau, which contained

---

1 When an adult's death is announced, everyone in the village participates in public mourning. Thus, when a man dies, it is not just his own wives who will mourn publicly. Someone who refrains from mourning is assumed to have participated in the person's death.
2 i.e., had engaged in sorcery to bring about his death.
3 The "witch" is, in fact, a witchhunter. She detects witchcraft by "counting" her beads in the way Muslims do when praying and by uttering various formulas.
3 This song either represents nonsense syllables or is in a language other than Vai. It does not *sound* Vai.

innumerable humbugs.[1] He was a plain-faced man, unassuming, without that pomposity and ostentatious display which characterize the men of his profession. Upon entering the room, his first act was to prostrate himself flat on the ground, going through many mutterings and grumblings; then he sends one of the lads for water with which he bathes his face and hands, and repeats the above. Whereupon he takes out his beads, counts them, grumbles again, commands both boys to stand in front of him with arms folded, while he invokes the spirit of the dead man, winding up with:

"Yam bah oh, yam bah oh,
Kali mufáye ma zhe yé! etc.[2]

He then lifts the mat, bids the youngsters bring more water, washes his face and hands, comes out into the Court where the women are, and makes the following announcement:

"Hear ye, my countrymen, ye who have regard for the ancestral Gregrees. Ye bade me consult the spirits to ascertain which of these women are guilty of witching this nobleman. The spirits were angry with us, and I had to pray and supplicate, going through the whole curriculum of prayers and performances before they would give me their ears. They are certainly angry with us because of the great sin we have committed. Oh, Kai Denu (fellow citizens), guard against this evil in the future. We have almost incurred the wrath of our guardian Gregree, who can only be appeased by giving the cup of sassa wood* to the two guilty women."[3]

---

* A very poisonous drink, which is distilled from certain herbs, roots, etc., and which inevitably brings death.

---

1 While this is a reference to the *gregree*, the use of the word "humbug" to refer to amulets seems idiosyncratic.
2 *m* "my " + *bá* "mother" + *ò*, i.e., "O my mother!", is a common expression of grief. The second line of the song begins *kài* "man" + *mú* "relative-clause marker" + *faá* "die," i.e., "the man who died ..." However, we have been unable to reconstruct the rest of the line.
3 More often "sasswood" or "sassywood" in modern times, it is "a concoction made from the bark of the *Erythrophlaeum guineensis*" (Warren d'Azevedo, *Some Liberian English Usages*, S-2). Walters's note implies that drinking sasswood is always fatal. In fact, drinking sasswood is a form of trial by ordeal. A person who drinks sasswood and survives is deemed innocent of the charge, while a person who drinks it and dies is presumed to have been guilty.

Whereupon he points out two of the innocent women, and condemns them to drink the fatal draught. He also commands that the others be kept a while longer in the pepper, until sufficient water had been extorted from their eyes; saying that this would serve for an example, that the women hereafter might show sympathy for their deceased husbands.

He also enjoins upon the Zobah present to be more diligent in instilling in the minds of the Borneys under their care their duty to their husbands. "For the welfare of the State and nation," says he, "and the continued supremacy of the Veys depend upon the women adhering strictly to the customs of their forefathers."

With fiendish cruelty they dance around the victims, making faces; and committing little acts of cruelty on their persons.

The command is given to strip them of their clothing, and to lead them into the medicine-grove.

Zobah with their band are there, and the crowd soon becomes hilarious in their wild demonstrations. The drums beat, the horns blow, the cymbals clash, the string-instruments sound forth their harsh strains. Notes discordant and inharmonious, clashing with terrible collisions, vibrations wild and barbarous—one jarring commingling of heterogeneous sounds—music unfit for the ears of Beelzebub.

This lasts several hours, and one would think ceased only when fatigue and exhaustion had set in.

I have heard a full chorus of my fellow-students bellow our college yell, and the developed lungs of good old '93 roar our soul-stirring whoop,[1] but these put together on a day when the atmosphere is most conducive to the distention of the vocal organs, would fall way below par compared with this chorus in the medicine-grove.

Finally, the frenzy ceases. The women are asked to stand, when they are again pointed to as an object lesson.

The younger cries, and makes a pathetic appeal to the chief for acquittal. Her cries and appeal could have moved the heart of a stone, but with contempt they spurn her. Whereupon the older says: "My friends, we are helpless, and in your hands. We have done nothing to merit this cup which is being prepared for us. The charge is, that in as much as we didn't cry on the death of that man, we

---

1   A reference to the Oberlin College Class of 1893, of which Walters was a member. This is one of the few places where the author introduces personal details into the text.

witched him. Did he deserve our tears? Had he treated us well, we would have loved him, and upon his death tears would have been a natural, inevitable sequence. *Tears are natural and spontaneous things, bursting from their closets only for the deserving.* Why this scar on my face which will last me to my grave? This girl," pointing to her fellow-sufferer, "was always weak and sickly. Does any of you know what she suffered from that man when she was once in a most helpless, pitiable condition? *Any man who can have the heart to abuse his afflicted wife is worse than a dog.*" The last is hardly out of her mouth, when she is kicked by a burly brute, and the poison is ordered to be brought immediately.

The younger woman again pleads and begs. Her condition is a sad one; her delicate health and weak constitution makes her case exceptionally serious. But a deaf ear is given to her cries. The bowls of the fatal draught are brought; they are commanded to drink them to the dregs. The older lifts the bowl to her mouth, throws back her head, empties it without a murmur, and dies without a struggle.[1] The younger, amid bitter sobs and heart-rending cries, drinks part of her share. It is enough, she cannot finish it. She kicks and screams, and in her death throes speaks tender words of caresses to the one whose cradle is his grave, then dies.

---

1 The death of this woman and her co-wife would be seen by the Vai as evidence that they had indeed caused their husband's death.

CHAPTER XI.
THE BEAUTIFUL SCENERIES.

It goes without saying that the above scene pierced our Borneys to the quick; so then, as soon as possible, they turned their backs upon the great, historic parliament, and took the "big road" trusting nature, the source of solace and comfort, to bring them back to their normal spirits.

It was a day well calculated to cheer and vivify the crest-fallen. It was as though spring, the season of color and song, had just gloriously opened. The balmy, bracing mountain-air, sweet-scented flowers pouring forth their wealth of fragrance, a thousand voices mingling and blending into sweet, harmonious chorus, like a full-voiced orchestra swelling along the winding hills and valleys; the chatter of the frisky, prancing "blue Jack,"[1] the babble of brooks, a stretching landscape of silken verdure, sprinkled here and there with spicy wild roses, every sprig adorned with a diamond of the first water; here and there glittering among the dewdrops and dancing among the leaves, are little birds of glorious plumage filling the air with gladsome carol; trees of imposing trunks whose spreading branches are apparelled in beauty and gorgeously laden with masses of foliage—in a word, all nature below appears elaborately ornamented with the grandest devices.

Not satisfied with this scenery the girls climbed the hills which sentinelled the country for miles around, to see the sun pass through a gate-way of chromatic glory and solemnly set into the crimson west, leaving the horizon encircled with a low streak of livid purple with a line of gold on its ragged edge. Off toward the right stand two hoary summits side by side, shaking their heads in bold challenge for superiority; from whose bases trickle two crystal streams with gladsome voices, which enlarge as they flow until like two warriors clashing their armor in joyful salutation they form a mighty confluence stretching out like a placid sheet of molten silver sharply outlined against a luminous sky. The wide heaven is delicately glowing in all its parts with soft harmonies of dusky red and blue, while in its higher zone the finest net-work of pearl-white clouds, suffused with

---

1 A pygmy antelope (*Neotragus pygmaeus*), called a *jack* in modern Liberian English (Warren d'Azevedo, *Some Liberian English Usages*, R-1). The "frisky, prancing" refers to a sequence of springing leaps, a characteristic of the animal.

a silver radiance, chase each other in rapid succession along the glorious crimson path.

Presently, the moon peeps from the gorgeous window of the east, like the true queen of the night, illumines the unshorn heights, flooding the landscape with her silvery light.

Following her, company after company of stars, pearls of the sky, beaming down like the eye of God, striving to add new luster to the already superfluous refulgence.

How admirable! How wonderful! How stupendous are Thy works, O Lord, God Almighty! Truly the heavens *do* declare the glory of God, and the firmament showeth his handy work.

CHAPTER XII.

CAUGHT.

The girls were not affected by the lovely scenery as one would suppose; for having lived amid similar scenes so long, it was natural that they should be the least appreciative of it.

I have seen men and women in that country, when all nature was thrilling in transport, to pass along with downcast eyes and crestfallen brows, unable to catch one bright suggestion from the lark's whistle or the waterfall's dash. The rose has for them no lesson, the flowers no word of warning, the grass no voice of hope.

With a resigned air, the Borneys left this blissful locality, and after passing through secluded groves, isolated nooks, and a multitude of tortuous meanderings, they found a well-beaten road, which led in the direction toward the lake they had seen from the hill. Following the narrow path, they came in a few hours to a cosy little village, barricaded, and full of plantain, orange, banana, and other tropical fruit trees.

Here they found a cordial reception, and were in high spirits, until just as they were taking their leave of the family to go to their room for the night, in walked a modest-looking fellow, who as soon as he had crossed the threshold, surveyed Guanya Pau from head to foot with a suspicious, supercilious look: dropped his head upon his breast, as if trying to place her, then with a familiar smile advanced toward the trembling girl with outstretched palm, as he said: "This is Guanya Pau, I believe." Guanya Pau recoiled without speaking. Fortunately she had the presence of mind to know that a word might betray her. She retreated hastily to her room, where Jassah soon joined her.

It was at once decided that after they had consulted their hostess as to who the stranger was, they would secretly make their escape.

Acting upon this resolution, she summoned the lady to their room, who told them that she was ignorant of the stranger's identity, that the first she had seen of him was a few days since, when he came to her house, asking for lodging, saying that he was on his way home, to a village in the neighborhood of Gallenah.

When it had grown dark, all the family being in bed, while the boisterous rooster was giving his first alarm of the night, the Borneys crept stealthily out of the house, took the big road, and were soon beyond the town's limits. Of course, in doing this, they had provoked the town's people—that is, by leaving the town in the night, as they are strangers. This would imply to these superstitious people that they were bearers of evil omen to their city, and consequently they would chase them. Therefore, the girls kept a sharp look-out as they went, their hearts jumping at every rustle of leaf or sigh of wind.

That night they covered such an expanse of territory as would astonish the ordinary pedestrian.

How we can travel, or work, or do the most irksome task when we are conscious that upon this effort depends the safety of our life or that of those near and dear to us. Our exertions seem superhuman. They are. In an exigency the feeble arm lifts a hundred pounds, or throttles the savage lion. The feet that usually become tired and sore after walking five miles, cover fifty at one stretch, wholly unconscious of the distance traveled or the possibility of their sustaining fatigue. A weak, delicate woman is changed into an amazon, and faces the thundering cannon, or breasts the billows of the storm-tossed sea. In times of great religious interests (would to God they were more frequent), when the servant of the Lord feels a deep, earnest solicitude for souls, when, with his spiritual eye, he sees thousands of his fellow men standing on the brink of the awful abyss ready to take the mad plunge, his soul catches fire, his tongue becomes loose, and he preaches as he never preached before.

How grateful we should be that our Heavenly Father has thus endowed us. If this were not so, wrecks upon life's tempestuous sea would be more frequent and appalling. Every unusual surge would sweep the poor, fainting soul far out into the broad chasm. Do not then tell me that there is none of the Divine in man.

If there is one thing, which I believe most thoroughly, it is the declaration of the Old Testament that God made man in His own image, and after His own likeness.

Day dawned, and the girls to their joy saw no sign of pursuers. But it is too early. The people are hardly aware of their flight. The sun hastens on his course in the heavens, but still no human forms loom up in the distance. The king of day reaches the zenith. It is growing intensely warm, and traveling is becoming more and more irksome.

Guanya Pau addresses her comrade: "Jassah, I think we can afford now to slacken our steps. I don't believe they intend to pursue us after all." She had hardly spoken, when Jassah exclaimed: "Guanya Pau, we are done for! Just look yonder to your right!"

Sure enough, there were six men, armed with knives, coming across the fields, in a direction from which they had not expected them.

There were no bugbugs here in which they could hide, as they were in an open field, with grass only knee-deep, with here and there a tree. But concealment now was of no use, for they had been seen long before they were aware of their pursuers.

The girls stood still, feeling sure that the worst had come. The men came up, displaying their knives, and talking in a hurried, excited voice. When they were within a few yards of the girls, Guanya Pau noticed one of them to be the man who had addressed her the night before and because of whom they had fled. She, therefore, became still more alarmed; but this man soon proved himself a blessing to her.

No telling what deed of wickedness these superstitious wretches would have perpetuated upon the two helpless maidens, were it not for this man, who protested that he knew Guanya Pau, that she was of the royal family of Gallenah; but her traveling without a male escort and in this fashion, so far from home, was a mystery that he couldn't solve.

As they came up to the girls, who had by this time recovered from their fright, standing prepared for almost anything, this man came up to Guanya Pau and said, "I know you, therefore you need not try to disown yourself; and just now it is wholly to your advantage to identify yourself. I am a native of Gallenah, the prettiest city on the Marphar, and so are you. Your father was the greatest king of the whole Marphar. Your name is Guanya Pau. Do I not speak the truth?" Guanya Pau still refused to answer. "Well, then," said he, "if you won't speak you must bear the consequences. The truth is, Guanya Pau, these men would have abused you as soon as they caught you, had I not told them that you are the daughter of the late King Kai Popo. Now my eyes don't deceive me, I can swear that you are Kai Popo's daughter, for many times have I eaten corjalley at your house,[1] and it is less than three years since I last saw you with Zobah at the celebration on the death of your father's successor."[2]

Guanya Pau being now assured of his sincerity, gave him an affirmative nod. Whereupon he further interceded with the men for their safety, and so they were taken back to the town without having their hands bound behind them or suffering any other inhumanity.

---

1 Traditionally, when strangers pass through a village, a resident will invite them in (particularly the chief) to rest and will give them water and food, most often "korjally/corjalley," i.e., country bread. See p. 96, note 2 regarding country bread.

2 A reference to a funeral feast, ordinarily to one held forty days or more after the person's death. Masked figures such as the Zobah would be in attendance at such an event.

Chapter XIII.

Escape.

As the party drew near the town they could hear the clash of cymbals, drum beatings and other expressions of rejoicings on the event of their capture, while the road, for a quarter of a mile beyond the town, was lined with curious spectators.

When they came into the town the noise ceased, they were carried into the women's department of the court.[1]

Both the departments of the court were thronged with eager listeners while Zobah put these questions to the girls:

"Who are you and where from?" Guanya Pau, knowing that no hiding the truth would answer here, replied frankly: "I am the daughter of the late Kai Popo of the town of Gallenah." But who would believe such a story?

Would Manja Kai Popo's daughter travel thus unattended and act as they had acted the preceding night?

Far be it from the truth. She is not a king's daughter and much less Kai Popo's; but some witch of evil omen, carrying about her person a bad Gregree to afflict the land. Upon this reply Zobah asked incredulously: "Manja Kai Popo's daughter? Where in the world have you heard about the great chieftain? Do you mean to lie to us, and have you contrived this scheme thinking that we shall let you go? Ah, my girl, you had better tell the right story, or you will soon wish you had."

In vain did Guanya Pau assure and reassure her that she was none other than Kai Popo's daughter, only to be slapped in the mouth and threatened with severer punishment.

How she wished now for that man to come in and confirm her testimony; but he was nowhere to be seen.

Finding her inexorable, Zobah continued: "Were you ever a Borney? if so, where and who were your teachers?"

Upon Guanya Pau answering that she had been a Borney at the well-known Gregree Bush near Gallenah, and naming as one of her teachers a Zobah who was a prominent figure there and whose reputation was known throughout the Marphar,[2] the Zobah began to

---

1 Guanya and Jassah are Borneys; as such, they would have been turned over to the Sande leadership.

2 In modern times as well, a Vai Sande initiate will cite her teacher as a way to establish credibility.

think that after all there might possibly be some truth in what she said.

But still it was shocking to think of Kai Popo's daughter acting as this girl had acted.

She went on with her questions, asking Guanya Pau all about her home and the Gregree Bush there, until she came to the great question what she was doing traveling alone so far from home, and why she left the town so stealthily the last evening.

Although Guanya Pau was expecting all the while these inquiries would come, she had not been able to frame as yet a suitable answer.

After a moment she said that she and her companion had strayed out in the woods and lost their way, and that they had left this town so suddenly because they were afraid of arousing suspicion by staying and loitering around.

A few more questions of secondary importance were asked, and the girls were given over to the chief, who commanded them to be immediately put into the stocks, while he dispatched a messenger to Gallenah to ascertain the truth about them.

Guanya Pau and Jassah were accordingly put into the stocks and left by themselves in the chief's large hall.

Nothing now seemed more certain than that they would soon be on their way back to Gallenah, where the most, cruel punishment awaited them.

But hope had not forsaken the brave girls and, besides, necessity is the mother of inventions.

Being women it was deemed unnecessary to place a guard over them during the night, and so they were left in the spacious hall all alone by themselves.

They spent the forepart of the night discussing plans of escape. They could hit upon none advisable, until at last Guanya Pau with her inventive mind threw up her hands in ecstasy and exclaimed, "Jassah, I have it, let us try fire!"

The "stock" is a large stick of wood which the prisoner can lift only by exerting all his strength to the rope tied at both ends. His right foot is laid over the middle of the wood where an iron spike is driven over the small part of the leg near the ankle, strings tied to both ends of the log enable the prisoners to move about.

The scheme Guanya Pau formed was this: There were iron rods around, which were used for boring holes, after making them red hot in the fire.

When everything had become quite still the girls secured the rods, heated them in the fire and bored into the wood next to the places where the spikes were riveted in, until they became loose, when they pulled them out with ease and found themselves free again.

Then their first precaution was to procure as quickly as possible some of the dried meat and "sweets"[1] which were in the adjoining room, and hastily left the town, taking an obscure road which made an acute angle with the big road on which they were captured, thinking that one would hardly suppose that they, strangers as they were to the country, would risk themselves in such an uncertain path.

Now again the poor girls put forth superhuman efforts and sped on in a manner calculated to excite wonder.

A hungry tiger[2] once intercepted their path and roared upon them, but undaunted, they moved on doubly quick, counting the tigers behind more fatal than all the beasts in the forest.

When day dawned they found themselves about a mile distant from a delightful stream, which they reached and waded through before the sun was up.

Keeping close to the bank of the stream, which became ever larger, they soon came to a landing where there were fishermen with their harpoons[3] and other fishing tackle.

One of these, who was on his way home, kindly consented to take the Borneys with him to the town.

---

1 This might refer either to "country bread" ("korjally") or to a mixture of country bread with peanuts.
2 In nineteenth-century usage, "tiger" can refer to any large wildcat.
3 Vai fishermen use a sharp iron blade attached to a bamboo pole.

CHAPTER XIV.
THE MOHAMMEDAN MISSIONARY.

The Borneys felt jubilant as the canoe glided on to its destination. Wild ducks here and there flew out of the water to congratulate them, while a fresh-water turtle occasionally lifted his head above the turbid stream to tender his appreciation for their heroism. The sea-breeze was blowing a delightful gale which ever increased in intensity and force. Soon the little lake was white with caps and its tranquil surface rolled up into foaming billows.[1]

One would, no doubt, be led to think of these girls as the Melitans thought of St. Paul,[2] that though they had escaped the land, yet vengeance suffereth them not to live. But this sudden change foreboded no ill to the fisherman, who knew such to be common in that time of the year with their lakes and rivers. In the morning the stream is calm and placid as a sea of glass. The anxious mariner launches his canoe, hoists his sail, flaunts his penon[3] to the breeze, drums are beaten, horns are blown, and everything seems to betoken a prosperous voyage. But soon the scene changes. The wind wafts to the southwest, a cloud appears on the western horizon the size of a man's hand, which grows every minute larger and blacker. A gale comes rushing and crashing against the boat, and if the mariners have not been quick to haul down the sails and to set the canoe about, she may ere long with all her cargo be lying on the bottom of the lake.

It was nothing more than natural that the Borneys should be anxious, knowing the superstitions which their people cherish. What would hinder him from thinking that they had incurred the anger of some Gregree, who would now swamp his canoe in order to wreak their revenge? They were therefore alarmed at every cough, glance or turn the fisherman made. Every moment they were expected to be called to an account and to be hurled into the raving stream. And

---

1 Lake Piso is customarily calm in the morning and turbulent in the afternoon, but Guanya and Jassah are not yet on Lake Piso.

2 In Acts Chapter 28 Paul is cast up on the land of the Melitans (Malta) after surviving a storm at sea where his example had cheered the sailors and they had survived. When Paul is bitten by a poisonous snake, the Melitans assume that he is being overtaken by vengeance for a crime he had committed before beginning his voyage, but as he miraculously survives the bite they assume that he must be a god.

3 A banner, hence a small sail.

oh, for them no fish had been prepared who would kindly swallow and disgorge them high and dry upon the shore. But their fears were groundless. The fisherman had witnessed many such gales and could have told them of his narrow escape swamping but two days since.

The gale passed over almost as quickly as it had come, the lake hushed her ragings and again settled into a peaceful calm. After a few more strokes of the paddle they landed safely upon the wharf of a small fishing town called *Nea Sanja* (Fishtown).[1]

Most of the people, as one frequently finds in a Vey town during the day, had gone to their farms. Having expressed a thousand *E seh eh* (thanks)[2] to their kind benefactor, they began to stroll around to look at the town. As they were passing what they took to be the chief's house, they heard the sound of something like a mussulman[3] at prayers. Following their curiosity they soon found that their impression was a correct one.

Mohammedan missionaries had made their advent into the town to disciple all the men;[4] and here was one at his mid-day devotions. They watched him through the tedious formula; smiting himself on the breast, performing multitudinous genuflections, prostrations and supererogations.

The Borneys were on the eve of taking their departure for scenes more delightful, when a citizen of the town came up, lifted the mat and entered the room. The teacher gave him cordial greeting and a friendly grasp of the hand, intimating that he knew on what busi-

---

1 *nyíé* "fish" + *sànjà* "town."
2 *í séé.* The phrase for acknowledging a satisfactory job or gesture. While it is routinely translated into English as "thanks," Welmers suggests that colloquial English "nice going!" is more apt (*A Grammar of Vai*, 143). A different Vai word, *báíká*, is used to express gratitude for a gift.
3 Moslem.
4 While the Vai "were among the first people on this part of the coast to receive and accept" Islam, its practice among them was largely confined to people of higher status: "Until recently only the headmen nominally held to Islam while the majority of the people continued their traditional forms of worship" (Svend E. Holsoe, *The Cassava-Leaf People*, 136). Further, there was "a general attitude to Islam" such that "people accepted aspects which could serve as constructive additions to what they already had, but rejected elements which threatened to destroy existing beliefs." There was at times conflict between Poro/Sande and Islam, but for the most part Islam was incorporated into existing belief systems rather than supplanting them (Adam Jones, *From Slaves to Palm Kernels*, 177).

ness he had come and that he would soon be at leisure to hold him company.

After adjusting his many paraphernalia and having washed his face and hands, he called a servant, who came in at break-neck speed, and in similar haste executed his master's command. A thing which enables a close observer to form some opinion of the teacher's character. Then a woman with a thin, emaciated frame, like one upon whom ravenous consumption or some other fell malady was preying, and who would be willing to barter herself to any one who would consent to do her walking for her, came with a bowl of prepared palaver sauce, followed by a little girl with a gourd of water.

The teacher with true hospitality asked the citizen to participate in the frugal meal. He respectfully, or rather, wisely declined, assuring His Eminence that it hadn't been long since he partook of a roasted cassada and fish.[1] But recollecting the demands of custom he appropriated a half dozen spoonfuls of the delicious palaver sauce and emptied the gourd of water much to the sorrow of the little girl, who was thereby compelled to take a few extra steps for more. His Eminence did quick justice to the remainder and at its conclusion smacked his mouth rather unceremoniously, as though it would not have unfitted him for the evening prayers should he have taken a little more. When he had washed and had his pipe lighted, with his head involved in a cloud of smoke, he came up to the citizen and announced that he was ready for the *kru arbung* (business).[2] The citizen indulged in a few common-places, and expressed the purpose of his visit, dwelling enthusiastically upon the worth of the subject in question. But the teacher was apparently inflexible, and answered only by giving an occasional negative shake of the head.

"Well then," asked the citizen somewhat abruptly, "for how much do you reckon the woman, since you are not willing to give the amount I ask?" The teacher replied rather contemptuously, "Why, about as much as I would value a cow or mule. For many times have I found a cow or mule of vastly greater value than many a woman.

---

1 If one arrives at someone's house while the person is eating, Vai hospitality dictates that the host offer food to the person arriving. If that person has just eaten, it is permissible to decline, using that as the reason. In this case, it is not clear why the citizen's declining the offer of food was done "wisely"; probably this is a comment on the quality and amount of food in the teacher's "frugal meal."

2 *kúlɛ̀à* "voice" + *bûŋ* "speak," i.e., "speak up (with the reason for the visit), give a report."

It is risky; for it all depends upon what kind of a woman you get in the bargain. It too often happens like the children's play, 'she won't work, she won't eat (?) and must be cast upon the dunghill.' My good friend, I have had serious experience with some of these fickle Borneys, who are good for nothing else but gossip and giggle; and besides, our women to-day have lost their pristine vigor." At this point the teacher stopped, refilled his pipe, applied the fire coal[1] and continued: "We shall never more behold such warriors in our land as in the past; men who fought our battle and freed our land from slavery. I, the true teacher of Islam, bewail the sad state of things which the future has in store for us."

"Well, Reverend Teacher," asked the citizen, "what can we do? You who are wont to advise us and whose advice is always wise and helpful, what remedy would *you* suggest?" The teacher lifting up his hand exclaimed: "Allah ha ku bolu!"[2] Then went on: "The girls must be taught early that they have no other reason for existence than to serve their husbands. *That is the prominent, fundamental idea of our life.* They must learn that they have no preferences; these must be instilled in them bright and early before they are grown up and have imbibed sentimental notions from various sources. In the name of my Holy Koran," continued the teacher enthusiastically, "that man ought to be drummed out of the country who allows his wife to do as she pleases. Oh, Allah, to what are we coming? World-renowned once for our valor and bravery, we have gradually dwindled to mere dwarfs. Almost any of our neighbors could now lord it over us. Where is that lofty patriotism, those inspiring war songs, that largeness of soul, that genuine love for country and freedom? These died with the last generation. And why was this? Nothing more than that we have allowed our women to come above their sphere. We have, I repeat it, my good friend, we have to our own detriment licensed our wives and daughters too far.

"I have come here to teach the truths of our Holy Koran, but if I shall only be able to impress this truth upon the minds and hearts of the men of this village, I shall consider my coming among you to have not been in vain."

"Again, Holy Teacher," asked the citizen, "how is it that you and your brethren give all your time instructing us men out of your Koran about Allah (God); but never teach our women?" "Allah ha

---

1 A burning piece of charcoal.
2 Local pronunciation of Arabic *Allah akbar* "God is great."

ku bolu!" again exclaimed the teacher, "I say again, women are not like men. Her inferiority is self-evident. I shall not say that they have no soul, which I almost believe, but I *shall* say that they are stupid and insusceptible of improvement. Our religion teaches their inferiority, and that they are subject to men.[1] So Allah ordained it, and it is not in our power to alter his decree."

---

1 *Contra* Walters, it seems unlikely that the presence of Muslim clerics would have significantly affected marriage among the Vai or the attitudes of Vai men regarding it Moreover, Walters's presentation of the Muslim cleric's reading of the Koran misrepresents the Koran's overall attitude to women. While as in many sacred texts, including the Bible, it is possible to find misogynistic and patriarchal statements, the Koran also contains many positive statements about women and about the rights and responsibilities that men have towards them.

CHAPTER XV.
ON THE FARM.

The Borneys were up betimes the next morning, dressed themselves like the working women of the town and with them started for the farms three miles away.

The party was a merry one. What with songs and story-telling, and anecdotes, and a general tendency to boisterousness, they soon forgot their hard lot and the work awaiting them.

And herein lies the life and soul of the Negro. The day may be dark and dreary, his life one unmitigated series of oppressions, the world and even God may seem to have forsaken him, yet amid it all he finds opportunity for song and praise. That is why the Negro, torn from his native land and carried to foreign shores, shorn of his manhood, subjected to the vilest cruelty, is never exterminated.

To the contrary, instead of pining he *grows.*

Almost any other race would succumb. But that susceptibleness of character, the ability to accommodate himself to circumstances, the conforming to the shifting scenes of life, the power to adjust his life to suit his surroundings, his flexible nature, his aptitude to find in the bitter cup of suffering a healthful tonic, mirth, fun, hilarity too often savoring of the boisterous, these I take to be the characteristic elements of this race which conserves his vitality and betokens his perpetuity if not his superiority.

But above all it argues that God has some good in store for this people. "For your shame ye shall have double."[1]

What of the wrongs and indignities heaped upon these poor women? They are abused, disrespectfully handled, sold as cattle, their womanhood bedraggled in the pandemonium of a polygamous home; yet amid it all, "*Felah bor ton Dumbor*"—life is a song.[2]

Mirth and fun, laughter and joviality, so pervade their whole existence that a casual observer would say their life is not so hard as missionaries and others would have us believe. But "one may smile and smile and be a villain."

It is nothing unusual to see a woman along the street with a baby on her back and a basket on her head, whose countenance bespeaks anything but happiness, singing a jolly song and apparently in great glee.

---

1 Isaiah 61:7.

2 *fèlà* "breath" - *bɔ* "go out," i.e., "exhaling" + *tɔ̀ŋ* "is" + *tɔ̀mbɔ́* "dancing, playing," i.e., "life is a dance."

There is an old adage among them which runs something like this: "Be sunny even on a cloudy day; for 'tis good and healthful."

It was not long before the Borneys were at the rice farm, and for once in the course of their wandering they experienced a genuine *Fala-sah*—(heart lay down*). [1] They are escorted by their friends from one end the farm to the other, given the little hoe, which they used with astonishing dexterity.

The king's daughters do not exhibit soft hands unused to work. By the way, soft hands are rather the prerogative of the superior masculine.

In true "scratcher's"[2] fashion the girls apply their utensils so assiduously that soon they are surrounded by a crowd of curious observers, who give them a hearty "*E seh eh*"—(thank you),[3] ignorantly plying them with questions about their home and lovers.

Toward eleven o'clock, under a temporary shelter, the clean rough mat is spread where the nearly famished party sit two by two around each laden bowl, and with no other means for eating than that with which Providence has provided them make a brisk dispatch of the savory palm butter.

In the meanwhile cracking jokes and telling tales of "The Monkey courting the baboon's sister" and the "Race between the Fullingtonga[4] and the Groundhog," etc.

When the meal is near its end, a Jonkai comes in, on whose broad shoulders is a capacious demijohn.[5] "*Ena niah na kai eh, Ena*"— (come in, my good man),[6] unanimously cry the women as soon as they have caught sight of the vessel and caught a whiff of its odor.

In obedience to their command he enters, puts down his burden at the feet of the laughing women and kindly offers his assistance.

The gourds brought, the Jonkai unstops the demijohn and the

---

* These two words are used to express satisfaction of any kind.

---

1 *fàlà* "liver (seat of the emotions)" + *sâ* "lie down," i.e., "contentment, satisfaction."

2 A planter. "To scratch" rice is to plant it.

3 See p. 129, note 2.

4 A kind of small antelope, possibly a Maxwell's Duiker, *Cephalophus maxwelli* (Svend E. Holsoe, "Notes on the Vai Sande Society in Liberia," *Ethnologische Zeitschrift Zürich* 1 [1980] 101).

5 A narrow-necked glass or stoneware bottle, usually holding one to five gallons.

6 *í* "you" + *nà* "come" + *níè* "here" + *ná* "my" + *kàí-è* "man-the" + *í* "you" + *nà* "come," literally "come here, my good man, come."

fragrant palm wine[1] is poured out until each has her gourd full, when one of the older women more lively than the rest undertakes to toast the two strangers in their midst. "Fellow women," says she, "we are as happy and as merry as jaybirds. Why should we not make our whole life a song, as 'tis said: "*Felah bor ton Dumbor*," ah, the truth is obvious. But I must not stop here in this hour of mirth to throw a dampness on the scene, I must direct my words to the two young women in our midst. I believe they are Borneys, and if so, may their lot be a happy one and may they be successful in falling into the hands of a worthy gentleman. We are a jolly, jolly party here to-day and we don't care for King Mussah[2] or any other dignitary. Let us sing, girls, 'Oh Kongo.'[3]

Then the old familiar song rings out sweetly in the air: "Oh Kongo! Oh, Oh Kongo! Be ma nya ya, Ya Ka che nyo, Fa nyang be."

This song has justice done to it only when it is sung by ladies and gentlemen in concert. These are all the words of the song, which are repeated over and over again.

The peculiarities of their songs is that they can weave into them whatever words are necessary to suit the occasion.

For example, I was accompanying a missionary to a Vey village where he would preach. While crossing in the canoe over to the town, the paddlers behind us, with one of these common songs paid the following tribute to the missionary:[4]

"Oh God man, your face is white, your hair is straight, you can read and write and speak God palava.[5] My face is black, my hair is curly, I can neither read books nor write letters nor speak God palava. But, by the devil, if the canoe upsets I know who would get first to land. Oh white man, you better learn to swim, you had better learn to swim."

At the cool of the day toward evening at the signal of the owl that "tasks done or not done 'tis time to go home," the party packed up their little bundles, secured their utensils and took the big road for the town.

---

1 "The sweet sap of the raffia and oil palms. It is drunk both fresh and fermented" (Warren d'Azevedo, *Some Liberian English Usages*, P-2). The palm wine is intended here to give more strength to the workers.
2 It is not clear to whom the woman is referring.
3 This is a Mende work song.
4 See the discussion of this incident in "The Extent and Nature of the Mission Control of *Guanya Pau*" in the Introduction.
5 A term in Liberian English (and pidgin English more generally) meaning "affair, matters related to."

Chapter XVI.
OUT A-FISHING.

That night it was decided that Guanya Pau should go fishing the next morning, whereupon the women made a collection of nets and baskets.

But while the women were speaking in gleeful anticipation of the projected fishing expedition, with their hands busily plying the twine, a gentlemanly figure minus the person[1] made his introduction into the room, and demanded of one of the women an account of the day's work, and having learned, he sullenly expressed his dissatisfaction at the amount of work accomplished, assuring her that they had indulged in too much play in work-time, and that in the future he would see that they did better.

When he had stalked his disagreeable presence out of the room, Guanya Pau asked about him, and learned that he was an ordinary citizen of the village, who had six wives, and the woman whom he had addressed was his head wife.

Bright and early the next morning the women arose, equipped themselves, and started for the river.

It had rained in torrents the previous morning, contrary to the wish of the women, and the river was therefore swollen high up the banks.

As they proceeded down the stream to find a suitable place to launch and cast their nets, a young man was seen running behind them, waving his hand, as though he had some important message for them.

The women halted until he came up, almost out of breath, who, when he had recovered sufficiently to speak, told them that they would find the banks in the direction they were going gradually yielding to the influence of the swelling waters, and that no good fishing-ground could be found.

Upon this information they bent their course down the stream until they came to the sacred pond. This is a body of water of the size of an ordinary pond emptying into the Marphar river, whose source is from under a huge rock five miles inland.

The pond swarms with beautiful fishes, but no one is permitted to touch them, they are the property of the dead.[2] No one is permitted to put his hand or foot into the stream.

---

1 Apparently, this means someone with the size and appearance of a gentleman who was not, in fact, gentlemanly.
2 Such ponds continue to exist in the Vai region; Muslims do not generally observe the prohibition on eating the fish, but other Vai do.

Of course such sacrilege the spirits would avenge.

Upon its bank the spirits of the departed held meeting at night, and voted to take vengeance for affront against their holy stream.

Every night, at a certain hour, lights can be seen on the bank when the spirits are said to be in council.

No sooner had Guanya Pau come to the water in front of the others in her haste to cross over, not seeing a bridge anywhere near, and being too much engaged in her own thoughts to notice the innumerable bunches of Gregree suspended on the tree around, she plunged in to wade through.

The splash of the water grated on the ear of her companions, who, as soon as they had become fully conscious of what had happened, threw up their hands in despair, while they cried: "Oh, my Borney, what have you done! Have you no reverence for the dead? Can it be possible that you have cursed both yourself and us? Oh, horrors! ten thousand horrors!"

Then the whole party screamed so loud and piteously that Guanya Pau and Jassah become anxious, and were afraid they would be reported to headquarters and sentenced to immediate doom.

So far as the curse from the dead was concerned Guanya Pau would ten times have preferred it to that of the stern, relentless living.

The women continued to stand bewailing their fate, praying the dead not to implicate them all in the offense. "Oh, inexorable fate! What mortal prayers or oblations can induce thee to let the offender go free! Against thy sacred laws has she transgressed, upon thy hallowed precincts trampled, polluted feet have recklessly fouled thy holy stream! Surely thou wilt avenge most speedily this unpardonable guilt. If not, why, the woody Kong[1] will take up a weeping, the full chorus of disordered waves will rend the air with lamentations, the lowly valleys will shriek unutterable woes, the loud thunderings and subtle lightnings will blend their voices in a chorus of grim melody. Yea, wilt thou, O spirits of the departed, not avenge this deed? Then the powers of earth and air, to thy shame, must do it.

"The palms near the water's bank stand in lofty majesty, waving their branches as though against them the offense has been committed.

"The sun buries his face beneath a black cloud, as he fears his light will be tarnished by the miasma.

---

1   *kɔ̃* is the Vai word for "tree," but the reference here—possibly to a sacred tree—is not clear. Among the Vai, a tree can be sacred, particularly a cotton tree.

"Surely all nature is angry at the deed. The heavens are in mourning, covered with a veil of sombre blackness."

Silence! The Gregrees speak. Heaven opens. A flood of water pours forth from its bosom. What, rain now, when thirty minutes ago there was no sign or vestige of a rain-cloud? Well, but what is strange about that? Why should it cause such wonderful comment when at this time of the year such occurrences are frequent?

But the women are blind to this fact, and nothing can account for it but Guanya Pau's mad plunge into the hallowed pond.

After ten minutes the rain ceased, the women likewise ceased, and continued their march along the river's bank, keeping Guanya Pau always in front, so as to keep their eyes on her.

They soon came to a fishing pond where they secured no small supply of fishes—grunters, tawneys, perches, etc., etc.,[1] and what was remarkable, was that at the close of the fishing Guanya Pau's basket was fullest of all; certainly the Gregrees had no control over the water, or this girl would not have succeeded so well. But they knew that they had.

This incident, of course, re-established Guanya Pau in their favor, and she was again given her liberty, and permitted to go in and out among them without suspicion or oversight.

The fishing ended, the women took the way for home along the river's bank.

It was about twelve o'clock, the sun was shining at his best, producing a heat that was almost intolerable.

The women had to pass another holy scene.

This time it was in the person of a deity of exquisite grace and beauty (?)—a leviathan monster, in short, an alligator of tremendous and scaly proportions.

This was their war-god, to whom they prayed when about to encounter the enemy, and whom they worship by placing in his way a sheep or goat. I have learned from good authority, that in cases of extreme peril, when to all appearances the enemy seems the more powerful and sure of victory, mothers have not hesitated, at the

---

1   Grunters are a Liberian salt-water fish, and they are found in the brackish waters of Lake Piso. Tawneys and perches are not names used in Liberia.

advice of the medicine-man, to give their children to make his Holiness a supper.[1]

At this hour he was lying high and dry upon the bank, with his huge jaws distended, which would close now and then like a prodigious steel-trap when a sufficient number of flies, bugs, and other flying insects had stored themselves therein for safety or shelter.

The women kept at a safe distance, all except, of course, Guanya Pau, who advanced closer to him than the rest, and, by a childish noise, caused him to shut the chasm prematurely, when he lifted his head, switched his tail, and glided down into the stream.

Guanya Pau was told that nothing but an offering would appease his anger, and naturally her first impression was that she herself would constitute the offering. But her fears were allayed when the leader of the party said that as soon as they reached the village she would send a Jonkai with a lamb or kid.

Nothing more was heard of Guanya Pau's irrevocable sin, and so the girl made herself comfortable on that score, and after a consultation with her companion, it was decided that they would leave the following morning to try their fate in parts unknown.

---

1 The crocodile (Walters's alligator) has a special status among the Vai. In the coastal village of Sugary (Vai *sòuí*), for example, a tame crocodile has been part of village life for over three centuries. Holsoe identifies crocodiles as being believed to be embodiments of ancestors ("Slavery and Economic Response among the Vai," 291) Accordingly, in Sugary the ritual feeding of the crocodile—in which the animal is given a chicken as well as palm oil, rice, and gin—is carried out by the head of the village, in his capacity as head of the clan. The attestation of infants being fed to crocodiles in the nineteenth century (see the discussion of "Domestic Slavery among the Vai" in the Introduction) involves infants taken from their enslaved parents, never infants whose mothers had voluntarily given them up.

Chapter XVII.

GOOD NEWS.

The Borneys had scarcely lain down that evening, when there was a gentle swinging of the mat which served for the door of the room, and to their summons to enter, a young man with an intelligent face popped into the room, apparently striving to make as little noise as possible.

"Well, who are you, and what do you want?" demanded Guanya Pau. Without answering her question, the young man began to pay a tribute to her worth and heroism, assuring her that her trials were at an end, as she would see from his message. After a good deal of flattery and circumlocution he told his errand:

Guanya Pau's lover had gone from the beach to her home with more than money enough to buy her; who when he learned of her running away and the other things connected with it, became prostrated, and for a while his condition was serious. But he finally rallied and resolved to prosecute a search for her, secretly employing this young man to aid him. He, the young man, had left him at a village fifty miles away, but was ignorant of his whereabouts at present; however, he would find him. His finding the girls happened as follows: On the previous evening he chanced upon where they were last, and got a clue as to the route they took. He added further that Guanya Pau's lover had offered him a large reward to find and to escort her to him.

For a while the girls were overcome with joy; but on reflection Guanya Pau checked herself and friend, saying that perhaps this fellow is an impostor. They therefore asked him for testimonials. Whereupon he produced from under his cloth a well-known knife which Guanya Pau had seen and handled many times. There was now no doubt of the messenger's veracity, and after indulging in another spasm of ecstasy Guanya Pau took him into the "big room," commended him to the lady of the house, who provided him with food and lodging.

She returned to her room, but it is useless to say that no amount of coaxing could induce Morpheus to take possession of their eyelids. Anticipations of soon meeting Momo, in whose embrace she would tell of her weary wanderings and misfortunes, ever filled her soul. Visions flitted before her of their union and going to a country where she would be the sole possessor of his affections, and live in civilized style.

"Oh Jassah," she said suddenly, "it seems as though the Gregrees whom I offended this morning have brought me good fortune instead of an evil one. But, Jassah, our success comes from our own persistence. It is truly said that whatever woman has in her head to do, she will do in spite of anything. And why not? The truth is, *men are ever exercising their prerogative to the letter, and we accept it without a question; but as soon as we assert ours, they brand us with transcending our sphere.* So long has woman been deceived that her condition seems to be *organic.* I may not even now succeed; but, Jassah, *the day will come,* THE DAY WILL COME. But pardon me, my friend, for reverting to these unhappy thoughts. Let us rather rejoice that our deliverance has come. Say, did I not tell you that *na Plading* (my sweetheart)[1] was as true as the glistening dewdrop? There isn't another man like him in the world. Momo is true to the core. And, Jassah, you shall live with us, as long as you live, my home shall be yours. What a season of happiness I shall enjoy together with you and my h———."

"O love, be moderate, allay thy ecstasy,
In measure rain thy joy, scant this excess;
I feel too much thy blessing; make it less,
For fear I surfeit!"[2]

"Ha, ha, they say it is not for us to 'love,' and to have 'preferences.'" These two words Guanya Pau pronounced with much of her characteristic irony. "Jassah, is there a woman in this world so low in the scale of being who is not endowed with these greatest of all blessings? May Heaven pity such a one! But there is *no* such individual. Why, that is putting us below the beasts!"

"Guanya," interrupted Jassah, "since we can't sleep and you are inclined to talk, will you change the conversation and give me an epitome of your love experience, beginning with your first meeting with Momo? I don't think you have ever told me where you first met him, and under what circumstances."

"Why, yes," responded Guanya, "most gladly shall I comply with your request to converse on a subject so full of romance and poetry. But I must not soar so high. I think it best to use the colloquial, commonplace, every-day speech. How I remember the first time I

---

1 *ná* "my" + *kpìlà* + *léŋ* "child," "boy-friend, sweetheart; lover." Welmers and Kandakai note that, while the term can imply sexual relations, it need not (*A Vai-English Dictionary* [Monrovia: The Institute for Liberian Languages, 1974] 59).

2 Portia in *The Merchant of* Venice, III.ii.111-14.

met him, as though it were yesterday. I was at home on a visit, Momo was employed by my mother to assist in making our oil.

"One day, while sitting on the mat as usual after his morning work, he noticed me trying in vain to break a stout piece of wood. He came up to me quickly and offered his assistance. With his strong, muscular arms he snapped the wood as though it were a twig. I smiled, thanked him, and said coyly: "I wish I had your muscles, Momo." He replied: "I haven't any objection to your having them, Borney, I'm sure." Now, my poor, fickle, little heart had to flutter because of that off-hand expression. Of course, as you know, Jassah, that, coupled with the honesty which shone from his face, meant lots to me. If men only knew how much joy or pain their carelessly spoken words cause us, they would be more sincere and *say only what they mean*. Well, when we had indulged in a pleasant chat, I went into the house. Ever after that he made it his duty to assist me with my wood and water, saying that somehow he felt a peculiar pleasure when near me. All the time, as you know, adding fuel to the flame; and I for my part could never go to the spring but I looked behind, hoping Momo was following; or go to gather wood, but I was eager to catch a sound of his footsteps. How many times I passed by when he was at his work, or standing in his yard, so as to attract his attention, I leave for you to guess. And, behold, they say that it is a monstrous thing for a girl to fall in love! Jassah, *I warrant that there isn't a woman in this whole Vey country who couldn't tell a story similar to mine.*

"Well, have you got that epitome you ask for, or would you have me end the chapter down to date?"

"Down to date," shouted Jassah.

"And so," continued Guanya Pau, "it went on day after day, week after week, month after month, and year after year. I thought (and do so yet) that there was nothing else in this world but Momo. Of course, Jassah, you are excepted," she said with a laugh. "I saw him in the moonshine, in the rainbow, and, above all, in my sweet dreams. He was the last one on whom my thoughts rested at night before my eyes lulled to sleep, the first object that met my gaze on awaking in the morning. If I were as diligent in thinking of the Gregrees as I am in thinking of Momo I would be a most devoted servant. But I feel that without him life is not worth living; and, my dearest Jassah, I mean what I say, when I declare that I would drown myself before I would suffer that ungainly Kai Kundu to get me, or anybody else, except Momo.

"Well, when this had gone on over two years, one evening about twilight, when I had finished my work, I went and sat under the cola-tree behind our house and pretended to be stringing my beads. But my true object was soon realized. Momo soon joined me and sat down by my side. Who can picture our feelings as that evening we sat beneath the shadows of that stately cola, in the clear moonlight? We sat side by side on the green grass, talking little nothings. By and by he took a long breath, somehow I felt anxious just because of that sigh. He then took both my hands in his, sending a thrill clean through me. Planting his frank, honest eyes on mine which soon were directed to the ground, he said: 'Guanya Pau, *nah Edear* (I love you);[1] *ya in dear wah?*' (Do you love me?)[2] What could I say but to whisper faintly: '*Da Keker*' (with all my heart).[3]

"After I had recovered from the fright, I thought it time that I be practical. I said frankly, 'Momo, I am compelled to condition the answer I gave you. Will you comply with it?' He replied magnanimously: 'Guanya Pau, I shall do anything you ask of me, feeling sure that you will ask nothing beyond the range of my ability.' I thanked him and said that from my early girlhood I had always looked at polygamy with extreme antipathy, and had vowed never to come into the possession of a man who will have another wife. He pressed me to his heart, saying that he had cherished similar ideas, and had planned to leave the country, as soon as he could conveniently do so, for the Beach where he could put his plans into execution.

"All was settled. We are enshrined in each other's affections, and if the Gregrees do not frustrate our plans, there will soon be a couple as happy as any the sun has ever looked down upon."

---

1 *ná* "I" + *í* "you" + *líà* "love," "I love you."
2 *yá* "you" + *n* "me" + *líà* "love" + *wá* "question," "Do you love me?"
3 *làhííkà* "entirely, thoroughly." The same word appears on 110, spelled *da hi ka.*

CHAPTER XVIII.

GUANYA PAU'S TWO DREAMS.

The girls talked way into the night, and after Jassah had told her short love experience, which, happily for her, was only like a soap bubble, they fell into a sweet slumber, and were at once carried to the land of dreams. But our dreams at times are so inconsistent with our feelings. Guanya Pau, instead of meeting her lover, and for joy fainting in his arms, met instead a squad of ghosts, who demanded reparation for her pollution of their stream. They were loud and vehement, and threatened to bury her alive if she would not as quickly as possible meet the demands. Her fears were intensified, when, from out of the very pond she had defiled, came a spirit, more terrible than the rest, with his eyes flashing fire, and smoke issuing from his mouth and nostrils.[1] He waved his hands, commanding the other spirits to give way, that he might devour the girl. With a scream Guanya Pau awoke. Her heart was beating fast, and she felt tired and frightened. Her screams had also awakened her companion, who jumped up, and asked what the matter was.

She sleeps again, and dreams that she is sailing on a lake. The propitious breeze fills the canvas, and the canoe glides mildly along. As it approaches its destination she hears in the distance the silver notes of bells, and wonders what it means. Soon the canoe comes to land, and her first inquiry is about the ringing she heard while on the lake. Her escort asks her to look out upon the streets.[2] In every direction she sees people on their way to some place, she knows not where—a man and woman walking arm in arm, children passing in high spirits and with bright faces, dressed as for a holiday. There is something strange, too, about the day itself. The air is balmy, the sun's rays are gentle, the grass looks like emerald, the sky is clothed in saffron, everything seems to be in gala day.

Again a sound similar to that which she had heard on the lake, rings out clear and sweet, in perfect harmony with the scene, and as

---

1 Dreams are freed from the constraint of accuracy, but the dragon in Guanya's dream is decidedly western in conception, not at all recognizable in a Vai context.

2 In this case the dreamer is envisioning a place unlike any that she has ever seen before. The Liberian community that Guanya sees in her dream–based on its proximity to a lake–is Robertsport. See the discussion of "The Settlers" in the Introduction.

at the last it tolls a stroke every few seconds, Guanya Pau thinks it must be the voice of a spirit.

Her escort then takes her into a house, large and capacious, where several hundred people are sitting. A man rises in the aft of the building, on an elevated stand, holds a book in his hand, and reads something from it. Then there follows a noise, as of a small thundering, accompanied by the whole audience, who quickly rises to their feet, and to her uncultured ears make a great noise. The congregation sits, bows their heads, while the man on the platform kneels down, and with his face directed to the ceiling, speaks many earnest words. He gets up from his knees, reads from a big book before him, when another song is sung. At the conclusion of this piece he stands up again, opens the book, reads a small portion from it, stands before the congregation, and with hands and head and mouth seems to pour forth his soul.

Guanya Pau is now attracted by the low cry of a woman, who sits in a seat in front of her, and can not refrain from asking her escort the cause. He tells her that the young lady is a sinner, that the minister's words had touched her heart; and in a low whisper he repeats to her his text: "For God so loved the world, that he gave his only begotten Son, that whosoever believeth in him should not perish, but have everlasting life." Guanya Pau is astonished beyond measure; but she sits perfectly still, with her eyes fixed on the preacher, though she understands not a word he says.

The preacher takes his seat, and after another song a man is seen bearing to the altar a bowl of water, when a young man clad in a suit of grey, whose face seems familiar, rises up from a front seat.

Guanya Pau looks eagerly, for she is sure that she has seen the face some time somewhere. She tries to place him, but what acquaintance can she have here in this strange land? Her eyes certainly are deceived.

The preacher reads from a little book which he holds in his hand, asks the young man a few questions, dips his hand in the water, and sprinkles it on the young man's head. As the young man gets up from his knees, he turns around, exposing his whole face to Guanya Pau. "Great Heavens! Can my eyes be trusted? Am I mad? No, no, it cannot be, it cannot be!" The minister kneels down, while the people bow, and offers the closing prayer; then standing up with his hands extended, commits the congregation to the care and keeping of their Heavenly Father.

Now there is motion in the aisles, greetings and hand-shakings. The preacher comes down from the pulpit, warmly presses the hand of the recently baptized young man, while many others, both men and women, repeat the same with congratulations.

The young man turns to come up the aisle. His eyes fall upon Guanya Pau. He stops, and looks more curiously, as if doubting his eyes. Then, as if to prove the accuracy of his ocular organs, he takes a step further. The people in the meantime, who are going out one by one and two by two, are so occupied in their expressions of their feelings and impressions of the sermon, and their joy to see the lost sheep brought into the fold, with other communications and conventionalities appropriate for the Lord's house and day, that they do not notice the young man's strange action. And again, as he had a reputation among them of being a thoughtful, earnest person, had they observed it, they would, no doubt, have thought that he was reflecting over the solemn vow he had just taken.

The young man advances nearer, after consulting with his own heart, laying aside all decorum, he looks the girl squarely in the face. She smiles, revealing her pretty teeth and the dimple in her cheeks. It is enough. "Guanya Pau!" he cries, and folds her in his arms. Amid sobs and tears the fainting girl lisps, "Momo," and awakes.

It was broad daylight, the sun was two hours high. Jassah had arisen, and quietly left the room. Guanya Pau felt weak and faint, so she decided to remain lying until Jassah returned.

Chapter XIX.
A SUFFERER.

It was not long before Jassah came tipping into the room, and expressed surprise that Guanya was still lying down. Guanya apologized by telling her wonderful dream. "O you great dreamer," remarked Jassah, "was I with you when you went into that house, and there before all those people how did I conduct myself? And you were not ashamed to fall into your lover's arms in so public a place?"

But Guanya Pau's evangel, who put his head in at this time to tell them that it was high time to be going, put an end to Jassah's questions.

Guanya got up, executed her toilet, ate a hearty breakfast on the strength of her dreams; and soon the three were out on their way to the next town.

When half the distance had been covered, as they were passing a palm grove, they heard a noise in the thickets, accompanied with pitiful groans.

Guanya, satisfying herself that it was a human being, dispatched their guide to ascertain who it was. He soon returned, saying it was "nothing but an old woman" who had run away from her master, with her foot still bound to the log; and that he had had a great mind to "lick" her for running away.

This made Guanya Pau fearfully indignant. "You wretch, you scoundrel, you low, base, unprincipled fellow," said she, "how can you have such a heart! Go away from me, I want nothing to do with you." "Come, Jassah!" and they made a direct line for the spot from which the groans came.

A miserable sight met their eyes. A thin face, wan complexion, swollen feet and ankles—a woman almost starved.

The man came up behind them; for though he was angry, and would have liked to knock Guanya Pau down for hurling those epithets at him, yet he dared not for Momo's sake, but especially for the sake of the reward which he was promised. He came, and offered his service. Guanya Pau would have refused, but seeing that his was possibly the only strength which could wrench the cruel iron and free the prisoner, accepted the offer without so much as looking to the place from which it came.

Suppressing his feeling, the man worked away with marked assiduity until the poor woman escaped with only a few scratches.

The released showered upon her rescuers a flood of *E seh eh,*[1] *Kanabah Ebowle* (Thank you, may God bless you);[2] then after a few words were exchanged relative to her welfare and the country, they parted.

The three reached the town, when the guide entered to make inquiries about Momo, leaving the girls in the road. But he had not gone far when Guanya Pau recognized among a crowd of men coming up the same man whom she met some time since at another town. They therefore retreated with all possible haste, till they came to the waterside, where finding an empty canoe, they launched out into the deep.

---

1 See p. 129, note 2.
2 *kàmbá* "God" + *yè* "let" + *í* "you" + *bálò* "bless," i.e., "May God bless you."

CHAPTER XX.

SUNSHINE AND STORM.

The next morning the Borneys found themselves on Tosau Island, in an old quaint town of grim history.[1] Much of the town was in a state of neglect and dilapidation. The houses were mostly circular, culminating into a point, built of bamboo and wattling, daubed with yellow clay. The roofs were of thatch and leaves, dried almost to a crisp, making an easy prey for the flames. The floor was of dirt, beaten and pounded until it was hard and solid. The houses were close together, and, like the typical African villages, there were no fences to cut off one neighbor from another, indicating lack of confidence in one another, and nothing for doors except mats. The yards were scrupulously clean, and in all the avenues where the women had the care and oversight, there was cleanliness and order.

Like other Vey towns, Tosau had its innumerable Gregrees and "Medicines," and manifold other indications told that they too were bound hand and foot by the chains of hoary superstitions.

The girls made acquaintances with some of the women, who took them along to the farm to share their work and hospitality. The Tosau people are especially celebrated for their hospitality, so the Borneys soon felt at home.

But the girls dared not tarry here long. Ah, will they never again have a season of rest, a home? Is it their fate henceforth to wander as vagabonds over the earth? No, the journey will soon end; but until then they must walk the path fate has marked out for them. It is theirs to obey and to be silent.

On the morning of the third day after their arrival, they made all hasty preparation to leave in the chief's big canoe for a town on the other side of the lake.

After expressions of gratitude to their kind hostess for their cordial reception and entertainment, and profuse adieus to the other members of the family, they went to the wharf and took passage in the capacious canoe, which had already one other passenger, a Vey gentleman, apparently of noble birth, with sandalled feet, calico breeches, which came as far as the knees, with legs of tremendous proportions; falling gracefully over this was a white, shirt-like gown, bordered with red tape, open in front half way down the breast.

---

1 *tóòsɔ́*. See "A note on topography and toponyms," in "Introductory Notes to *Guanya Pau*," above, p. 65.

Upon his head set a red cap, covering only the crown. He was quietly sitting upon a beautiful rattan chair, with a pipe in his mouth, adding his mite of tobacco smoke to the canopy beyond. Near by stood his flask of palm-wine, out of which he took between every dozen puffs a long draught. As further indication of his prestige, he had a curiously twisted rattan staff, and across his shoulders suspended a string of those beads which only men of rank wear.

He eyed the Borneys rather suspiciously as they got into the canoe, but betrayed no anxiety, and soon gave himself up to smoking and palm-wine drinking.

When they were well upon the bosom of the lake, Jassah addressed her friend: "Guanya, after all it seems to me that we shall be no better off because of our traveling. I'm afraid we shall never see Momo again. Now, you know that wherever we go in this country, whether on the Marphar or the Pisu, we shall find the same system prevailing respecting woman. Have you thought what we had better do, my friend, shall we———?" Here Guanya interrupting her, said: "But, Jassah, I failed to tell you of a discovery I made night before last in Tosau. My reason for keeping it a secret was through fear that your joy might intensify mine, and so lead us to act imprudently. You know that I secured the full confidence of our hostess. When you had retired that night, I opened my heart to her, and prayed her assistance. She sympathized with me, laid my head upon her bosom, called me a brave little girl, and imparted to me this good news: Down the Beach, where I told you Momo went to work, and where I too went a few nights ago in my dream, is an American (Liberian) settlement; there a man has but one wife, and woman is held in the highest esteem and respect. All that I saw in my dream is correct. They are God's people, who have God-men to do nothing else but to speak God palaver to the people. She said that even if a slave runs away and goes to them, his master dare not go and ask for him. She told me that she has helped some girls of my spirit to go there, and hear that they are in school, learning to read and write, who have given up their Gregrees and medicines, and have laid their hearts down to the American religion.[1] She then advised me to accept a passage in the king's big canoe, which leaves for Bendoo,[2] where we can get an easy opportunity to go to the Beach."

---

1 i.e., "have accepted the American religion and found happiness thereby."
2 *bèndù*, the largest town on the north shore of Lake Piso.

After giving thanks, the girls indulged in a playful criticism of Kai Kundu's short, ungainly figure, flaunder nose, and two-pound lips; contrasting Guanya Pau's features with his, asking what the two look like together.

But just then the passenger in front moved uneasily in his seat. The girls didn't see it; for Guanya Pau at the same time cried out: "And who knows but what we may meet Momo there!"

Chapter XXI.
THE END.

> "In the unreasoning progress of the world
> A wiser spirit is at work for us,
> A better eye than ours."[1]

In a few hours the canoe came to land. The girls, after briefly surveying and discussing the situation, and having asked a few questions of the townspeople at the wharf, started for the town. But, alas! The town so near but yet so far! Only one more short day's journey of twelve hours and they would have seen what Guanya Pau saw only in dream—church steeples, those monitors of heaven, rising in their majesty, and pointing to the skies! On heaven's threshold, but cruel destiny permits them not to cross! When victory flashes its resplendent rays, then must they suffer defeat! On the eve of basking in the sunlight of liberty they must be incarcerated in the dungeon of despair!

Alas, those sweet chimes of the Sabbath-bell, the heavenly strains floating down the aisles of the tabernacle, the thrilling, soul-stirring words from the God-man's lips, these will never greet their ear, nor fill their soul!

As the unsuspecting girls turned to go up the street to which they were directed, that gentleman of note—their fellow-passenger, came up suddenly behind them, and without ceremony laid his hand roughly upon Guanya's shoulder, saying in a dictatorial tone: "Guanya Pau, you are my prisoner. Kai Kundu has sent men into all parts of the country to apprehend you. Come, go with me."

The girls answered not a word. They couldn't.

So elated was he over his success that he immediately hired a canoe, and they embarked for a port farther up the river.

He would have secured Guanya Pau, had he heard her threat. No doubt, it is well that he hadn't.

The canoe glided gracefully on. The lake was as tranquil as a sea of glass. The breeze was light and genial. The sky was bright and cheerful. The receding woods were soon robed in a garment of misty blue.

That evening, as the last vestige of the sun sank beneath the western waters, there was a splash two feet from the canoe; when Jassah

---

1 Wordsworth, *The Prelude*, Book V, ll. 359-61.

exclaimed with her usual calmness: "I shall never leave you, Guanya!" there was another splash. The two girls were in the yawning deep!

After a minute Guanya Pau came to the surface and said pathetically: "This is preferable to being Kai Kundu's headwife."

Then she sank to rise again at the last day, when the seas, and lakes, and rivers shall give up their dead.

FINIS.

Appendix A: From Sir Arthur Helps, Friends in Council *(1853)*

From Sir Arthur Helps, *Friends in Council: A Series of Readings and Discourses Thereon* (Boston & Cambridge, MA: James Munroe & Co., 1853; rpt. Leipzig: Bernhard Tauchnitz, 1873) Vol. 1, Chapter 8, 122–28

[The quotation that appears in the original on the frontispiece page facing the portrait of Queen Ranavalona is from Sir Arthur Helps's *Friends in Council.* The book was in the library at Oberlin in Walters's time.

The relevant chapter reflects the slightly ambivalent tone of the quotation. Helps is clear that, although women's capacity for reasoning needs enlarging, it is not to be "supposed that men and women are by education to be made alike." He is also clear that "a boundary line exists between the intellects of men and women which, perhaps, cannot be passed over from either side." In effect, here as elsewhere, Walters is both of his time and in some ways ahead of it. Overall, his view of women is deeply imbricated with Victorian attitudes despite the startling modernity of his tone in places. We ought not to assume easily that his advocacy is for an education that is "liberationist" in any modern sense. But there is evidence from the text that Walters's view is more advanced than the book from which this quotation is taken, as a reading of the chapter from which it is drawn will easily show. Since Helps's text was written almost half a century before Walters's period at Oberlin, it is not surprising that Walters's views on women are more advanced, especially in the light of Oberlin's leading role in advancing the cause of women's education.]

EDUCATION OF WOMEN.

It seems needful that something should be said specially about the education of women. As regards their intellects they have been unkindly treated—too much flattered, too little respected. They are shut up in a world of conventionalities, and naturally believe that to be the only world. The theory of their education seems to be, that they should not be made companions to men, and some would say, they certainly are not. These critics, however, in the high imaginations they justly form of what women's society might be to men, forget, perhaps, how excellent a thing it is already. Still the criticism is not by any means wholly unjust. It appears rather as if there had been a falling off since the olden times in the education of women. A writer of modern days, arguing on the other side, has said, that though we may talk of the Latin and Greek of Lady Jane Grey[1] and Queen Elizabeth,[2] yet we are to consider that that was the only learning of the time, and that many a modern lady may be far better instructed, although she know nothing of Latin and Greek. Certain it is, she may know more facts, have read more books: but this does not assure us that she may not be less conversable, less companionable. Wherein does the cultivated and thoughtful man differ from the common man? In the method of his discourse. His questions upon a subject in which he is ignorant are full of interest. His talk has a groundwork of reason. This rationality must not be supposed to be dulness. Folly is dull. Now, would women be less charming, if they had more power, or at least more appreciation, of reasoning? Their flatterers tell them that their intuition is such, that they need not man's slow processes of thought. One would be very sorry to have a very grave question of law that concerned one's self decided upon by intuitive judges, or a question of fact by intuitive jurymen. And so of all human things that have to be canvassed, it is better, and more amusing too, that they should be discussed according to reason. Moreover, the exercise of the reasoning faculties gives much of the pleasure which there is in solid acquirements; so that the obvious facts in life and history will hardly be acquired by those who are not in the habit of reasoning upon them. Hence it comes, that women have less interest in great topics, and less knowledge of them, than they might have.

Again, if either sex requires logical education, it is theirs. The sharp practice of the world drives some logic into the most vague of men: women are not so schooled.

But, supposing the deficiency we have been considering to be admitted, how is it to be remedied? Women's education must be made such as to ensure some accuracy and reasoning. This may be done with any subject of education, and is done with men, whatever they learn, because they are expected to produce and use their acquirements. But the greatest object of intellectual education, the improvement of the mental powers, is as needful for one sex as the other, and requires the same means in both sexes. The same accuracy, attention, logic and method that are attempted in the education

---

1 Lady Jane Grey (1537-54) reigned as Queen of England for nine days in 1553. She was renowned for her precocious learning and mastery of languages.

2 Elizabeth I (1533-1603) was Queen of England from 1558 to 1603.

of men, should be aimed at in that of women. This will never be sufficiently attended to, as there are no immediate and obvious fruits from it. And, therefore, as it is probable, from the different career of women to that of men, that whatever women study will not be studied with the same method and earnestness as it would be by men, what a peculiar advantage there is in any study for them, in which no proficiency whatever can be made without some use of most of the qualities we desire for them. Geometry, for instance, is such a study. It may appear pedantic, but I must confess that Euclid[1] seems to me a book for the young of both sexes. The severe rules upon which the acquisition of the dead languages is built, would of course be a great means for attaining the logical habits in question. But Latin and Greek is a deeper pedantry for women than geometry, and much less desirable on many counts, and geometry would, perhaps, suffice to teach them what reasoning is. I dare say, too, there are accomplishments which might be taught scientifically; and so even the prejudice against the manifest study of science by women be conciliated. But the appreciation of reasoning must be got somehow.

It is a narrow view of things to suppose that a just cultivation of women's mental powers will take them out of their sphere: it will only enlarge that sphere. The most cultivated women perform their common duties best. They see more in those duties. They can do more. Lady Jane Grey would, I dare say, have bound up a wound or managed a household, with any unlearned women of her day. Queen Elizabeth did manage a kingdom: and we find no pedantry in her way of doing it.

People who advocate a better training for women must not, necessarily, be supposed to imagine that men and women are by education to be made alike, and are intended to fulfill most of the same offices. There seems reason for thinking that a boundary line exists between the intellects of men and women which, perhaps, cannot be passed over from either side. But, at any rate, taking the whole nature of both sexes, and the inevitable circumstances which cause them to differ, there must be such a difference between men and women, that the same intellectual training applied to both would produce most differing results. It has not, however, been proposed in these pages to adopt the same training: and would have been still less likely to be proposed, if it could be shown that such training tended to make men and women unpleasantly similar to each other. The utmost that has been thought of here, is to make more of women's

---

1 Euclid (325-265 BC) was the most prominent mathematician of antiquity, best known for his treatise *The Elements.*

faculties, not by any means to translate them into men's—if such a thing were possible, which, we may venture to say, is not. There are some things that are good for all trees—light, air, room—but no one expects by affording some of the similar advantages of this kind to an oak and a beech, to find them assimilate, though by such means the best of each may be produced.

Moreover, it should be recollected that the purpose of education is not always to foster natural gifts, but sometimes to bring out faculties that might otherwise remain dormant; and especially so far as to make the persons educated cognizant of the excellence in those faculties in others. A certain tact and refinement belong to women, in which they have little to learn from the first: men, too, who attain some portion of these qualities, are greatly better for them, and I should imagine not less acceptable on that account to women. So, on the other side, there may be an intellectual cultivation for women, which may seem a little against the grain, which would not, however, injure any of their peculiar gifts, would in fact carry those gifts to the highest, and would increase withal, both to men and women, the pleasure of each other's society.

There is a branch of general education which is not thought at all necessary for women; as regards which, indeed, it is well if they are not brought up to cultivate the opposite. Women are not taught to be courageous. Indeed to some persons courage may seem as unnecessary for women as Latin and Greek. Yet there are few things that would tend to make women happier in themselves, and more acceptable to those with whom they live, than courage. There are many women of the present day, sensible women in other things, whose panic terrors are a frequent source of discomfort to themselves and those around them. Now, it is a great mistake to imagine that harshness must go with courage; and that the bloom of gentleness and sympathy must all be rubbed off by that vigor of mind which gives presence of mind, enables a person to be useful in peril, and makes the desire to assist overcome that sickliness of sensibility which can only contemplate distress and difficulty. So far from courage being unfeminine, there is a peculiar grace and dignity in those beings who have little active power of attack or defense, passing through danger with a moral courage which is equal to that of the strongest. We see this in great things. We perfectly appreciate the sweet and noble dignity of an Anne Bullen,[1] a Mary Queen of

---

1 Anne Boleyn (1507-36), the second wife of Henry VIII, was executed for treason (alleged adultery).

Scots,[1] or a Marie Antoinette.[2] We see that it is grand for these delicately-bred, high-nurtured, helpless personages to meet Death with a silence and confidence like his own. But there would be a similar dignity in women's bearing small terrors with fortitude. There is no beauty in fear. It is a mean, ugly, disheveled creature. No statue could be made of it that a woman would wish to see herself like.

Women are pre-eminent in steady endurance of tiresome suffering: they need not be far behind men in a becoming courage to meet that which is sudden and sharp. The dangers and troubles, too, which we may venture to say they now start at unreasonably, are many of them mere creatures of the imagination—such as, in their way disturb high-mettled animals brought up to see too little, and therefore frightened at any leaf blowing across the road.

We may be quite sure that without losing any of the most delicate and refined of feminine graces, women may be taught not to give way to unreasonable fears, which should belong no more to the fragile than to the robust.

There is no doubt that courage may in some measure be taught. We agree that the lower kinds of courage are matter of habit, therefore of teaching: and the same thing holds good to some extent of all courage. Courage is as contagious as fear. The saying is, that the brave are the sons and daughters of the brave; but we might as truly say, that they must be brought up by the brave. The great novelist, when he wants to show a coward descended from a various race, does well to take him from his clan and bring him up in an unwarlike home.[*] Indeed the heroic example of other days, is in great part the source of the courage of each generation: and men walk up composedly to the most perilous enterprises, beckoned onwards by the shades of the brave that were. In civil courage, moral courage, or courage shown in the minute circumstances of everyday life, the same law is true. Courage may be taught by precept, enforced by example, and is good to be taught, to men, women, and children.

---

[*] See *The Fair Maid of Perth* [an 1828 novel by Sir Walter Scott. The villain Conachar is brought up outside his clan, and proves a coward when confronted in battle by the hero at the end of the novel].

---

1 Mary, Queen of Scots (1542-87), daughter of James V of Scotland, was executed for treason (alleged conspiracy against Queen Elizabeth).
2 Marie Antoinette (1755-93), Queen of France, was guillotined by French republicans.

Appendix B: Charles C. Penick, "The Devil Bush of West Africa" (1893)

Charles C. Penick, "The Devil Bush of West Africa," *Fetter's Southern Magazine* 2.2 (1893): 225-31

[More than ten years after returning to the US, Bishop Charles C. Penick published "The Devil Bush of West Africa" in a Louisville publication, *Fetter's Southern Magazine*. As was typical of Penick's writings from the period, he claimed that his knowledge of the Vai furnished him with an understanding of African Americans that others, if they had never been to Africa, could not hope to match.

Given that the institutions in question are innately clandestine and closed to non-initiates, the question arises as to the source of Penick's information about them. For the Sande, he acknowledges his source as being another missionary. For the Poro, on the other hand, he claims to have received his information from mission boys who "grew up and learned to trust me." However, Penick wasn't at the Cape Mount Mission very long, and he left finally in October, 1882. Thus, it seems likely that the source of his information on the Poro came from those whom he had brought to the US, either Walters or Pela Penick or both. (Lewis Clinton, the third African in his charge, was Bassa, an ethnic group whose Poro appears to be considerably less powerful than that which was found among the Vai, Mende, and Gola.)

Penick's description of the "Woman's Devil Bush," i.e., the Sande, relies on another missionary's account of two events. One involves the missionary's being taken inside the sacred fence, where the leader of the Sande put the students through a dance routine. If the missionary did in fact go inside the sacred fence, this is surprising. Whether he did or not, he recognized that he had not seen anything exceptional while there. The second part of what he observed, the torture and death of a man who had shown disrespect to the Sande, was *meant* to be public, to be a lesson to all other men.

While Penick acknowledges that the "institution is not wholly an evil to man," his account emphasizes its power, exoticism, and "cruel vengeance." Similarly, his presentation of the "Man's Devil Bush," i.e., the Poro, focuses on cruelty: death to any boy who inadvertently acquires a scar while in the bush school, death to any boy who sees and speaks to a female while in the school, and death to any female who happens "to wander within the confines of the 'Devil Bush'." (We cannot confirm Penick's allegations about scars; certainly the bush school was set up and conducted in such a way that the occurrence of either of the two latter events—a Poro student seeing a woman, or a woman happening onto the site of the bush school— was exceptionally rare.) What we find especially significant about Penick's account of the Poro and Sande is that, even as he condemned them jointly as "an institution so superstitious and relentless in its execution," he nonetheless acknowledged that the Poro was "an institution for instructing every man in the tribe as to his duty to the commonwealth." In this, Penick echoes Walters, for whom the Poro was the "noteworthy" product of the alliance among the Vai that Guanya Pau's father had forged (84). Here at least, Penick seems to be taking his cue from Walters.]

"THE DEVIL BUSH OF WEST AFRICA"

At the north end of Liberia, on the west coast of Africa, a beautiful mountain rises out of the sea to the height of 1,060 feet. It seems to have been thrown up by a volcano at some distant period and rose from the bottom of the sea, for just at its base the depth of the sea has not been sounded, and on the east side of the mountain lies a lovely lake, evidently fenced off from the ocean by the uprising of the mountain. This lake is interspersed with many a green island, and over its waters float in lazy flight strange, beautiful birds, with snowy clouds of white storks, crimsoned here and there with the deep color of the flamingo. Through the dense evergreen forest, whose boughs are all woven together by vast unbroken stretches of vines, so deep and dense that the sunlight never reaches the damp earth, flow three rivers into the lake. Along the banks of these rivers and through the depths of these dark woods roam elephants, leopards, bush cows, hippopotami, a great variety of deer, numerous and rare species of monkeys, and many other varieties of game.

It is here that the "Vey" (pronounced "Vi") people have their homes. They are evidently a mere remnant of once great people ; but now have dwindled to a few thousand. They are of a brown or walnut-wood color, with ever fresh live looking skins. In stature they are a little below the medium size, but with a grace and beauty that I have never seen equaled anywhere. Their limbs are small boned, tapering, and as muscular as those of the trained athlete. Their lips are not thick nor heavy, and for the most part open with a pleasant smile. Their foreheads are narrow and high. Their eyes are intelligent and animated, but usually mild or playful instead of sharp or fierce. They have many little arts that have not been discovered by the rest of the tribes on the "West Coast," such as spinning and weaving cloth, working iron, and making silver ornaments; but that which has raised this tribe and set it up above all the tribes of Africa is the fact that they have invented for themselves an alphabet and have a written language among them, entirely in their own characters. One of the strange features about this writing is that some very striking likeness has been found between it and one of the forms of writing in Northern China, so I was informed by one of the representatives of the Philological Society of London.[1] Altogether this little tribe forms a very important study for those interested in the pathway that man treads out of darkness into light, or out of light into darkness. My object, however, at this time is to give the world some idea of one of those mysterious and sacredly guarded institutions for which Africans are so noted, and the schooling in which enabled them to pass through three hundred years of slavery, living, as it appeared to their closest observers, two separate and distinct lives; one, that which was seen and known to the whites, the other, known and understood to the blacks alone. And just here I would say it is the existence of this dual life that has so puzzled the conclusions of that multitude of superficial students who undertook in a day to study, know and write the negro and his disposition, and in so doing started many well-meant efforts to aid them, on principles so utterly false that they soon came down with a crash. To know the negro means much patient investigation both here and in his home in Africa, and then wise comparing of the truths gathered, so as to trace the shaping and molding influences that have wrought this mysterious people into what they are. Of all the institutions among the negroes on the "West Coast" I found none that appeared to exercise more influence over them than the "Devil Bush."

What is the "Devil Bush?" you are ready to ask; and so were we, but the question though asked a thousand times over died away unanswered. At its sound every native would close his lips, and veil even his eyes with an impenetrable expression. We would be walking along a path, when suddenly the guide would stop, point to a small handful of grass taken on each side of the path, bent over and tied across it. That just meant you had to turn back, for a little fur-

---

1 The Vai script, presented in Appendix D, was created in the 1830s. Any resemblance to a form of writing in northern China is strictly coincidental.

ther on was the "Devil Bush," and to intrude into those sacred precincts meant—ah, well, he never told you what, but from his manner something as terrible as death. Men would bring their children to school, and the more honest and open of them would say, "Daddy, I leave my gal in your hand until time for her to go in 'Devil Bush.'" Others would give you no such warning, but about the time the girl reached her eleventh year or a little later, she would receive word by a hurried messenger to come at once, her mother or father or grandmother was ready to die, or as they expressed it, "live die." They, of course, left hurriedly, never to return to the mission again save as somebody's wife, after two or three years' absence. Upon asking them why they did not return sooner as they invariably promised to do, the one answer came, "I have been in 'Devil Bush.'" Nor was the success with the boys much greater. The nearer a boy was united to a noble family the more certain was he to be torn from the mission on one pretext or another, whether he were willing or not, and once in the confines of the unknowable thing, the "Devil Bush," you would see him no more for months, and sometimes years. Of course this formed one of the gravest hindrances to the efforts of the missionary, for no sooner did he begin to get a hold upon his pupils than they were spirited away. It, therefore, became a matter of first importance to know this "Devil Bush" and to do what we could to utilize or counteract its influences just as they were with or against Christianity. The first man I met who had made any headway was the Reverend David A. D——, a born missionary, full of energy, tact, courage and common sense. Let me say right here, if there is any place under heaven where a fool, indolent, weak, or cowardly man or woman is not of use, that place is the "Foreign Mission field." The Rev. D—— had, by some providential move, gotten the son of the "Queen of the Woman's Devil Bush" into his school. Being a strong, winsome character, the missionary soon won its way into the confidence and love of the boy. As the home of the "Woman's Devil Bush" queen was one hundred and fifty miles interior an opportunity to get this boy and place him in the "Man's Devil Bush" did not occur for a much longer time than usual; the Rev. D—— used this time with all his might, so when the boy was called home the missionary had his heart. In course of time, therefore, came an invitation from this young prince for his old friend to visit them in his home. This invitation was quickly accepted, and soon the missionary stood within the barricade of the town of the "Queen." But this meant nothing, so far as learning the secrets of the organization was concerned. In vain did he seek to ingratiate himself into the favor of the queen; she was very agreeable and very talk-ative on all subjects save the "Devil Bush," whose mysterious enclo-sure stood walled-in outside the town. He finally told his old pupil and friend to go and tell his mother he wanted to see inside the "Devil Bush," a request no male African dared make. The answer came back an emphatic "No!" But D—— was not to be outdone so easily; he had in his pocket a new, bright silver dollar; this he placed in the hands of the prince as a present to his mother, with the request again repeated, "to see the 'Devil Bush.'" Would you believe it? Away back there in the jungle of heathen darkness the dollar charm worked. The queen looked at the glittering coin a while, then took it in her hand and felt it caressingly, an expression of relenting came in her face, and she answered the prince and her court: "He is noth-ing but a fool American, and has not sense enough to understand it anyway; we will let him in." This seemed to be scoring a success, but it is just such a success as the over-confident white often scores in his dealings with the African heathen.

We have not the documents to prove it, but there is still lurking in our minds a strong suspicion that the "Devil Bush" was doctored to suit the occasion, and though the American was far from being the "fool," as she said, he was duped a little on that occasion. After much ceremony he was led into the enclosure, where were gathered hundreds of girls for the training of the institution; these the queen called around her and had form in a large circle; she then took a long whip and made them dance and leap around her, very much as a ring-master of a circus would do. This she protested most solemnly was what she was teaching the girls, and not one other thing could D—— get out of her. Baffled and discouraged, he left the confines where no other man had trod, knowing little more than when he entered. But a strange disclosure came most unexpectedly. Late that afternoon a native from a distance entered the town intoxicated, and began to make quite an uproar; he was remonstrated with and told to keep quiet, for this was the town of the "Queen of the Devil Bush." He swore and told them he cared not for the "Devil Bush" or its queen. He was left undisturbed that night, but early next morning was taken before the queen, who said to him:

"My friend, when you came here last night you were in rum, and you did curse the 'Devil Bush.' Did rum do it, or did you really know what you said, and did you mean it?"

His answer was quick and insolent, saying:

"I meant it, and do not care for your cursed old 'Devil Bush.'"

These words were scarcely out of his lips when he was caught up by four strong women, hurried to an open space in the center of the town, stripped, tied, and so fixed that he could not move. Then many bunches of small rattan splits were brought, and strong, quick and skillful fingers began to wrap his fingers and toes, drawing the splits with all their might. In vain did he plead for mercy. They knew not the word in the "Devil Bush." On went the wrapping up each finger and toe; then up each hand and foot, more force being put on the splits, as they could hold the limbs firmer and let more women pull the cords. Pleadings broke into groans, groans into cries, cries into shrieks, which D—— said were the most heart-rending he ever heard. On went the wrapping up arms and legs to the body. It was now 12 m. Some five hours had been consumed in this terrible work, they were getting ready to wrap his body, provided his life remained in him long enough for them to complete the task. At this juncture a friend of the dying man arrived and ransomed him with a great price. Sullenly and slowly they unwound the rattan cords; but, alas, too late! He died at 4 p.m.

Such was the exhibition of the cruel vengeance of the "Woman's Devil Bush," as witnessed by my friend. There are other things ascribed to its members, with considerable probability of being true. It is said that if a man is unusually cruel to one of his wives (for he may have as many as he is able to buy) that the matter is brought before the "Woman's Devil Bush"; the case is tried, and if it is a true one the man is condemned to die; a person is appointed, skilled in the art, to poison him, and in due course of time he dies. The death is made a long and painful or a quick one, according as they wish to inflict greater or less punishment. Again, if the tribe decides to go to war, that declaration of war is not complete until it has been referred to the women and they pass upon and approve it. In addition to these powers that we see cropping out, it is certain that the women are instructed in all the arts that are considered necessary to a good wife and mother, ere she is permitted to leave the "Devil Bush" and be taken by her betrothed husband. Thus it will be seen that this institution is not wholly an evil to man, though it certainly is a "woman's rights" concern, and that with a vengeance.

When I sought information as to the "Man's Devil Bush," I found myself at first completely foiled. It was not until many of the boys grew up and learned to trust me that little by little I gathered the links which, when woven together, gave me some ideas of its mysteries. It is an institution for instructing every man in the tribe as to his duty to the commonwealth. It seems that no one can hold office until he has gone through the "Devil Bush." The diploma is not given on sheep skin, but on that of the graduate by a number of deep scratches from the back of the neck a short distance down the backbone. When these heal they leave rectangular scars raised so as to be distinctly seen and known. When a boy enters the "Devil Bush" he is stripped, and a most careful examination made of all his scars, and these are noted in the records. But it is said that the "Devil" never lets one in his "Bush" get hurt or scarred saved [sic] with the diploma mark. This is a most unfortunate assertion and has cost many a life. Should a boy get hurt in any way, it matters not how, he is carefully watched and every effort made to heal him without a scar; but should these efforts fail, and scars be left, those scars seal his doom. He is killed, and his family is notified in the following way: Whenever the inmates of the "Devil Bush" wish to obtain food they disguise themselves so as not to be recognized by any one; they then make a raid on the nearest town, blowing a peculiar note on a trumpet made of an elephant's tusk, with a lizard's skin so stretched over it as to produce weird vibrations. At this sound the inhabitants of the town hurriedly place food out in the streets and entering their houses close their doors, so as not to see the "Devil." The whole raiding party then pass through the town, taking charge of all the food they find, and leaving a broken earthen pot at the door of the mother of the boy who has been killed. That broken pot says: "Your part is spoiled and broken;" or in other words, "Your boy is dead." This is all she ever learns of the fate of her boy; just the story the jagged lips of a broken earthen pot tell. Henceforth she mourns with a great void of heart, facing the deep mysteries of the terrible "Devil Bush."

There is another thing bringing certain death. Should one of the boys chance to see and speak to a woman or a girl while he is in the "Devil Bush" (save when he is out on furlough), it is death. This was described to me as follows, by an eye witness:

"We were near the outer border of the encampment one day (I think we were six in number) when suddenly we heard the voices of girls talking; we listened and then all ran away save one boy who recognized the voice of a girl from his own town. He stopped and asked her how all were. He then followed us and we went to the lecture court. The boy told some one that he had heard from home and how he did it. This was soon carried to the "Head of the Devil Bush." The boy was called and made to confess it. So soon as this confession was had the entire company of inmates was assembled, and formed in a circle around a pole lying upon the ground. This pole was about the size of a large telegraph pole, such as we see in cities. Long bamboo ropes were tied to one end of this so that it could be easily raised upright. The boy was led to the end where the ropes were tied, and then made to hug the pole with both arms and legs, then tied securely in this position. The pole was then lifted perpendicularly by all laying hold of the ropes and pulling steadily; as it stood the appearance was that of a boy who had climbed to the top of the pole. Then came a moment of awful suspense, all held their breath awaiting the fatal signal from the "Head of the Devil Bush." It was given, and simultaneously every hand let go the ropes; one instant the pole stood in mid air, then came sweeping to the ground with a dull thud, and all was over. The calculation had been so made as to let the pole fall on the boy, and it had crushed him, body and head, into a lifeless mass. All because he dared to let the outside world hear him speak from the mysterious confines of the "Devil Bush."

Should a girl or a woman chance to wander within the confines of the "Devil Bush" their doom is sealed. They are brought before the "head officer" and examined as to how they chanced to get in there. It makes but little difference what answer they give, they are finally told some of the boys will show them a place to sleep, and that is the signal for them to be led away by anyone who pleases, for they are abandoned to the will of the inmates, and left at their mercy with no appeal, until the time for moving the encampment when they are put to death. This, it is said, is done to prevent any woman from ever giving information as to what is within the dreaded confines.

In addition to the regular duties taught every prospective citizen, the accomplishment of the "black arts" is also taught as a post graduate course to those who may select it. How far this approaches the skill of our own sleight of hand performers I can not say, but am told that they do some clever tricks, and have witnessed performances that were sufficiently clever to puzzle me.

Such are the fragments of knowledge I have been able to gather by years of patient trying and waiting, and I leave the reader to judge as to the tremendous influence an institution so superstitious and relentless in its execution must exercise on molding the habits of an enlightened race, and how difficult it must be to break them up.
The Rt. Rev. C.C. Penick, D.D.

Appendix C: Excerpts from three books by Thomas Besolow (1890, 1891, 1892)

[Thomas Besolow was a Vai man brought to America at about the same time as Walters, though by the Methodist not the Episcopal Church. Besolow published his first book, *From the Darkness of Africa to the Light of America, the Story of an African Prince*, in 1890. But he withdrew it from circulation and issued it in a revised edition with a different publisher the following year. The problem seems to have been that the book had received negative reactions from some of its white American and Settler readers. In the 1891 preface, Besolow blames the 1890 "errors" on a white female amanuensis he had hired, whom he claims altered his text without his permission. It is difficult to determine how true this is. It may well have been an excuse, and it seems likely that it was the negative reaction he had received from some early readers that caused him to withdraw the text and alter it. In the 1890 text he had inveighed against the racist treatment he and his fellow Africans had received at Lincoln University. In the 1891 book, he revised this section, evidently in response to the strong reaction of the President of Lincoln University. Besolow seems to have been mainly concerned with how this and other controversy might affect the success of his book with his white American audience. In particular, judging by the revisions made to the 1891 edition, readers had been disturbed by the implications in the 1890 edition that a sacrifice of slave babies to sacred crocodiles was performed by his mother in Besolow's presence and on his behalf. The 1890 text also implies that she sacrificed adult slaves to ensure that her son not be sent to the mission by his father. In the 1891 edition this section is much modified. Walters also has an account of a crocodile sacrifice, but he implies that it is free children whose mothers sacrifice them voluntarily. This seems unlikely, as we record in the notes to the text (139). In comparison, though, Walters's version is restrained, and does not dwell on the horrors in the way Besolow does. Besolow was seemingly learning quickly both how to titillate his audience with such accounts of pagan monstrosities and how to distance himself personally from them. A comparison of the 1890 and 1891 accounts below will show how he managed this.

In 1892 he published a second book *The Story of an African Prince in Exile*, which, although it shared part of the title with the earlier work, was a wholly new and different work. Much of the long introduction to this is taken up with an attack on Besolow's detractors in America and Liberia.

What makes Besolow of special interest is that he quotes the 1891 *Guanya Pau* in several places in his 1892 work. In one place the material is placed in quotation marks, though the reference is not acknowledged to Walters (p. 179). This and the dates prove that it is Walters who is the prior source. Besolow attributes a quotation from *Guanya Pau* to "an eminent writer on Western Africa." It is possible that there is an earlier source for both, but this does not seem likely. We reproduce the places where he directly quotes Walters in the section below.]

Walters, Besolow, and the Crocodile Sacrifice

[From Thomas E. Besolow, *From the Darkness of Africa to the Light of America, The Story of an African Prince* (Boston: T.W. Ripley, 1890) 19-21.]

She [my mother] had many animals killed and offered to the Moon and Carnabah,[1] beseeching them to permit her son to remain in Bendoo. In a town of her own, quite a large and prosperous one, northwest from Bendoo, she had two prisoners killed and used as offerings to Carnabah. Beside all this, several of the slave women were compelled to take their newly born babies, and to come with mother and me to Lake Peso, where the sacred crocodiles were kept. As the medicine man in his long, floating, white woolen cloak, led us to the water's edge, I can see now in my mind's eye, as plainly as I did then, the red, hungry eyes of the animals as they swam within a dozen feet of the shore. Their great, gaping, slimy mouths, with the white, shiny, fang-like teeth, opened as though they were eager for the expected feast.

Mother and I knelt together with the slave women and their infants, while the priest stood in front of us, and delivered a long harangue to the animals. I remember distinctly of seeing tears drop from the eyes of one of the women, as she bent over her little babe who was cooing and throwing its little hands in the air, happily all unconscious of the horrid fate awaiting it. She quietly brushed the tears away, however, for if caught in the act of weeping for her child, in all probability her own life would have paid the penalty. What

---

1 Walters's *Kanabah*; see the note for p. 93 of *Guanya Pau*.

honor greater could be conferred on a slave woman than to be asked to offer her child as a sacrifice to the gods! It *should* be happiness supreme; but, after all, the wide world over, human nature is the same, and mother love is mother love, be it in the breast of an English queen or in that of the untutored savage.

After the priest had finished his long address, he took the babies from their mothers' arms, one by one, and anointed their naked little bodies with fragrant oils and salves.

Then the mothers, in their supposed joy at the proceedings, were expected to dance and caper about, and sing a propitiatory song to the gods, in which they fervently hoped that the sacrifice would please them, and be sweet and tender and toothsome.

Looking back upon it now, I see how dreadful it was, and what a strain it must have been to those women, to have pretended joy and pleasure, when, in reality, they must have been wretched and miserable beyond expression. Bravely they hid their feelings, and danced about, throwing their arms into the air, and screaming shrilly, perhaps in this way venting their grief, as one after another of their infants were cast into the waters of the lake, to the waiting, greedy animals. I watched with fascinated eyes, as the little black bodies disappeared in the cavernous mouths of the crocodiles, leaving a long train of crimson blood dyeing the still waters of the lake. Distinctly on shore, could we hear the monsters as they cracked the bones of the unfortunate babes, whose pitiful cries of pain might well have touched a heart of iron; and all the while the mothers danced and sang madly. At last it was over, and only the red eyes and cruel heads of the monsters looking for more prey to devour, and the blood-crimsoned waters, bathing the shores, remained to tell of the scene just enacted.

Young as I was, and used as I was to such scenes, which were as much a matter-of-course as your Sunday morning sermon, I remember that I felt a throb of something very like pity, as I saw those mothers walk dejectedly before us—*with empty arms.* As I write about it now, man grown as I am, and it comes to my mind with all its fearful significance, I cannot keep back the tears. May the one just, kind, and merciful God, free my native land from a custom so horrible! May He endow me with such strength and grace that I shall be able to help in abolishing a system at once so cruel and debasing!

[In the second edition, the passage has been changed. From Thomas E. Besolow, *From the Darkness of Africa to the Light of America, The Story of An African Prince* (Boston: Frank Wood, 1891) 32-34.]

My mother told me, before going, that she should offer prayers to the gods to prevent my father from sending me away, and also that it was a very fortunate thing for me that the sacrifices were to be offered at this time, as she believed that the crocodiles would listen to and grant the prayers of a loving mother to her son.

I will tell this story with some comments, as nearly as I remember it told to me.

The hour for the sacrifice was at hand. Suddenly a deep silence fell over all. Fifty or more medicine-men were approaching the shore. They wore long, floating, white robes, and looked very sober and solemn indeed.

About a dozen feet from the shore could be seen the red, hungry eyes of a half-hundred crocodiles. Their great, gaping mouths were opened greedily, as if they were eager for the expected feast. The low, drawling voices of the medicine-men were heard for a half hour or more in an unintelligible harangue; then through the crowd there pushed their way twenty-five slave women with their naked babes in their arms. At this point the musicians began to play upon their instruments—the dancers began to execute some wild, fantastic dances—the singers began to howl, for no other word expresses it—the voices of the medicine-men grew louder and shriller, and amid all this, the spectators with many a prayer and promise to the gods fell upon their knees and rocked themselves to and fro as though in mortal anguish; and all the while the gleaming eyes of the crocodiles seemed to dilate and grow larger, and their capacious, horrible mouths seemed to look more greedy and expectant. The only quiet ones in the crowd were the slave mothers and their babes. To look upon them was a sight never to be forgotten. The tears were silently dropping from eyes as they bent over their little babes, who were cooing and throwing up their little chubby hands into the air, happily unconscious of the horrible fate awaiting them. The mothers quickly and quietly brushed away the tears, however, for if caught in the act of weeping for their babes, their own life, in all probability, would have paid the penalty.

These babes were to be offered as sacrifices to the crocodiles; and what greater honor could be conferred upon a slave woman than to be asked to offer her child as a sacrifice to the gods? After the priests had finished their long harangue, they took the babes from their mothers' arms, one by one, and anointed their naked little bodies with fragrant oils and salves; and then the mothers, in their supposed joy at the proceedings, were expected to dance and caper about, and sing a propitiatory song to the gods, in which they fervently hoped that the sacrifice would please them, and be sweet, tender, and tooth-some. How dreadful it was! What a strain it must have been upon those mothers to have pretended joy and pleasure when, in reality, they must have been wretched and miserable beyond expression. Bravely they hid their feelings and danced about, throwing their arms into the air, and screaming shrilly, perhaps in this way venting their grief, as one after another of their infants were cast into the waters of the lake, to the waiting, greedy animals. The crowd watched with fascinated eyes the little black bodies disappear into the cavernous mouths of the crocodiles, leaving a long stain of crimson blood dyeing the waters of the lake. Distinctly on shore could be heard the monsters as they cracked the bones of the unfortunate babes, whose pitiful cries of pain might well have touched a heart of iron; and all the time the mothers danced and sang merrily. At last it was over, and only the eager eyes and cruel heads of the monsters looking for more prey to devour, and the blood-reddened waters bathing the shores, remained to tell the scene just enacted.

Though I was young, and accustomed to terrible scenes, yet when this scene was pictured to me, I remember that I felt a throb of something very like pity, as I thought of those poor women who had sacrificed the lives of their babes, but as I write about it now, man grown as I am, it comes to my mind, with all its fearful signif-icance, I cannot keep back the tears. May the one just, kind, and merciful God free my native land from a custom so horrible! May He endow me with such strength and grace that I shall be able to help in abolishing a system so cruel and debased.

[In *Guanya Pau* Walters treats the same aspect of Vai society as fol-lows, pp. 138-39.]

The fishing ended, the women took the way for home along the river's bank.

It was about twelve o'clock, the sun was shining at his best, pro-ducing a heat that was almost intolerable.

The women had to pass another holy scene.

This time it was in the person of a deity of exquisite grace and beauty (?)—a leviathan monster, in short, an alligator of tremendous and scaly proportions.

This was their war-god, to whom they prayed when about to encounter the enemy, and whom they worship by placing in his way a sheep or goat. I have learned from good authority, that in cases of extreme peril, when to all appearances the enemy seems the more powerful and sure of victory, mothers have not hesitated, at the advice of the medicine-man, to give their children to make his Holiness a supper.

At this hour he was lying high and dry upon the bank, with his huge jaws distended, which would close now and then like a prodigious steel-trap when a sufficient number of flies, bugs, and other flying insects had stored themselves therein for safety or shelter.

The women kept at a safe distance, all except, of course, Guanya Pau, who advanced closer to him than the rest and, by a childish noise, caused him to shut the chasm prematurely, when he lifted his head, switched his tail, and glided down into the stream.

Guanya Pau was told that nothing but an offering would appease his anger, and naturally her first impression was that she herself would constitute the offering. But her fears were allayed when the leader of the party said that as soon as they reached the village she would send a Jonkai with a lamb or kid.

The Overlap between *Guanya Pau* and Besolow's 1892 Book

[In Besolow's 1892 text the name Pandama-Pluzhaway is used as it is in Walters, but in Besolow it is identified as the founder of the Poro (male association) not the Sande (female association). From Thomas E. Besolow, *The Story of an African Prince in Exile* (Boston: Frank Wood, 1892) 175.]

Sometimes the boys from these places visit the town, and the king-devil, who is commander-in-chief of the forest, Pandama Pluzhaway, the devil's brother-in-law, leads the procession, and when he blows his horn it seems as if ten thousand ivory horns were sounding. According to the laws of the tribe, students attending this institution have the liberty to kill any cattle, and take anything eatable, when they enter town.

When this devil blows his horn the second time, intense silence reigns for about half an hour; then multitudinous voices mingle in the air, and as this host runs to and fro throughout the town, the ground seems to tremble under foot. All those who do not belong to this devil's institution, or have not hitherto joined, will fly to their homes for refuge; for the members of this institution will kill every animal they see. Members of this body will paint their faces with chalk and cover their heads with mud, so that their mother and father will not know them.

[The direct quotations from Walters in the Besolow 1892 edition are contained in the following excerpt; we have italicized them, pp. 178-81.]

A man in this part of Africa, when his daughter returns from the devil bush, if she is fine looking, is sure of his $150, or $200 for her. Last year I wrote to Africa for a girl, and I tacitly understood that I was to pay a certain sum of money for her. My sole object was that I might educate her as a teacher for my proposed institution, and her parents were informed that the king's son wanted a wife. And the parents being impressed that my father was formerly very rich, and knowing I was in the white man's country, where all the money is, they naturally enough thought that I was rich; so her father said that I could have the girl, and he counted it a great honor to him and his family; but I must still abide by the laws of the land, and send him $500. Of course I did not have the money, so the negotiation was not completed; as I said, it was not the wife that I wanted but to educate a teacher for my institute. I would advise American young men—especially the poor ones—if they expect ever to live in that part of Africa, to procure their wives on this side, where they can be secured without a money value, at least.

Zobah, the principal of the institution, often lectures to the young women on matters of practical importance, which are wholesome and beneficial. The reason why the Liberians call Zobah the devil, is as follows: her barbaric habiliments resemble the image of the Evil One, which consist of a false face and a black gown reaching to the ground, and to complete all, she has a headdress two or three feet long, and a tremendous wand in her hand. I remember when Meh's father died, Zobah came in town and danced at the time of his burial; she only came in town when there was a wedding or death of a nobleman. We natives believed that she was not human, but the Devil. *"An amusing story is told of how an American was affected on meeting Zobah. There was some celebration at a certain town, when he was eager to see the whole; but in his curiosity he ventured outside the prescribed limit, and of course one of the Zobahs started for him. Fortunately the American had his gun with him, and after retreating a few steps stopped, and with an oath, for which the average American is famous, made the devil halt, turn around, and march back to her quarters."* Of course the American had to pay a fine for his indecorous act [cf. *Guanya Pau*, 89]. "Borney," or gregree bush girls, are under strict laws and rules. They never are allowed to dance with men or boys; and while they wear the talisman about their neck, before they assume their dress, are not allowed to hold conversation with men.

If men insult them, the gravest punishment will attend the offender. If one of these borney is detected in a falsehood, she is severely punished. Young boys, for stealing, have straw tied about their hands and set on fire; but if they break into a house they are often thrown into the river with a large stone tied about their necks, or are burned to ashes. If a stranger comes to visit you, the very best house you have must be vacated and given him, or the use of it, while he is with you, and also feed him free of charge. Men who are addicted to falsehood are burned alive. If the American people were to adopt such measures for a while there would not be bogus notes in circulation; liars would become scarce; money-sharks would move farther into the Atlantic to find their prey; we who are very credulous would not fall into their hands as often as we do. The writer understands fully that there is a tendency to partiality in treating on subjects in which he is concerned, but his words can be verified by eminent writers on Western Africa. The natural superiority of the Vei people has fallen from a pinnacle of greatness to the lowest scale of degradation. The Vei people were once noted for their prowess and warlike stamina, but those days have passed away.

Hear what an eminent writer on Western Africa says: *"The Vei princes were ready to respond to the peal of the clarion. These were the watchwords of the once patriotic Veis, 'Give me liberty, or give me death.' The Veis of to-day are but pigmies to what they were once. The martial spirit has waned; the patriotic sentiment, the undaunted heroism, the 'give me liberty, or give me death' principle, the contempt for the coward, and praise for the brave, have dwindled to an alarming degree. It has been truly said that a nation is great in proportion as it has great men. The Veis were at their zenith in the days of Prince Manoh, Ballah (Hole in the Head), King Sand-fish, Prince Marranah, Kaipopo, King Freeman, King Grey, and Armah, son of Zodimah. These men were of superior fiber, in strength Herculean, in statesmanship brilliant, in principle uncompromising. With these kings liberty was man's supreme and Divine right, and he had no reason to live except in the full, untrammeled exercise of it. No threat could baffle them, no sudden appearance of an enemy on the frontier could intimidate them; no amount of money could bribe them. But one reason for the present degradation of the Veis is due to their alliance with Liberia, who fight their battles for them; secondly, the damnable, diabolical rum which has been sent from England, Germany, and Holland, has ruined our people.*

"*Prince Manoh, the writer's grandfather, was the one who led the victorious legions through the turbulent struggles with Bessie and Madina, the most memorable battles of the Veis. My uncle, Ballahkaipalley,* came in contact with the combined forces of the Corsohs, Hurras, and Phan tribes, near Fisherman's Lake, and gained a triumphant victory, which brought liberty to Gallinas and freedom to Marpha. Prince Ballah was excellent in martial prowess and in statesmanship. Had this African been born under the benign sky of monarchical and republican Europe, or of the Great Republic, his name would have been immortalized in history beside that victorious conqueror of Wagram, Montebello, Austerlitz, Jena, and Boridino, Napoleon Bonaparte, who lives in the heart of every Frenchman even to-day, or the indomitable Washington, Grant, and Von Moltke. Then let us call Gray as the poet of the hour:—*

"Full many a gem of purest ray serene
The dark, unfathomed caves of ocean bear;
Full many a flower is born to blush unseen,
And waste its sweetness on the desert air." [cf. *Guanya Pau*, 81-82]

[We might note that Besolow changes the second part of this, altering the fictional lineage Walters had devised for Guanya Pau to accommodate and celebrate his own ancestry.]

---

* I find at this late hour that Ballah was my father's brother only by adoption, and was not a blood relative. The Vei people have a strange way of claiming relationship which is sometimes entirely unfounded.

Appendix D: The Vai Writing System

[The Vai script was developed in approximately 1833 by Momolu Duwalu Bukele. While Bukele apparently knew that writing systems existed (and most likely had seen people make use of Arabic and English writing), the system he devised is entirely original; its principles are different from those that underlie Arabic and English, being instead similar to those used in the Cherokee writing system.[1]

Roughly speaking, the script is a syllabary, with almost every character signaling a consonant-vowel sequence. While the script has 210 characters (according to the chart given on p. 178, produced by a conference in 1962 at the University of Liberia), most literates find a knowledge of 40 to 60 of the most commonly occurring characters to be fully adequate. The script continues to be used today, primarily for correspondence and record-keeping.]

SAMPLE OF VAI

	Transliteration:	mbe-i	3	de	di-fi-ye	lo	nã	ki-ba-lo-mũ	ke	a	me
1.	Transcription:	mɓéì		dè	dìfí-ɛ́	lɔ̀	ná	kìɓálò	mù	kɛ́	à	mè
2.	Gloss:		May	3	day	night-the	in	I	dream	REL	do	it	this

	nã	ku-lu-ṅ	mũ-su	wa	fe-le	a	nã		ṅ	ba-la
1.	ná	kúlúŋ	mùsú	wá	fèlè	à	ná-à		ŋ́	ɓàlà
2.	I	Kru	woman	EMPH	see	she	come-COMP		me	to

	ṅ	wo-ha	mbe	a	ti	nã	kpe-la-de-ṅ	ko	ke-wu-ye	lo
1.	ŋ́	wòló-à	mɓè	à	tì	ná	kpìlàdéŋ	kó	kèù-ɛ́	lɔ̀
2.	I	want-COMP	I	her	be	my	lover		be	dream-the	in

'The night before May third, this is the dream I had: I saw a Kru woman. She came to me. In the dream I wanted to her to be my lover.'

— From a journal originally in the collection of Oldman Gbondo Senwan in the village of Laa, Tombe Chiefdom, Grand Cape Mount County, Liberia. The journal dates from the beginning of the twentieth century. In it the author recorded business transactions, major events, and dreams. Sample, translation, and analysis provided by Mohamed B. Nyei.

---

1 Holsoe raises the possibility that there was a Cherokee connection to the development of the Vai script but leaves the matter unresolved. Svend E. Holsoe, "A Case of Stimulus Diffusion? (A Note on Possible Connections Between the Vai and Cherokee Scripts)" *The Indian Historian* 4.3 (1971): 56-7.

TABLE 54.1: *The Vai Syllabary, 1962 Version*

Translit.[a]	Value	e	i	a	o	u	ɔ (ǫ)	ɛ (ę)
p	[p]							
b	[b]							
ḅ	[ɓ]							
mḅ	[mɓ]							
kp	[kp]							
mgb	[mgb]							
gb	[gb]							
f	[f]							
v	[v]							
t	[t]							
d	[d]							
l	[l]							
ḍ	[ɗ]							
nḍ	[nɗ]							
s	[s]							
z	[z]							
c	[c]							
j	[ɟ]							
nj	[nɟ]							
y	[j]							
k	[k]							
ṅg	[ŋg]							
g	[g]							
h	[h]							
w	[w]							
–								

ɤ Syllabic nasal

Nasal syllables

		ĩ	õ	ũ	ɔ̃	ɛ̃
hʋ	[ɦ]					
m	[m]					
n	[n]					
ny	[nj]					
ṅ	[ŋ]					

a. The transliterations are not official or standard, and reflect typographic convenience.

From John Victor Singler, "Scripts of West Africa," *The World's Writing Systems*, ed. Peter T. Daniels and William Bright (New York: Oxford UP, 1996) 593-98.

Appendix E: Letters and Articles by Joseph Jeffrey Walters

1. To Mrs. Louise Wood Brackett, a teacher and the wife of the Principal of Storer College, 5 October 1888 (WVU, A&M 2621, Box 1 FF2)

Oberlin,
Ohio, Oct. 5th 1888.

Mrs. Brackett,

My Dear Friend:

This will inform you of my arrival to Oberlin college. I made the senior preparatory[1] as expected, and being two weeks late am working most assiduously to make up back lessons. Daily recitations are marked.

There are over 1100 students in school and it surprises me to see how the faculty keeps everyone in his place. The religious force is very good. There are class prayer meetings on Fridays, Bible classes Wednesdays and college prayers at 5 p.m. daily.

I feel much assisted by the influence of the school—everything uplifting. Before commencing each recitation a prayer is offered or a hymn is sung. Last Friday the subject of the meeting covered an incident I experienced in Africa which I related. At the close a young lady made her way through the audience to me, shook hands telling me she was born in Africa—I presume her parents were missionaries there. I shall visit them tomorrow, D.V.

Mission spirit is very strong here; and the cause is held in high esteem.

Permit me to tender you and Prof. many thanks for your efforts of summer before last to get me in college. I feel much indebted to you. I shall try to attest my appreciation for your kindness by improving my time.

I presume the neighborhood around feels very much the loss of Mr. Kirk. For my own part it is impossible for me to become rec-

---

1 Walters spent his first year at Oberlin in the final year of the preparatory (pre-college) program.

onciled. I never had a relative whose death affected me more than Mr. Kirk's. It seems to me as if Storer loses one of her best sons every year—for the last four years.

The organist here I think is Prof. Rice of whom you spoke to me before leaving the Ferry
[end of second page of letter; the rest of the letter is lost]

2. To the Editor, *Oberlin News* (7 April 1892)

ARE COLORED CHURCHES NEEDED IN OBERLIN?

Such a question was asked me a few days ago by a white friend who had been solicited in behalf of the Colored Baptist Church which is now in process of organization. After careful and deliberate consideration as well as painstaking observation for more than three years, I am compelled to answer No: and these are my reasons:

In the first place I am surprised at those Oberlin pastors who say that it is high time to establish colored churches here. Why is this more so now than it was twenty-five years ago? If education and intelligence determine our fitness for the white churches then at no other time in Oberlin's history were we better fitted for these churches. Or, do they mean to say that because of our qualification we ought therefore to be by ourselves? To this we answer that intellectual fitness alone does not constitute a right to organize churches, that there are many other considerations which must contribute.

Secondly, a large majority of the colored people of Oberlin repel the idea, considering it an attempt to draw the color line, and who would prefer going to no church at all before uniting with a church designated "colored." Not that they have less of race pride or are so anxious to identify themselves with their white friends, but because the system savors so much of the Southern prejudice which is so opposed to principles taught in this *par excellence* of American institutions.

Thirdly, an experiment has been made and failed. Rust Church which was organized several years ago is an example of the utter futility of such efforts. Ever and anon there is a threat of capsize; her few members are ever at war among themselves, and the best of these have become dissatisfied and joined other churches. Her young people, as they are converted, almost invariably unite with the other churches. Her pastors who have not always been intelligent, Christian men, have done much to hasten her doom which now seems inevitable.

Fourthly, it is claimed that such a church is needed for those of the people who are unlearned, and who cannot understand the services of the white churches. Are all the white members who come in from the country around intelligent people? Would not the same argument hold good for them to congregate by themselves? But, alas for the church that does not tone its services to suit the least in its congregation. These ignorant people will come in when the sermons are patterned after those Jesus preached, and the Spirit of Christ pervades the worship.

Lastly, for the colored churches to meet the demands of the times they must have educated ministers, and such the few who would congregate by themselves are unable to secure because of their inability to support them. To have such ministers and services as some of them have had is a disgrace to Oberlin. Let once more the Gospel idea of the brotherhood of man and the Fatherhood of God possess the hearts of the Christians of Oberlin and colored churches will be a thing of the past. Let us have here above all things and all places a Church of Christ—broad, democratic, apostolic. A Church above the mincing sentimentalities of the social aristocracy.

JOSEPH J. WALTERS.

3. To the Rev. William S. Langford, General Secretary of the Board of Missions of the Episcopal Church, 15 May 1893 (AEC, RG 72 69)

42 Vine St.,
Oberlin, Ohio
May 15, '93

Rev. Dr. Langford,

My Dear Sir:—

I have been in communication with Bp. Ferguson, of West Africa, to the effect that I should prepare myself to take a chair in Epiphany Hall, Cuttington.[1] With this in view I have paid special attention to

---

1 Epiphany Hall, Cuttington, in the Cape Palmas region of Liberia, was founded by Bishop Ferguson as an institution of higher learning to train Episcopal priests and teachers. The cornerstone for Epiphany Hall, the school's first building, had been laid in 1889. In keeping with Ferguson's vision for the school, in 1897 it was renamed the Cuttington Collegiate and Divinity School (D. Elwood Dunn, *A History of the Episcopal Church in Liberia, 1821-1980* [Metuchen, NJ: The Scarecrow Press, 1992] 135).

the New Testament language & a few other theological studies; but am most proficient in the Greek & Latin languages.

I shall receive my degree (B.A.) from Oberlin College next June, D.V. I have not had a full theological course, the state of my health being such renders it inadvisable for me to continue longer at school. I have had sufficient in this course to enable me to complete the work independently & if necessary can graduate from some Seminary either here or in England, in the future.

I am a special friend of Bp. Penick, late of Africa, who is my advisor & father in the Gospel.

Wishing to hear from you soon,

I am, yours faithfully,

Joseph J. Walters.

P.S. I shall be ready to start for Africa about August next.

4. To the Rev. Joshua A. Kimber, Secretary of the Board of Foreign Missions of the Episcopal Church, 2 June 1893 (AEC, RG 72 69).

42 Vine St.,
Oberlin, Ohio
June 2d, 1893

Rev. Joshua Kimber,
22 Bible House, N.Y.

My Dear Sir:—

What I intended to ask at the hands of the Board in my letter of May 15th is that it will please meet the expense of my passage to Liberia. Necessity compels me to ask this favor inasmuch as I have been dependent upon myself for my support in the prosecution of my preparatory & college courses & especially because of my recent protracted illness which renders me unable to follow my customary means of support.

It was my intention, at the completion of my college course the 21st inst. to enter the "General Theological Seminary" next fall, but owing to my state of health I am advised to return to Africa as soon as possible.

I may be able to pursue my course there and when well again return here to complete them.

I should like to leave for Africa early in July.

Yours faithfully,
Joseph J. Walters.

5. To the Rev. Joshua A. Kimber, 12 October 1893 (AEC, RG 72 69)

Cape Mount
Liberia, Africa
Oct. 12, 1893

Rev. Joshua Kimber
22 Bible House
New York

My dear Sir:—

On my arrival to Cape Mount I find the Veys of this section on the point of starvation because of the native wars which have reduced them. I have therefore written an article for publication in a few of the American papers in their behalf,[1] & have asked those who are willing to contribute anything to send their contributions to you, trusting you will favor us by buying rice with the same & send us.

Their condition now is worse than that of the "Pahn War" when Bishop Penick appealed to his country & friends for [aid].[2]

I hope you will favor us in our deep affliction and do all in your powers to alleviate the suffering in this quarter. Our work here is lagging because of the famine, as we are sometimes afraid to approach men & women about their souls' salvation because we know the first thing they need is food for the body.

Help us and help us speedily for God's sake.

Yours fraternally,
Jos.

---

1 One version of the article to which Walters refers was published in the 30 November 1893, edition of the *Oberlin News* and is given below.

2 The page is torn; there is room for one word, and our guess is that it is *aid*.

6. "An Appeal for Help," *Oberlin News* (30 November 1893)

The writer of the following was a native and graduate of the Class of 1893, Oberlin College, since which he returned to his native land.

Cape Mount, Liberia, Africa

Several years ago when the "Pahn War" was raging in this part of Africa there was so much need and suffering that Bishop Penick, one of the greatest white men that ever trod West Africa's soil, and one who is ever ready to help suffering humanity everywhere, appealed to his Christian people in the United States and received a liberal and cheerful response. Were he here now I can imagine how urgent would be his appeal.

Today we are in worse distress and I venture to appeal to the kind friends of America for help.

Since my arrival in Cape Mount a few weeks ago I have longed to go to some of the surrounding villages to preach; but what reception can the gospel find among a hungry people. Their bodies must be fed first.

The people for whom I am soliciting are the Veys, a tribe of Africans I introduced to my Oberlin friends in my little book "Guanya Pau." They are an industrious, intelligent people, producing and controlling much of the commerce in this section. The interior tribes have always been jealous of them and there has been no end of wars and rumors of wars. Their present enemy are the Zophao and the Hurou, two powerful, warlike tribes from the interior who are bent on destruction of the Veys. Large and flourishing towns that a few months since were doing a great business in palm kernel, oil, wood, rubber, ivory, &c., are today reduced to ashes, and their inhabitants, those that escaped the sword or slavery, reduced to the utmost necessity. They all rush down upon Cape Mount for help and protection, and so general now is the suffering that Liberians and natives alike are reduced. Many have pawned their children for food, and women offer to barter their honor for one meal of rice. Herbs, roots, and leaves hitherto food for the wild beast alone are now devoured by these famished people. It was a little amusing to see three Vey men chase a snake, hem him in, catch him, throw him into the fire and eat him before he was well done. Ten youths recently died at a town a few miles from here, from swallowing persimmon seeds. Fruits and vegetables are not permitted to attain half their growth. The people of Cape Mount who are an agricultural people, raise nothing, for theft and robbery are wholesale and rampant.

The Veys are no feeble, emasculated people. Their enemy is simply their superior, whose vocation is war, while the Veys are a peaceable, agricultural and commercial people.

I appeal to the Christians of Oberlin and elsewhere in their behalf. Send us rice and please send it as quickly as possible. As it is inconvenient for each contributor to secure rice I suggest that you give your contributions to Professor Chamberlain or President Ballantine and he kindly oblige us by sending the same to Rev. Joshua Kimber, 22 Bible House, New York, who will buy the rice and send us. Help us in this our deep extremity, and God will reward you richly for doing this for his name's sake.

Joseph J. Walters

7. From "A Letter from Africa," *Baltimore American* (21 January 1894)

[In late 1893 and early 1894, Bishop Penick, Walters's "advisor and father in the Gospel," went on a speaking tour in his capacity as Agent for the Commission of the Protestant Episcopal Church for Work Among the Colored People. The Penick Archives at St. Paul's Church in Winston-Salem, NC, contain newspaper articles reporting on his sermons in Baltimore, Boston, Cleveland, Memphis, and Philadelphia. The article that appeared in the 21 January 1894 issue of the *Baltimore American* had the following headline:

THE AFRICAN AT HOME,
BISHOP PENICK'S OBSERVATION
IN LIBERIA
What He Saw There Gave Him a
Clearer Insight Into the Nature
of the Colored Man and Will
Help Him in His New
Line of Church Work,
The Future of
the Race
Here.

The following is an excerpt from the *American* article.]

A LETTER FROM AFRICA

Bishop Penick has just received a letter from an African prince, Momolu Massaquoi, son of the King of the Vey tribe, which may be of interest to readers of *The American* from its graphic story of the condition of one of the famine-stricken districts of Africa. The writer is one of three natives, who were brought to this country by Bishop Penick and afterwards educated by the Episcopal Church.

The letter reads as follows: "Since my arrival in Cape Mount a few weeks ago, I have engaged to go to some of the surrounding villages to preach: but what reception can the Gospel find among a few hungry people. Their bodies must first be fed. The people for whom I am soliciting aid are the Veys, a tribe of Africans who lived in the towns and villages on the Cape Mount and Marphar Rivers and Pisu Lake, an industrious, intelligent people, producing and controlling much of the commerce in this section. The interior tribes have always been jealous of them, and there have been no end of wars and rumors of wars. Their present enemies are the Zophar and the Huraw, powerful and warlike tribes from the interior, who are bent on the Veys' destruction. Large and prosperous towns which a few months since were doing a great business in palm kernels, oil, wood, rubber, ivory, &c., are today reduced to ashes, and their inhabitants, those that escaped the sword and slavery, reduced to the utmost necessity. They all rush down upon Cape Mount for help and protection, and so general now is the suffering that Liberians and natives alike are reduced. Many have pawned their children for food, and women offer to barter their honor for one meal of rice. Herbs, roots, and leaves, hitherto food for the wild beast alone, are now devoured by these famished people. It was a little amusing to see three men chase a snake, hem him in, and catch him, throw him into the fire and eat him before he was well done. Ten youths recently died at a town a few miles from here from swallowing persimmon seeds. Fruits and vegetables are not permitted to attain half their growth. The people of Cape Mount who are an agricultural people, raise nothing, for theft and robbery are wholesale and rampant.

The Veys are no feeble, emasculated people. Their enemy is simply their superior, whose vocation is war, while the Veys are a peaceable, agricultural and commercial people.

I appeal to the Christians of the United States in their behalf. Send us rice, and please send it as soon as possible.

As it is inconvenient for each contributor to secure the rice, I suggest that you send your contribution in money to Rev. Joshua Kimber, 22 Bible House, New York, who will buy the rice and send us. Help us in this our deep extremity, and God will reward you richly for doing this for his name's sake.

[The *Oberlin News* article by Walters and the *Baltimore American* letter—ostensibly by Momolu Massaquoi—are essentially identical, with most of the differences between them straightforward, e.g. the presence of Oberlin-specific references in the Oberlin version only.[1] Presumably it was Bishop Penick who excised from the Baltimore version the author's characterization of the Bishop as "one of the greatest white men that ever trod West Africa's soil ..."

What is baffling is the apparent attribution of the letter in the *American* article to Massaquoi rather than to Walters, its actual author. While it is possible that this is a reporter's error, the degree of Penick's involvement in the production of the articles that reported on his speaking tour makes it more credible that he is the one who introduced the confusion.[2]

Late in 1893 Massaquoi traveled from Liberia to the US. On December 28, 1893, he wrote from Williamstown, Massachusetts, to the Rev. Kimber to ask for Bishop Penick's address. This creates a plausible scenario, though not one flattering to Bishop Penick, to account for the attribution of authorship in the *American* article. By it, Walters wrote the letter to Penick and then gave it to Massaquoi, asking him to mail the letter upon arriving in the US. If Massaquoi did so, Penick was then able to say, strictly speaking, that he "had just received a letter from an African prince, Momolu Massaquoi." Crucially, however, the person from whom Penick received the letter (Massaquoi) and "the writer" (Walters) were different individuals.

---

1 We have not seen an actual copy of the November 30, 1893, number of the *Oberlin News* in which Walters's appeal appeared; however, the Oberlin College Archives provided us with a typescript version of the article
2 Three aspects of the situation appear unmistakable: Walters was the author of the letter that appeared in the *American* article, neither Walters nor Massaquoi claimed otherwise, and Penick knew that Walters was the author. The letter in the *American* is fundamentally the same as the letter to the Oberlin *News*, the authorship of which is not in doubt. Beyond that, the personal facts in the letter, e.g., "Since my arrival in Cape Mount a few weeks ago," describe Walters, not Massaquoi. Penick would have known this.

(Massaquoi was not brought to the US by Penick (Raymond J. Smyke, personal communication), but Penick can truthfully say that "the writer"—since it was Walters—was "one of three natives, who were brought to this country by Bishop Penick and afterwards educated by the Episcopal Church.")

It is certainly possible that it was a newspaper reporter who confused the letter bearer with the letter writer, but Penick's involvement with the writing of these newspaper articles points to the likelihood that Penick himself crafted the misleading wording. This raises a new question: why would he have done so? Our answer is speculative and is, of course, built on our suspicion that it was the Bishop's disingenuousness—not a reporter's error—that produced the misattribution. Simply put, Penick was dazzled by social standing. (There is ample evidence of this in Penick's writings on Vai society.) Massaquoi was Vai nobility, and Walters was not. Massaquoi is referred to as "an African prince, ... son of the King of the Vey tribe." Indeed, the Massaquoi family held a pre-eminent place among Vai aristocracy.[1] In contrast, Walter appears to have come out of poverty. From Penick's perspective, then, it appears that, not only does a plea from a prince carry greater cachet, the recipient of a letter from a prince is himself of higher status than is the recipient of a letter from a commoner.]

8. To the Rev. Joshua A. Kimber, 5 June 1894 (AEC, RG 72 69)

St. John's Mission,
Cape Mount
June 5, '94

Rev. Joshua Kimber,
My Dear Sir:—

I write to solicit your and others sympathy & aid in respect to certain books which I need to present & which I am unable to purchase.

When I came here last Febr. because there was no other accommodation I was domiciled in Bishop Penick's old house. The build-

---

1 See Raymond J. Smyke, *Massaquoi of Liberia, 1870-1938* (*Genève-Afrique* 21 [1983], No. 1).

ing being in a state of decay is infested with a bug (known to science, I believe, as the white ant) common to the country which have played havoc with some of my best books. My Hebrew lexicon with another good book are totally ruined together with several copies of the "Spirit of Missions," "Christian Herald" and other valuable papers. They have damaged a fine Psychology, Bible Dictionary, Botany & several of my school books. The only commentary I have is now of little use.

I therefore ask your assistance in the following books: Hebrew Lexicon & Grammar, Lexicon of the New Testament, a commentary on the Old and New Testaments, Butler's Analogy, French's Parables & Miracles, Schaff's Church History, some good work on the Prayer Book, Articles, Creed, Paley's Natural Theology, a volume of standard sermons, some Introduction to the Old & New Test., Biography of Spurgeon, Harmony of the Gospels, & what other books will be profitable for me in my course.[1]

We are now having much rain here in Cape Mount & vegetation is luxuriant.

I hope in the near future (D.V.) to ask for a small library for the station, such is becoming indispensable.

We are all fairly well.

I was much surprised & made uneasy on the night of the 2d inst. when someone made attempts at 12:30 o'clock to break into my room.

With many wishes for your continued health & labor in the cause,

I am, yours faithfully,
Joseph J. Walters.

---

1 The books Walters ordered include the following:
The Analogy of Religion, by Joseph Butler (1692-1752), first published in 1736; *The History of the Christian Church*, by Philip Schaff (1819-93), an eight-volume set first published in English in 1853, though shorter versions existed as well; and *Natural Theology*, by William Paley (1743-1805), first published in 1800. "Spurgeon" was Charles Haddon Spurgeon (1834-92), a renowned Baptist preacher in England; famed for preaching to crowds of 6,000 without amplification. (His 63 books of sermons are still in print.) Within a year of Spurgeon's death, four biographies of him had been published; presumably, Walters was referring to one of these. Finally, the "Harmony of the Gospels" integrates the four Gospels' presentations of events in the life of Jesus into a single chronology.

9. Annual Report and Scholarship List, Cape Mount Mission, received at Bible House, New York, 13 August 1894 (AEC, RG 72 69)

St. John's Mission,
Cape Mount,
Africa

My Dear Friends:

It falls to my lot to send you the report for this year & I do it with the feeling that you desire to know the whole truth that you may the more clearly see our needs & be in a better position to help us.

Upon my return here from the United States last September I was very anxious to visit my *alma mater* where three years of my life was spent when a boy & where I received the first incentives to a higher & nobler life. Like Caesar I came, I saw, but unlike him I was conquered. That is, I was disgusted at the general appearance of things & when on my return to my boarding place I was asked of my impressions of the mission, I flatly exclaimed: "Mrs. Brierley's (St. George's) department is the only school up there." But the cause of the irregularities I noticed was not far to seek. Institutions, like states, must have great men in their service in order to be great. Men of sterling integrity who will make their interests theirs, and their troubles & adversities their own.

St. John's needs one or two good teachers & *the need is imperative & paramount*. Men who will give their whole time to the work, whose hearts throb with a genuine love for & interest in these heathen children, but especially, men who are pronounced foes to tobacco & intoxicating liquors. It is high time that we learn to discriminate in the selection of those who are to train the young— especially the young of our heathens. The Bible incarnate in the teacher is worth more to them than sermons, precepts or creed. As is the teacher, so is the pupil—character begets character. But yet, the late incumbent of this station in an address some time since—the two departments being at variance, or rather, the incumbent being at variance with the other department—said, "Children, you must not do as we teachers do; but do as we tell you to do."

If teaching the lessons prescribed in text books is the whole of teaching then we can afford to employ any who are intellectually competent, but if the teacher is to build character, to instil in those young minds the great principles of truth & righteousness then it behooves us to be careful. That Bishop or Board is to be pitied that is compelled to take whoever they can find. But it seems to me ten thousand times better to close the doors of the schoolhouse than have the wrong kind of instructors.

Every year the Southern Colored Schools of the United States are sending out noble young men as teachers & preachers. I have no doubt but that there are some who would as soon serve their Master in Africa as in America if our needs were only presented to them. I have heard colored students, schoolmates of mine in the Northern schools, express a genuine desire to become missionaries to Africa.

Our day-school during the last half of the year has suffered much from unnecessary interruptions & the work on the whole has been unsatisfactory—at least, I am dissatisfied with mine. There are some bright minds in the school who need only the spur of inspiration & enthusiasm to make them shine in their fullest strength.

We are in great need of a suitable schoolroom with desks, blackboards, maps, charts & other necessary school apparatus. These we must have if in Africa Africans are to be thoroughly trained for the work.

Our Church and Sunday School have gone on regularly and the Christian young men of St. John's have organized a "St. John's Chapter of the Brotherhood of St. Andrew." This society contemplates among its few interests paying special attention to all newcomers, making them feel at home & thus preventing a poor home-sick boy from running away.

We have had a reduction in the number of pupils owing to the fact that when the late incumbent was removed from the station he took with him all those under his immediate care, some of whom he redeemed from slavery here, as it was thot, with the mission funds for the mission. But we hope soon to have the vacant places filled.

You will notice in the scholarship list that eight of the pupils are from St. George's Hall. They are excellent representatives of that department & show the quality of work being done there. Too much cannot be said in praise of Mrs. Brierley & her co-workers. Especially, the former whom I consider one of the noblest missionaries that ever came to Africa. That deep, abiding interest; that enthusiasm for the cause; that intense love for the work & yearning for souls, these distinguish her & make her work sublime. And these characteristics must distinguish all who would see the Kingdom of Christ advanced in the world. "May she go late to Heaven."

We are now beginning to feel the need of a small library. There is no better way for our boys and girls to learn to speak the English language well than to have them read good books in this language.

Therefore please, friends of the school, send us such books as would interest & instruct the young people in America. Books of travel & adventure, biographies, histories, novels, poetry, a few reference books & a good dictionary. Will some one not kindly send us the "Youths' Companion" for a year? Back numbers of papers will also be gladly received. We have here every variety of tastes & temperaments as is seen abroad—from the lover of light, funny stories to that of works more sober & grave.

I feel assured that none of our generous, noble-hearted supporters & friends will become discouraged because of the picture presented above. I rather believe it will increase your interest in us & call forth such hearty & loving response that will place the work in a better condition of usefulness. "We must pass through fire & water before we come to a wealthy place.["] Speedy efforts are being made to correct evils, & with the proper forces at work, we hope sooner or later to come to that "wealthy place"; when, well-trained & disciplined, our young men & women will go out from this institution to carry the Gospel to the regions beyond. We therefore ask you, each supporter & friend, to pray earnestly for us.

Very sincerely yours,
Joseph J. Walters

St. John's School

"David Livingstone" (advanced) scholarship; *Henry T. Gross*, assistant student teacher, continues at his post and tries to do his duty.

"Poughkeepsie Memorial" (advanced) scholarship: *William F. Sherman* is growing into a fine young man, but not yet thoroughly established in character. He is the largest boy on the mission & the humblest when corrected for a fault. He is our chorister, carpenter, & general reliance.

"Jesse H. Campbell" (advanced) scholarship: *Charles Johnson* is reliable and quiet, a matter-of-fact young man, lacking quickness of intellect, but anxious to learn, especially how to write letters. He is very inaccurate in his counting & as assistant in the mission store has always to be assisted when the cloth to be measured exceeds twenty yards.

"Susan Carrington Clark" (advanced) scholarship. *Henry Marsh* was transferred from St. George's Hall. He is the smallest boy and the finest reader in his class. Has quite a knack for making palavers with the little ones; is a tease.

"Lewis W. Burton" (advanced) scholarship. *Philip Watson* is one of the advanced pupils. He has a hard time with the ancient languages, but is good in English studies, especially Geography. He is reliable and firm & has been appointed "Clothes Monitor."

"Bishop Whitaker" (advanced) scholarship; *James Jackson* is from St. George's Hall. He is very studious, bright & promising. Of him we cherish great hopes.

"J"(In Memoriam) (advanced) scholarship; *Alexander Mackay Smith* is a kind affectionate boy, studious & ambitious, but has great difficulty with the English language. He has the ministry in view.

"H" (advanced) scholarship. *Richard Campbell* is from St. George's. He is a fine student with good ability & high aspirations. Of his future usefulness we are quite confident. His aim is to become a teacher, but his father is somewhat in favor of the ministry for him. George Penick reported last was taken away by the Rev. Mr. Shannon.

"Frank" (advanced) scholarship: *Alfred D. Sherman* has good intellect and a loving disposition & makes marked progress in his studies. His chief fault is his dislike for manual labor. He likes to play the gentleman.

"Williams" (advanced) scholarship: *Albert Z. Roberts* is good tempered & studious, stands well in his class, is capable of doing excellent work when he has a mind to; but, unfortunately, he is not always in the mood.

"Jennette H. Platt" scholarship: *Thomas Emmons* is from St. George's Hall. He is a fine little reader, very fond of the pots of whose contents he likes to carry about on his clothes ocular evidence. A little fussy & consequently forever in trouble.

"Orlando Crease" scholarship: *Charles Williams* is ever at the foot of his class, studies very little; a passionate lover of good clothes.

"Pauline Beck Henson" scholarship: vacant. We hope soon to have these vacancies filled.

"William A. Fair" scholarship: *Thomas Kekoolah Clark* is a good easy-going lad with a reckless abandon in person & dress. He is troubled with a disease known here as "kracraw."

"Ten Broeck Memorial" scholarship. *Lewis Burton Shannon* is very quiet, slow & dull & exceedingly fearful of the rod. His father, Mr. Gray, is very anxious about his boys here & is a model of heathen parents in this respect.

"C.C. Hoffman" scholarship: *James Bishop* is steady & reliable with a "touchy" disposition, but will always yield to reason; very neat in person & dress. His story respecting his disbelief in the contents of books as read to him by mission boys before coming to the mission is very amusing.

"Staten Island No. 1" scholarship: *Lewis McCauley* was once good in his books, but has recently relaxed his hold & fallen behind. He is obedient & kind, ever ready to do his duty when told.

"Staten Island No. 2" scholarship: *Dansanah* is now away, but expected back soon. He is spoken of by the boys with much confidence & they all seem to love him.

"R.H. McKim" scholarship: *Horatio Gray* is a bright boy, has studious habits, very playful and of a quarrelsome disposition which involves him in occasional palavers.

"Wright Waddell" scholarship: *John Gayah Freeman* is from St. George's. He is a remarkable boy, a good scholar, & excels in Scripture studies, is peaceable & cleanly.

"Solomon Memorial" scholarship: *Edward Molleybone Davis* is bright & active, has an impressive & intelligent little face & is well calculated to hold his own among the larger boys. He is "Bell Monitor."

"Christ Church Sunday School" scholarship: *Thomas Momo Gray* is an indolent, careless student, with little or no ambition save to be decked out in the best attire the mission can afford. He tries hard to ape the "dude."

"J.A. Gambrell" scholarship: *John Hunter* has returned to us & thinks now he will stay since his brother has come back home to care for his widowed mother.

"William F. Petit" scholarship: *Damani* is too fond of play to do much in his books.

"Faith Blind" scholarship: *Claudinsley Osborne* once excelled in his studies & gave great promise, but for some unknown cause has become rather dilatory of late. He dislikes work & gives trouble during work hour. Many of these boys are gentlemen's sons with soft hands unused to toil, because at their homes the slaves do the work while they indulge in sports & parades. So when they come to us they find it hard to do the very work they were accustomed to assign to a slave.

"Putnam Memorial" scholarship: *Jacob Ziah Gross* is a boy for whom we have some anxiety. He is wilful and obstinate, overbearing in disposition, always troubled with sores, & a little addicted to swearing. He is such a boy as they would send in America to the "House of Correction."

"William W. Farr Memorial" scholarship: *William Robert Brewer*, last reported, has left.

"Bishop Starkey" scholarship: *Josiah Jackson* is a member of the advanced class. He is an earnest student, works hard & is making progress. His composition last term on "Coffee" was the best of the class. His great fault is slovenliness in dress.

"Rev. S.C. Hill" scholarship: *James Dandah Noble*, last reported, has left.

"Thomas S. Savage" (In Memoriam) scholarship: *Joseph Moore* is from St. George's. He is now at home on a visit.

"St. George" scholarship: *Ernest Z.B. Shannon* has steady & regular habits; is hard-working & conscientious. He is the best in his class.

Nancy B. Low scholarship: *Charles Varney Diggs* makes good progress in his studies, is kindly dispositioned, honest & trustworthy. He is much hindered by an impediment in his speech.

"Wharton" scholarship: *Daniel Johnson*, last reported, has left.

"St. Paul's" scholarship: vacant.

"Kate Blake" scholarship: *Wm. Boiama Gray*, once one of the first in his class, has grown careless & delinquent. He has a violent temper and became so indignant at a boy for telling the teacher that Boiama's sickness on examination day was due to the examination that Boiama threatented [sic] to cut him.

"Clara Emily Penick" scholarship: *Thomas Lloyd*, reported last, made so little improvement in his studies that his father took him away to try him at farming.

"Mrs. Caroline W. Bragg" scholarship: *Wm. Hall Johnson* is one of our best vocalists, a good, earnest & painstaking student, but decidedly lacking in self-respect. And this is a fault so common among our children. Half the battle is in getting them to be decent & cleanly in person & in dress. Dirt & filth are essentials to heathenism, & they can show no better sign of having put off the old man & his deeds than by assuming a neat & tidy appearance.

"Lily B. Ferry Memorial" scholarship: *Henry Neely* is very fond of arithmetic & is inclined to devote his study hours to that alone. He possesses a kind & quiet disposition; never complains when assigned his task.

"Waldburg No. 1." scholarship: *Alexander Taylor* has an uncontrollable passion for fighting. He loves his books withal & applies himself with much assiduity.

"Waldburg No. 2." scholarship: *Henry Stanley* is from St. George's. He is a good cook & likes the business. When transferred to St. John's he sent word to his friend in that department that the continuance of their friendship would be conditioned on his allowing him to superintend the kitchen at St. John's.

"Waldburg No. 3." scholarship: *Alexander Jackson* is a small Congo boy who came to us a week ago. He is below the size required for St. John's, but because his brother is here who with his father was very [anxious] to have him begin his studies early & at St. John's. I took him.

"Waldburg No. 4." scholarship: *Walter Jordan* is from St. George's. He deports himself becomingly, is diligent in his work, & like some others from St. George's is quite an adept in culinary affairs.

"John Sharp Foster Memorial" scholarship: *Henry Foster Shannon*, last reported, was a boy redeemed by the Rev. Mr. Shannon whom he took away when he was dismissed from the mission.

"Rev. August P. Stryker Memorial" scholarship: *Amos Bye Freeman* is from St. George's. At St. George's we are told that he was studious & bright, but the transfer seems to have lessened his ambition & he has joined the ranks of delinquents.

"Bishop Huntington" scholarship: temporarily vacant.

Joseph J. Walters

10. To the Rev. Joshua A. Kimber, 17 September 1894 (AEC, RG 72 69)

Cape Mount
Sept. 17, '94

Rev. J. Kimber,
My Dear Sir: –
Enclosed please find a small order for myself. I sent the same to Mr. Sherman but he failed to send it on the grounds that I am not an ordained missionary. But my case I beg to be made exceptional. The articles can be secured here only by paying an exorbitant price & the state of my health is such that I am in absolute need of them & the small stipend, tho' acting Supt., will not allow me to get them here together with the medicines which cost me $4 & $5 per mo. Please favor me in this & let the articles come by the first opportunity.

I have suffered much since I came here for the want of things suitable to my condition. Were I well I could put up with almost anything, but since I am not I must be careful & seek such conveniences as will enable me to live.

Yours faithfully,
Jos. J. Walters

(Personal Order)
½ Bbl Flour
½ " Sugar (granulated)
1 Ham
1 Breakfast Bacon

Appendix F: Obituaries of Joseph Jeffrey Walters

1. From *The Storer Record*, Storer College (February 1895) Vol. 12, No. 2 (WVU, A & M 2621, Box 14, FF 14)

Among Former Students

It is with extreme sorrow that we record the death, on the 13th of November last,[1] of Jos. J. Walters, '85, at Cape Mount, Liberia. His health, which had become completely undermined while he was in this country, did not rally as was hoped when he returned to his native land. He was permitted little more than a year of service at his chosen work in Africa. We shall speak of him more at length in the next number of the RECORD.

[While this announcement promises a longer obituary in the next number, the three issues of *The Storer Record* that were published subsequently in 1895 contain no reference to Walters.]

2. From *The Oberlin Review* (6 February 1895)

IN MEMORIAM

JOSEPH JEFFREY WALTERS, born at Cape Mount, Liberia, W. Africa, date unknown, educated at Cape Mount School and at Harper's Ferry, W. Va.; entered Oberlin College in the Senior Preparatory class of '89; graduated from the Classical Course in '93; returning to Africa became Superintendent of Cape Mount Mission School of the Protestant Episcopal Church; died Nov. 12, 1894, of consumption.

JOSEPH JEFFREY WALTERS, '93 O.C., died at his post in the Vei country, W. Africa. A genuine and heartfelt sorrow comes, I am sure, to every one who knew Mr. Walters, at the mention of this sad news. Perhaps no one of the many students who have come from heathen countries and received in Oberlin that training in Christian education which might make them a blessing to their darkened homes,

---

1 The source of the date of Walters's death is Dr. Sarah Walrath. Her letter to the Rev. Joshua Kimber (AEC RG 72 68, 13 November 1894) seems to suggest that Walters died on the 12th of November, not the 13th. See "Walters Returns to Liberia" in the Introduction.

has come into closer and more intimate association with the general life of the College than Mr. Walters. Perhaps no one of them has so influenced the life and thought of his classmates toward the development of truth, not only in regard to the condition and needs of Africa, though that was a subject very dear to his heart, but as well toward all noble conceptions of justice and religion. And I think I may say truly that there was no one of the class of '93 who deserved or received a larger share of the respect and esteem of his classmates than Mr. Walters. I remember how he lay for many weeks, during his Senior year, so ill that his life was for a long time despaired of. I know there were many prayers offered in our class prayer-meetings for his recovery, and his appearance again among us, weak and enfeebled though he was, seemed an occasion for genuine thanksgiving. Mr. Walter's life was one of genuine helpfulness to those whose hearts were open to read its lessons. He never put himself forward. He was a most perfect gentleman, refined, courteous, modest and retiring in the presence of those whose prejudices forbade an intimate acquaintance. But he was always ready to speak for what he considered the truth, and his burning eloquence frequently stiffed the souls of his hearers, whether in the society hall[1] or the larger public assemblage. In all his work, Mr. Walters was thoroughly conscientious. His class work, his society work, everything he put his hand to, showed earnestness and devotion. To have known Mr. Walters well was to have obtained a stronger and clearer faith in the practicability of Christianity and civilization for the world, and especially a keener sense of sympathy in the great work of redeeming Africa. It is almost unnecessary to say that Mr. Walters' whole life was consecrated to this work. He had planned to carry on his studies

---

1 Society Hall was a building on the Oberlin campus, completed in 1868 and torn down in 1917. "As originally designed, the first floor contained three lecture rooms, while on the second floor there was a society room, from which the building took its name" (http://www.oberlin.edu/~archive/resources/photoguide/society_hall.html). The "society room" would presumably have referred to literary societies like the one to which Walters belonged. As noted in "Walters in America: Oberlin College" in the Introduction, literary societies provided a setting in which students developed their oratorical skills. Hinman's reference to Walters's eloquence in "the larger public assemblage" may suggest that he lectured publicly at churches or other assemblies. However, we have no other evidence that he lectured on a public circuit to raise funds, as his contemporary Thomas Besolow did.

after graduation, taking a Theological course here, and some special preparation for missionary work, in Germany. But doubtless the weak state of his health, among other reasons, prompted him to return at once to his home, in the hope that his native climate might restore his vigor. There is no report of his work. He had planned great things, but they were not to be accomplished. We only know that he died, Nov. 12, 1894, at Cape Mount, W. Africa, at the head of the Episcopal Mission School. Why could not his life have been spared and he have been allowed to use to their full extent for the salvation of Africa, his rich endowments, till perhaps he might indeed have become an African Neesima?[1] God knows best; only let us pray that his place may be speedily filled and many more drawn to the work to which he had consecrated his life.

George W. Hinman.

---

1   Joseph Hardy Neesima (1843-90) was, according to information provided by the college he founded in Japan, "the first Japanese person to receive a degree from a Western institution of higher education" (http://ilc2.doshisha.ac.jp/users/kkitao/doshisha/Neesima/chronology. htm). Born near Tokyo, he fled Japan as a 21-year-old "so he could study Western science and Christianity." Neesima graduated from Phillips Academy, Amherst College, and the Andover Theological Seminary. (As was to be the case with Walters, ill health made Neesima's studies more difficult: "His rheumatism made it difficult to work for the last six months of his time at Amherst College.") After being ordained a Congregational minister, Neesima returned to Japan and–with funding from the American Board of Commissioners for Foreign Missions–founded Doshisha Eigakko (Doshisha College), later Doshisha University. Neesima received an honorary doctorate from Amherst in 1887. Beset with chronic ill health, he died in 1890. Neesima's life story would have been well known at Oberlin in Walters's day.

Bibliography

African Repository. Vol. 5 (1829).

Anthony, Kate J. *Storer College, Harper's Ferry: Brief Historical Sketch*. Boston, MA: Morning Star Press, 1891.

d'Azevedo, Warren. "Some Historical Problems in the Delineation of a Central West Atlantic Region." *Annals of the New York Academy of Sciences* 96 (1962): 512-38.

———. *Some Liberian English Usages* [a revision of his 1967 work by Michael Evan Gold]. Typescript. Monrovia: The United States Peace Corps, 1971.

Barnard, John. *From Evangelicalism to Progressivism at Oberlin College, 1866-1917*. Columbus: Ohio State UP, 1969.

Bergeron, Susan, and Gloria Gozdzik. *A Historical Resource Study for Storer College, Harpers Ferry, West Virginia*. Typescript. Morgantown, WV: Horizon Research Consultants, 2001.

Besolow, Thomas E. *From the Darkness of Africa to the Light of America, The Story of an African Prince*. Boston: T.W. Ripley, 1890.

———. *From the Darkness of Africa to the Light of America, The Story of an African Prince*. Boston: Frank Wood, 1891.

———. *The Story of an African Prince in Exile*. Boston: Frank Wood, 1892.

Biennial Catalogue of the Officers and Students of Storer College, 1889-91. Harper's Ferry, WV: The Board of Trustees, 1891.

Bledsoe, Carolyn H. *Women and Marriage in Kpelle Society*. Stanford: Stanford UP, 1980.

Boone, Sylvia A. *Radiance from the Waters: Ideals of Feminine Beauty in Mende Art*. New Haven: Yale UP, 1988.

Brooks, George E., Jr. *The Kru Mariner in the Nineteenth Century: An Historical Compendium*. Liberian Studies Monograph Ser. 1. Newark, DL: University of Delaware, Department of Anthropology, 1972.

Brown, Robert T. *Immigrants to Liberia 1843 to 1865: An Alphabetical Listing*. Liberian Studies Research Working Paper 7. Philadelphia: Institute for Liberian Studies, 1980.

Caine, Augustus F. *A Study and Comparison of the West African "Bush" School and the Southern Sotho Circumcision School*. Northwestern University MA thesis, 1959.

Caseley Hayford, J.E. *Ethiopia Unbound: Studies in Race Emancipation*. 1911. London: Frank Cass, 1969.

Comaroff, Jean, and John Comaroff. *Of Revelation and Revolution: Christianity and Colonialism in South Africa*. Chicago, IL: U of Chicago P, 1991.

Dapper, Olfert. *Naukeurige beschrijvinge der afrikaensche gewesten*. Amsterdam, 1688.

Donovan, Mary Sudman. *Women's Ministries in the Episcopal Church, 1850-1920*. Columbia University PhD dissertation, 1985.

Duino, Russell. *The Cleveland Book Trade, 1819-1912: Leading Firms and Out-standing Men.* University of Pittsburgh PhD dissertation, 1981.

Dunn, D. Elwood. *A History of the Episcopal Church in Liberia, 1821-1980.* The American Theological Library Association Monograph Ser. 30. Metuchen, NJ: The Scarecrow Press, 1992.

Dwyer, David J. "Mande." *The Niger-Congo Languages.* Ed. John Bendor-Samuel. Lanham, MD: UP of America, 1989. 47-65.

Edgerton, Robert N. *The Fall of the Ashante Empire: The Hundred-Year War for Africa's Gold Coast.* New York: The Free Press, 1995.

Ellis, George W. *Negro Culture in West Africa.* 1914. New York: Johnson Reprint Corporation, 1970.

Etherington, Norman. "The Missionary Writing Machine in Kwa-Zulu-Natal." *Mixed Messages: Missions, Textuality and Culture.* Ed. Gareth Griffiths and Jamie S. Scott. New York: Palgrave, forthcoming.

Fairchild, James H. *Oberlin: The Colony and the College. 1833-1883.* Oberlin, OH: E.J. Goodrich, 1883.

Fletcher, Robert Samuel. *A History of Oberlin College from its Foundation Through the Civil War.* 2 vols. Oberlin, OH: Oberlin College, 1943.

Gage, Matilda Joslyn. *Woman, Church and State: A Historical Account of the Status of Woman Through the Christian Ages; with Reminiscences of the Matriarchate.* New York: Truth Seeker, 1893.

Grace, John. *Domestic Slavery in West Africa, with Particular Reference to the Sierra Leone Protectorate.* London: Frederick Muller, 1975.

Griffiths, Gareth. *African Literatures in English (East and West).* Longman Literatures in English. London: Longman, 2000.

———. "Appropriation, Patronage and Control: The Case of the Missionary Text." *Colonies, Missions, Cultures in the English-Speaking World: General and Comparative Studies.* Ed. Gerhard Stilz. Tübingen: Stauffenberg Verlag, 2001. 13-23.

Hammond, Dorothy, and Alta Jablow. *The Africa That Never Was: Four Centuries of British Writing about Africa.* New York: Twayne Publishers, 1970.

Harley, George W. *Notes on the Poro in Liberia.* Cambridge, MA: Papers of the Peabody Museum 19.2 (1941).

Harris, John M. "Some Remarks on the Origin, Manners, Customs and Superstitions of the Gallinas People of Sierra Leone." *Memoirs read before the Anthropological Society of London* 2 (1865-66): 25-36.

Helps, Sir Arthur. *Friends in Council: A Series of Readings and Discourses Thereon,* 1853. Leipzig: Bernhard Tauchnitz, 1873. Vol. 1, Chap. 8.

Hi-O-Hi. Oberlin, OH: Oberlin College, 1894.

Hofmeyr, Isabel. *The Portable Bunyan: A Transnational History of 'The Pilgrim's Progress.'* Princeton: Princeton UP, 2004.

Holsoe, Svend E. *The Cassava-Leaf People: An Ethnohistorical Study of the Vai People with a Particular Emphasis on the TewO Chiefdom.* Boston University PhD dissertation, 1967.

———. "A Case of Stimulus Diffusion? (A Note on Possible Connections Between the Vai and Cherokee Scripts)." *The Indian Historian* 4.3 (1971): 56-57.

———. "Theodore Canot at Cape Mount, 1841-1847." *Liberian Studies Journal* 4 (1974): 163-81.

———. "Slavery and Economic Response among the Vai (Liberia and Sierra Leone)." *Slavery in Africa: Historical and Anthropological Perspectives*. Ed. Suzanne Miers and Igor Kopytoff. Madison: U of Wisconsin P, 1977. 287-303.

———. "Notes on the Vai Sande Society in Liberia." *Ethnologische Zeitschrift Zürich* 1 (1980): 97-112.

Holt, Dean Arthur. *Change Strategies Initiated by the Protestant Episcopal Church in Liberia from 1836 to 1950 and Their Differential Effects*. Boston University PhD dissertation, 1970.

Hosford, Frances Juliette. *Father Shipherd's Magna Charta: A Century of Coeducation at Oberlin College*. Boston: Marshall Jones, 1937.

Innes, Gordon. *A Mende-English Dictionary*. Cambridge: Cambridge UP, 1969.

Johnson, Jangaba. *Proverbs of Liberia: Vai, Gola, Grebo*. Typescript. Monrovia: The Liberian Information Service, 1963.

Jones, Adam. *From Slaves to Palm Kernels: A History of the Galinhas Country (West Africa) 1730-1890*. Wiesbaden: Franz Steiner Verlag GMBH, 1983.

Koelle, Sigismund W. *Outlines of a Grammar of the Vei Language, Together with a Vei-English Vocabulary*. London: Church Missionary House, 1854.

MacCormack, Carol P. "Sande: The Public Face of a Secret Society." *The New Religions of Africa*. Ed. Bennetta Jules-Rosette. Norwood, NJ: Ablex, 1979. 27-37.

Marchese, Lynell. "Kru." *The Niger-Congo Languages*. Ed. John Bendor-Samuel. Lanham, MD: UP of America, 1989. 119-39.

Martin, Jane J. *The Dual Legacy: Government Authority and Mission Influence among the Glebo of Eastern Liberia, 1834-1910*. Boston University PhD dissertation, 1968.

———. *Krumen "Down the Coast": Liberian Migrants on the West African Coast in the 19th Century*. African Studies Center Working Papers 64. Boston: Boston University, 1982.

Meredith, George. *The Ordeal of Richard Feverel: A History of a Father and Son*. New York: The Modern Library, 1927.

Murdza, Peter J., Jr. *Immigrants to Liberia 1865 to 1904: An Alphabetical Listing*. Liberian Studies Research Working Paper 4. Newark, DL: Department of Anthropology, University of Delaware, for the Liberian Studies Association, 1975.

Newell, Stephanie. *Ghanaian Popular Fiction: "Thrilling Discoveries in Conjugal Life" and Other Tales*. Oxford: James Currey, and Athens, Ohio: Ohio UP, 2000.

———, ed. *Marita or the Folly of Love: A Novel by A. Native*. African Sources for African History 2. Boston: Brill Academic Publishers, 2002.

Niebuhr, Berthold Georg. *The History of Rome*, 3 vols. London: Walton and Maberley, 1853.

Oberlin College. *First Circular of the Oberlin Collegiate Institute*. Oberlin, OH: Oberlin College, 1834.

———. *Oberlin College Catalogue, 1892-93*. Oberlin,OH: Oberlin College, 1892.

———. 1937. *Alumni Catalogue 1833-1936*. Oberlin, OH: Oberlin College, 1937.

Owen, Nicholas. *Journal of a Slave Dealer*, edited by Eveline Martin. London: George Routledge and Sons, 1930.

Penick, Charles Clifton. *Our Mission Work in Africa*. n.p.: n.d. [1881?]

———. "The Devil Bush of West Africa." *Fetter's Southern Magazine* 2.2 (1893): 225-31.

Protestant Episcopal Church in the USA, National Council. *Liberia: Handbooks of the Mission of the Episcopal Church, No. 4*. New York: National Council, 1928.

Schulze, Willi. *A New Geography of Liberia*. London: Longman, 1973.

Scribner, Sylvia, and Michael Cole. *The Psychology of Literacy*. Cambridge, MA: Harvard UP, 1981.

Shick, Tom W. *Emigrants to Liberia 1820-1843: An Alphabetical Listing*. Liberian Studies Research Working Paper 2. Newark, DL: Department of Anthropology, University of Delaware, for the Liberian Studies Association, 1971. Also available from Madison, WI: Data and Program Library Service <http://dpls.dacc.wisc.edu/Liberia/index.html>.

———. *Liberian census data, 1843*. Available from Madison, WI: Data and Program Library Service <http://dpls.dacc.wisc.edu/Liberia/index.html> 1973.

———. *Behold the Promised Land: A History of Afro-American Settler Society in Nineteenth-century Liberia*. Baltimore: Johns Hopkins UP, 1980.

Sibley, J.L., and D.H. Westermann. *Liberia—Old and New: A Study of its Social and Economic Background with Possibilities of Development*. Garden City, NY, Doubleday, Doran & Co., 1928.

Singler, John Victor. "Language in Liberia in the Nineteenth Century: The Settlers' Perspective." *Liberian Studies Journal* 7 (1977): 73-85.

———. "The Liberian *Guanya Pau*: Africa's First Novel in English." *Monrovia Daily Observer* (June 20 1989): 5.

———. "The Day Will Come: J.J. Walters and *Guanya Pau*." *Liberian Studies Journal* 15 (1990): 125-34.

———. "Scripts of West Africa." *The World's Writing Systems*. Ed. Peter T. Daniels and William Bright. New York: Oxford UP, 1966. 593-98.

Smyke, Raymond J. *Massaquoi of Liberia 1870-1938 Genève-Afrique* XXI.1 (1983).

The Spirit of Missions. Vols. 43-48, 59-60 (1878-1883, 1894-95).

Storer Record. Vols. 11-14 (1892-1897).

Viswanathan, Gauri. *Outside the Fold: Conversion, Modernity and Belief*. Princeton: Princeton UP, 1998.

Ware, Rachel J.N. *Episcopal Schools, Cape Mount*. Cuttington College, Liberia, Bachelor's thesis, 1954.

Walters, Joseph J. *Guanya Pau, A Story of an African Princess*. Foreword by Oyekan Owomoyela. Lincoln: University of Nebraska, 1994.

Welmers, William E. *A Grammar of Vai.* University of California Publications in Linguistics 84. Berkeley: U of California P, 1976.

Welmers, William E., and C.K. Kandakai. *A Vai-English Dictionary (preliminary draft).* Typescript. Monrovia: The Institute for Liberian Languages, 1974.

The Young Christian Soldier and Carrier Dove. Vols. 12-16, 23 (1879-1883, 1890).